DON'T STOP NOW

CLAIRE CAIN

Army Couple Photography by Rainbeau Decker.

Book Cover Design by Amanda Walker.

E-Book ISBN-13: 978-1-7327718-5-7

Print ISBN-13: 978-1-7327718-4-0

To the ladies!

CHAPTER ONE

Gabriel

THE BLONDE BUN in front of me was a perfect swirl of gold and yellow hues, the hair pulled tight and meticulously back from the woman's face. Her patrol cap was tucked into the pocket just above her knee, like mine. She was holding a plastic container packed with salad bar fixings—spinach, beets, peppers, cucumbers—a lot more, but I didn't want to peer over her shoulder and freak her out.

It was all I could do not to let my eyes run over the back of her uniform, but I was determined not to do that here, in the commissary, in front of two dozen other soldiers quite likely doing just that.

Ever since she came into the ER, I'd seen her everywhere. *Everywhere.* At the gym. At the commissary two days out of the last six. In her car driving in gate one last week. I swore I saw her at the movie theater last weekend, but maybe that was my imagination.

This wasn't uncommon. I'd been at Fort Campbell for about a year and a half, and since it was my first time working at an Army hospital—my first job after getting my bachelor's degree and then my master's in nursing and commissioning into the Army—I'd come to expect that sometimes after I took care of someone in the ER, they'd show up in all kinds of places.

But her... it was becoming a problem.

I'd treated her three weeks ago when she came in for abdominal pain after passing out at the gym. I'm not sure what happened after she left, but she hadn't come back in.

She stepped up in the lane ahead of me, the sign above our line claiming that soldiers had priority during the hours of 1100 to 1400, an unhelpful gesture considering everyone in the place was a soldier in uniform. She set a divider down on the little conveyer belt behind her salad and a bakery bag without looking up.

Part of me willed her to look up and notice me while the other part of me dreaded her doing that and not recognizing me the way I definitely did her.

I knew her by her light, golden hair, its uniform-perfect bun styled at the back of her head so unlike the loose, messy pile that had sprung out in all directions from the crown of her head as she'd stared straight in front of her while I took her pulse, my brown skin dark against her pale wrist as I counted her heartbeats to establish heart rate.

I recognized her compact body, despite being hidden in the looser-fitting Army uniform, much more concealed now than it was in just tight black shorts, a bright white sports bra, and a royal blue tank top that was less an actual shirt and more a suggestion of one. I remembered how her chest would rise and fall under my stethoscope as I listened to her heart, the thin skin visible there flushed from pain or exertion or anxiety.

Stop thinking about her chest.

I stepped forward too, placed my salad on the belt to the left of the divider, added a bottle of water because, like an idiot, I'd forgotten mine at home. The by-product of my Mexican parents was, at moments like these, I could hear my mother in my mind as if she were standing in front of me and not taking her own lunch break in the employee lounge at the Dallard's of Wyeth, Texas, where she'd worked for the last twenty years.

My mother hated wasting money, and she'd glare at me with her lips pinched in exaggerated disgust if she saw my plastic water bottle, rolling her eyes at my *throwing away money* just to hydrate at my convenience instead of finding a perfectly good drinking fountain somewhere.

Or a hose, for that matter.

I studied my salad through the plastic container, though my eyes wandered to the hand of my check-out line neighbor as her index and middle fingers alternately drummed soundlessly on the lid of her salad while the checker—Alice, said the nametag—handed the soldier in front of her his receipt.

"Hi there, how you doing?" Alice asked.

"Just fine, thank you. How are you? Hanging in there with the lunch rush?" She—Captain Jackson—responded with a calm, smooth voice.

Her voice had been shaky, unsure, in the ER. That made sense since she'd passed out twice in the span of two hours, and the second time it took her a few minutes to remember what had happened. Not unusual to be disoriented in a situation like that, but she'd been upset until she put all the pieces together.

"Are you two together today?" Alice asked, her eyes lifting to me with a Grade-A customer service smile, then pointedly looking back at Captain Jackson.

As Captain Jackson turned to look at who Alice was talking about, I smiled back at her and shook my head. "No, ma'am, we're not," just as that quiet voice also declared, "No."

Captain Jackson looked at me with a polite smile on her face—nothing more than her lips pressed together and slightly turned up—but before she stepped forward toward the payment console, her eyebrows raised. "Oh, it's you," she said, her cheeks reddening as she pulled out a wallet, a card, and swiped.

"Hi, ma'am. I hope you're doing better," I said because I couldn't very well ask her anything in detail—not without embarrassing her or violating HIPAA protocols.

"Yes. I am. Thank you." Her response was stilted, her hands shoving her card back in the thin, black wallet and grabbing her salad. "Thank you," she offered to Alice, and then stood there, facing the exit a moment before she walked to it and out the sliding glass doors.

Rae

Of course.

Of course the gorgeous nurse who'd seen me at my absolute worst was the man standing behind me in the commissary. Of course I blushed when I recognized him. Who wouldn't?

I shut my eyes and my grip tightened on the steering wheel, though my keys rested on my thigh and the car was silent. I thought of that awful day, the last time I saw him.

"I'm not sure when it started, but I know it has become increasingly... problematic in the last six months," I

explained, my fingers clenching the sheet resting over my legs on the hospital bed.

"Ok. And it seems to be related to your menstrual cycle?" The nurse's lips pronouncing menstrual cycle sent a flood of embarrassment through me. I wasn't ashamed of being a woman, or even having to describe the pain. But I was angry at being there in the first place—angry I'd passed out, angry I didn't know why the pain was getting worse, and angry I was spending my time in the ER instead of finishing my workout and heading home so I could get to bed on time.

"I think so? I'm not on my period now—shouldn't be for another two weeks." And that was the killer. The timing was unclear, unpredictable.

"Are you bleeding now?" he asked, his voice rich and smooth and completely at odds with his bright blue scrubs and the stark white of the hospital.

"I don't think so. I don't usually bleed when it happens." I flushed again, knowing my chest, neck, and cheeks were bright with embarrassment. Why couldn't I have had a female nurse?

"Are you currently pregnant or breastfeeding?" His brown eyes were directed at the laptop resting on his knees where he entered notes as he hunched on the small stool next to the bed. I huffed out a breath.

"Definitely not."

"You couldn't be pregnant?" I could see his dark, thick eyebrows were raised as he typed away.

"No."

"Not even a chance? Because that would be an important—"

"I haven't had sex for the better part of six years, so yeah. I'm certain." His head popped up when I said "six" and his *eyes were searching my face, his lashes blinking as if that might clarify things for him.*

"O-ok. Not pregnant."

I let out a breath and leaned back against the bed. What a humiliating topper to a magnificently mediocre day. Not only was my nurse the most beautiful man I'd ever seen, but now I'd just given him a brief tour of my sexual history in a spectacular example of what it meant to over-share.

A knock on my window sounded and pushed me out of the memory. I looked up to see a wall of green, tan, and brown uniform standing just outside my car door and a brown hand holding a salad container and a bakery bag.

My bakery bag. Mother effer.

I unclipped my seatbelt and pulled the door handle, stepping out of the car and forcing him to step back to avoid getting hit by my moving door.

The awkward attempt at conversation spilled out of my lips. "Thank you, so much." My words were unsure, my eyes not certain where to land between the bag and his face. He flashed me a white smile, his brows rising as I stretched out a hand toward my bakery bag.

"Are you feeling better, ma'am?" His voice was amused as he handed me the bag.

"Yes, thank you, Lieutenant," I said, my voice tight. I was squinting back at him, my sunglasses tucked in the center console of my car rather than saving me from the brightness, and I felt a rush of annoyance as he just stood there, looking at me.

"Good. I hope so." His water bottle tucked under one arm, the other holding only his salad now, he didn't move. I noticed he had an inordinate amount of shredded carrots topping his salad, and then felt another swell of annoyance. Why were we standing there? What did he want?

"Can I help you?" The edge in my voice was too much, I knew. I could easily sound pissed off, and that combined with my RBF was a dangerous combination, especially as a female leader in the ultimate boys' club.

"Uhh, no? I was just making sure you didn't miss out on your pretzel." His forehead wrinkled in confusion and the edges of his mouth turned down slightly.

"Well, thanks. That was nice. But listen, I don't date soldiers." I let out a controlled breath as I saw his head rear back and his eyes dart dramatically from side to side.

"Ok?" The question in his voice was clear, but I didn't need to explain myself. I was propositioned regularly, and I wasn't in the mood.

I gave an exaggerated nod as I put one leg back into my car, one hand on the top of the door, one on the top of the car. "Have a nice day, Lieutenant," I said, my tone final.

"Uhhh.... You too, ma'am," he said, his face still bewildered as he stepped back from the car.

I watched him walk away while my hand dove into the paper sack of its own accord. It pulled out the perfect, golden-brown pretzel, and I shoved a chunk of it into my mouth, gulping down the carbs and waiting for my pulse, my irritation, my embarrassment to slow.

I didn't see Lieutenant Marquez again for several weeks, but I'd been keeping my head down, and I'd had no more pain, which was a relief. On Friday afternoon, Lieutenant Colonel Basto, my battalion commander, emailed to say he needed to meet later that day.

"Afternoon, Captain Jackson. Have a seat." He hadn't yet looked at me since he was still typing on his computer, wrapping up one of what was very likely hundreds of emails for the day.

"Thank you, sir." I sat in the chair directly in front of his large, cluttered desk, my posture perfect.

"I know this meeting wasn't on the calendar for the week, so I appreciate you meeting me this late in the day," LTC Basto said as he swiveled in his black office chair to give me his full attention. He folded his hands on his desk and waited for my response.

"Of course, sir."

"You've been here with us in the brigade support battalion for, what, six months?"

"Yes, sir. I changed out of company command in late July and moved over to the support operations shop early August while I wait for my follow-on. I've been approved for a year-long advanced civil schooling opportunity and was accepted at Vanderbilt, so I'll remain in the area but move down that way come next fall."

"I know you had a stellar command. I was proud to have a logistician stand out amongst a bunch of infantry captains. I know the time in Afghanistan wasn't easy, but you can be proud of the work you did and the way you led your company. Obviously the Army has recognized your excellence and that's one reason you're heading to get your master's down at Vandy."

His words were unexpected. I knew I'd done well in command—my evaluations and counselings from Lieutenant Colonel Wilson, the Rambler Battalion commander, had made that clear. But I wasn't expecting to trade on the currency of my command forever, nor could I if I wanted to continue to be successful.

Getting the master's at Vanderbilt was checking a box on a goal I'd had since learning early on that to stay in past a certain point, you needed a master's degree. I was happy to have the Army pay me to go get one, but also happy enough to stay here at Campbell while I waited for that time to come around.

"Thank you, sir. I learned a lot in command."

"I'm sure you did. Even though it has been a decade or so since my company command, it was formative for me." I nodded my head in agreement, knowing he'd keep talking. "We're looking at a situation where I'm likely going to need someone to step in to be the SPO. Not sure about that just yet, but I'm thinking you're the obvious choice."

I swallowed audibly, or it must have been because my heart was kicking up its usual beat to the pace it keeps when I'm running sprints.

"Sir?" What else could I say? He was asking me to step into the SPO—Support Operations Officer—a job currently occupied by a major, a job I'd hold in three to five years, if things went well. Major Toms had done a good job from what I could tell, but he was on leave at the moment. Maybe he'd had a family emergency.

"Major Toms may need to step out."

Oh.

Oh. Something had happened.

"How can I help?" My voice shook a little from the adrenaline pumping through me, and I hoped he didn't notice.

"Just stay tuned. It'll be a few weeks, but I don't want it to be a shock if it happens, and I want you to be ready."

"Roger, sir. I will be." I stood and he nodded to me, then swiveled back around as I stepped out of his office.

Did that just happen?

I couldn't suppress the small smile that spread on my face—it should have been a thousand times bigger. It should have turned up the lights.

This is incredible!

What LTC Basto was offering was insane. It was terrifying. It was exhilarating. They must not have been able to get another major to fill the spot immediately, or maybe it wouldn't pan out. Likely, it wouldn't, because again, I was pretty sure Major Toms had done a good job with things, but still... Basto wouldn't be telling me it was a possibility unless the likelihood of changes were high.

After signing out of my computer and powering it down, I grabbed my keys, phone, and hat, waving to the few stragglers in the office. It was now seven o'clock, and I was going to be late to meet Ann and her friends for dinner.

Ann was my best friend, and she happened to live next door to me. We met during in-processing at Fort Campbell about two years ago, both destined for the Rambler battalion as newly-minted post-career course captains, her to the staff and me to Echo company. Better yet, it turned out we'd rented townhouses next to each other and ended up getting to know each other outside of work thanks to the proximity.

She was in the Rambler battalion as a signal officer, and she was awesome. Now that I was with the BSB—Brigade Support Battalion—we didn't see each other as regularly during the week, but we often worked out together after work and still hung out on weekends when we could.

She was the one to take me to the ER weeks ago when I'd passed out. While there, my attending physician caught her fancy, and after exchanging information that night, she and the doctor had gone for coffee and then planned a group gathering. After that, they'd been inseparable.

Ann and I had hardly seen each other since then, so

she'd asked me to join her at a dinner that night since Alisha, or Doctor Jordan as I knew her, had invited her to some kind of social for the hospital and suggested she bring a friend so she wasn't the only non-medical person there.

Though Ann was typically very reserved, much like I could be, she was surprisingly aggressive in terms of social engagements and pursuing people she was interested in—an approach I admired, though didn't understand. She was usually what dragged me from the familiarity of my little haven just off of Tiny Town Road.

~

Gabriel

After a long day in the ER, I was finally cleaned up and following as the hostess led me to a large high-top table in the back of the restaurant where five women and two men sat chatting and laughing. Other tables were full of my fellow hospital staff, and as I passed familiar faces, I waved or greeted them with a pat on the back or a handshake. I was sitting with some of the ER team, and I hadn't had time to find a date.

The event was a quarterly effort at teambuilding or morale—one of those buzzwords administration always busted out. Whatever it was, it worked pretty well—they gave out some awards and said nice things about people, and in the end we all had a good night out (except the poor suckers working who couldn't come). I found my table, moved to the last available seat on the end of the rectangular set up, and as I approached, my blood pressure spiked as I saw who was sitting at the end of the table. Her back was to me, but as I rounded the table and took my seat, smiling and waving down the narrow row at the others, reaching across to shake someone's hand, Captain Jackson's eyes were wide and glued to me.

"Captain Jackson," I said, a courteous nod in her direction.

"Lieutenant Marquez," she said, then turned her attention to Dr. Viraj who was telling an animated story, gesturing and boisterous as usual. His dark hair was long on top—far longer than mine, but he could get away with that being an MD. Robert, a fellow nurse, sat to my right and I gave him a "hey man" as I settled in.

I grabbed a menu and perused it with half my attention while covertly studying the woman across from me. Her long, bright blonde hair spilled over one shoulder, all the way down past her chest, past the alluring "V" of her black top. Her eyes looked dark in the low light of the restaurant, and I thought maybe she was wearing eyeliner or mascara, unlike when I'd seen her in the ER and at the store days ago. She wore a functional watch on one wrist, some silver bangles on the other arm, and long silver earrings that fell several inches down from her earlobes, drawing my attention to her neck.

She had one of those necks. A neck you'd call graceful or delicate or elegant, even though nothing in my interactions with this woman hinted at her taking kindly to those words as descriptors of her.

"Did I just hear you call each other captain and L.T.? No, no, no." Ann, the woman I'd just officially met sitting next to Jackson, though I remembered her from the ER too, shook her head and wagged a reprimanding finger at us. "Captain Jackson's first name is Rae. And you are?"

Rae.

What a perfect and improbable name for this woman.

"I'm Gabriel." I held out a hand across the table. "Nice to formally meet you," I said, waiting for her to take my hand.

I hadn't missed the dirty look she shot Ann when her friend said her first name, but she turned a blank face my way and took my hand.

"Nice to meet you Gabriel." She pulled her warm, small hand away and settled back on her chair while I bent and flexed the fingers of the hand she shook where it now hung by my side, chasing the little electric prickles that raced to the surface of my skin when our palms and fingers touched.

I made a point to study my menu again and made my choice, then closed it. Everyone else was taking turns talking, pestering Dr. Viraj about another crazy story he'd just told. I watched Rae as she looked down the table, a small smile playing on her lips until she noticed me looking.

"Did you need something?" She didn't have the same edge she'd had when she shut me down at the commissary by saying she didn't date soldiers, but it was the same general tone. The tone that said *I'm better than you* or *I'm out of your league* or *Don't even bother.* Why she'd decided to aim that attitude my way, I didn't know, and it rubbed me the wrong way.

"What do you suppose I'd need from you?" My voice was far harsher than it should have been, but her approach with me was *wrong*.

Her mouth opened, then closed. I saw the blush creep in from the top of her cheek bones, and based on what I knew, I guessed if I could see the color of her chest and neck in this low light, they'd be red too.

"Ok, listen. I'm sorry." She looked down at her hands resting on the edge of the table, holding on, then flicked her dark blue eyes up at me.

Oof, those eyes.

"Sorry for...?"

"I've been a jerk to you. I—it's a bad habit, but it didn't come out of nowhere. I'm sorry." She glanced up at me, her light brown eyebrows furrowed with concern.

"Not sure I'm following." I shifted in my seat, settling in to see what she'd say.

This was unexpected. She was easily the most beautiful woman I'd ever seen in real life. It was frankly more comfortable for her to be a bit prickly, verging on temperamental, than for her to turn out to be a genuinely nice person, too. If she'd stick with the stereotype of beautiful but frigid, that'd keep my interest at bay.

"When you gave me back my pretzel the other day, I had this horrible thought you were about to ask me out," she said and made a regretful frown.

Horrible thought. Ouch.

"Oh, yeah... No." I tried to say it lightly, because honestly, I had been thinking about whether I could ask her out and not be a creep since our first meeting was me reviving her from passing out on the ER floor. Even then, she was pretty, but I was working. Every time I'd seen her after that, far or near, I was in the uncomfortable position of recognizing she was rare and appealing—at least her face. Her hair. What I'd seen of her body.

I'd been leaning toward embracing that *No, I can't just ask her out* when she'd shut me down before I opened my mouth that day, and I was thankful she had before I'd embarrassed myself more than I already had by just standing there, looking at her.

"I'm getting that, and I'm sorry. It happens, uh... fairly frequently, and I didn't, uh, I didn't want you to..."

"Say no more. All is forgotten. I could never bring a girl

like you home to my mom, so, fear not," I said, a casual wave across the table like it wouldn't have even occurred to me to ask her out.

Her dark lashes fluttered, and then one side of her mouth quirked up. "A girl like me?"

"You know," I said, dipping my head like we shared a secret.

Her brow perked. "An older woman?"

Somehow her saying that sent a shot of heat through me, but I kept my benign smile and shook my head.

"Someone in the Army?"

I flashed her a bright, full smile—one that had often won me interest from women. I stood from my seat just slightly and leaned over the table. "A blonde girl," I said in a stage whisper.

Her lips pursed, then released into a delighted grin. "Is that so?"

"Yes, ma'am. So you're safe from me, Rae. I think we're destined to be friends."

"Perfect, Gabriel. I'd be very happy to be your friend." She beamed at me then, and I felt the conflicting sense that I'd lost something and gained something else.

CHAPTER TWO

WE'D BEEN SITTING THERE for an hour, everyone chatting and taking last bites, and the conversation and time spent across from Gabriel Marquez, first lieutenant, nurse, and maybe the most gorgeous man I'd ever seen, had done nothing to allay my interest in him.

But I wasn't interested in him.

I'd never date a soldier again—not ever. That was one rule in my life I wouldn't break. I hadn't known I needed a rule like that until I *did* date a fellow soldier, marry him, and within fifteen months, divorce him.

Consider the lesson learned.

But Gabriel.

Gabriel, what a perfect name for this guy.

I just couldn't stop looking at him.

He was talking with one of the nurses down the table whose name I'd forgotten in the flurry of introductions earlier. Gabriel was smiling as he spoke, and his full lips were shaping words, his white teeth all lined up perfectly behind them, bringing flashes of confidence and humor to his dialogue. His hands gestured now and then with perfect comedic timing, and as I watched, I felt a strange jolt of kinship with him.

He was entirely different from me in almost every way based on personality—I was more reserved, and he was clearly outgoing. I tended to come off cold and a little uptight or remote, but he was warm, welcoming, comforting, even when he just sat and listened.

He was settled into who he was. Maybe it was something about how he sat in the chair or the way he wasn't hesitant to speak up and share his ideas, or maybe it was the way he didn't seem phased by my assumptions of him and then my apology. Whatever it was, Gabriel struck me as a man who was comfortable in his skin.

"What do you think, Rae?" His warm voice spread over me from across the table, and I leaned in to regain the thread of the conversation.

"Sorry." *I spaced out while admiring your lips of perfection.* "What did you ask?"

"We were talking about favorite foods, places around here you love. I said Yamato outside gate one, and any Japanese steak house, because there's one on every block here. Ann said she loves Korean, and Shelby said she's all about the Catfish House. What's your favorite?" He smiled at me, like nothing was wrong in his universe.

"Hmm..." I said, running through my mental list of favorites.

"Don't tell me you don't eat out..." he teased.

"Why would you think that?"

"You seem like a woman who might be... particular in

her tastes," he said, his eyes squinting as he assessed me, his voice lowered a bit. I looked at the other faces and found they weren't listening to us—they were focused on Dr. Viraj again as he laughed boisterously and slung an arm around a blushing Shelby.

"That doesn't sound like a good thing." I chuckled lightly but felt the corners of my mouth tilt down. The familiar feeling of being *no fun* dripped from my head down to settle in my shoulders like cold water.

"Oh, it is." One side of Gabriel's mouth lifted and I saw his eyes widen.

"How so?"

"You clearly take care of yourself. I see a lot of bodies as a nurse." He said this like I'd know what that meant. My cheeks heated at his reference to having seen me in the hospital—I couldn't escape the embarrassment I still felt at having passed out. I'd been to the specialist and they'd determined I'd had an ovarian cyst burst. Great. Nothing to be done about it, nothing to suggest it would necessarily happen again.

"You see a lot of bodies..."

"Yes." He just looked at me, his deep brown eyes framed by thick eyebrows that made him look just a little sad or concerned in the way they turned down toward the bridge of his nose—this had the effect of giving him what someone might refer to as *bedroom eyes,* and although I never would have used that term before meeting him, Gabriel had those kind of eyes. They were perfectly at odds with his perpetually smiling mouth.

"Ok." I had no idea what else to say.

He cleared his throat. "So, your favorite kind of food. What do you get when you don't want to cook?" He leaned over the table on his elbows, shifting his water glass out of the way.

"I like a lot of things. I live off Tiny Town Road so it's easy to get whatever—"

"But if you had to choose. What do you want when you're starving? What do you crave when you're desperate for—"

"Definitely Mexican."

Gabriel's smile started small, but soon he was blaring his smile at me like a declaration, like he'd won something.

"What?"

"What you crave is Mexican?" he asked, leveling me with a serious stare even as he worked to hide his grin.

"Yes. I'd have it every day if I could. Probably three times a day." I bit my lip to keep from laughing at him.

"You'd *have Mexican* three times a day if you could?" His voice was amused and pleased and something else I couldn't quite pin down.

"Absolutely. I love the flavors, and it doesn't always have to be bad for you."

"Oh, this is true. Mexican can be very good for you."

Gabriel

I'd probably be dreaming about her *Having Mexican* for the next year. She couldn't have missed the innuendo, but maybe she had. That would be disappointing because she did seem serious.

But why was I analyzing her sense of humor?

Yes it was important in a friend, but I was evaluating her like I wanted to date her, and she'd already set me straight on that note. I checked the urge to put my hand on her lower back as we left the restaurant, resulting in an awkward swoop of my arm until my hand lodged into my pocket. Like a good friend, I kept my eyes off of her spectacular denim-clad backside as she walked in front of me and stuffed my other hand in my pocket to keep from touching her in some way like I itched to do.

She high-fived Ann, shook Dr. Viraj's hand, and I noticed he held her hand just a little longer than he needed to as he gave her his charming smile—no doubt he'd be interested since he was interested in anything with the right chromosomes in a very wide age bracket. Rae removed her hand and stepped back from him with a courteous smile, then waved at Dr. Jordan, Shelby, Rebel, and Callie. Robert had left a half hour earlier to make nightshift, which reminded me I was switching to nights next weekend.

I felt nerves slice through me as she turned to me, her hands holding her small black purse behind her back.

"It was... good to see you again, Gabriel. I'm glad we cleared the air." She rocked back and forth on her feet, which were wearing surprisingly high-heeled boots that I chose not to look at for fear of finding one more thing I'd be thinking about later, then she looked at the ground, and finally back up at me.

"Me too, Rae. Glad you're feeling better, and glad we've clarified that you have no interest in me because it would have been awkward for me to have to shoot you down if our friends start dating and we see each other all the time."

She chuckled and shook her head. "Yes, that would have been intensely awkward, which is a real rarity in my life, so I'm glad we avoided that." She grinned at me, and I thought I saw her shoulders sag a little in relief.

"Now that we've met, I can admit I see you everywhere. I'll be sure to say hi next time." My phone buzzed in my pocket, and I pulled it out so I could answer once she walked away.

"Please do. See you around." She turned and walked to her car, and I watched as I answered the phone.

"Vik. What's up, *hita?*"

"G, I'm sorry. I've got to get to work so I'll just say it. My scholarship check didn't quite cover my books this semester..." I heard the regret in her voice and my smile faltered as I made my way to my car.

"No problem. I'll send you some cash. How much you need?"

"You aren't even going to ask which classes I need the books for? What if I'm out buying cocaine or something?" Her voice rose in disbelief through the line.

I turned the ignition and the engine of my Subaru Forrester revved. It wasn't my dream car, but I'd bought it in college, used, and it was paid for.

"Yes, I'm very concerned that my valedictorian sister, my little overachieving she-devil, is shamming me out of my paycheck to buy cocaine. It's just that I can't acknowledge it, and I know if I don't fund your habit, you'll turn to the streets, so..."

"Did you just insinuate I'd become a hooker for blow? This escalated!"

"Oh, no, I don't mean you'd be a prostitute. I mean you'd start pick-pocketing like you used to when I was still home at Mom and Dad's."

"I took a twenty from your wallet *one time* without asking. Seriously, G, you have to—"

"*Hita*, I'm kidding. You know I love helping you out, and I'm so proud of you. I don't want you to hesitate to ask, and I trust that you won't, so tell me what you need, and I'll get it to you."

Victoria was younger by seven years and probably a genius. She was the youngest in our family of five siblings, and because she chose to attend Vanderbilt on a partial scholarship, she wasn't far from me while I was at this duty station since Fort Campbell was only a little over an hour from Nashville and the Vanderbilt campus.

We were close—we always had been. I was her default babysitter starting at about eight, and because I was the youngest boy, we were lumped together despite the age gap. My brothers Angel, Marco, and Tony were all off to work or college as I entered high school. I'd never bonded with them or grown out of my hero-worship of them while still at home, but with age came wisdom, and I could easily say there was no more worship to be had now.

But between four sons and one daughter, my parents and their very blue-collar paychecks wouldn't be able to fund Vik's dream of going away to school, of getting out of Texas, and getting a little distance. She'd been suffocated in high school since Angel and Tony had stayed in our home-town and taken it upon themselves to police her teen years and keep all potential dates well away from her—or so they'd thought. She'd hated this, and I always thought her drive to do well in school was only half-related to her desire to demonstrate her academic ability.

Marco withdrew from the family after high school. He went to college and walked on the soccer team at UT. The only thing that kept him in school was soccer, and he ended up leaving a year shy of graduation to go play professionally.

All that was to say, Vik and I were close, and when she ended up needing help with money, it seemed crazy for her to take out loans. I knew my parents couldn't help her.

So I did.

I helped her out with her apartment, and the occasional books or whatever. It was no big deal. I made good money in the Army, and living in Clarksville was cheap, plus I had hardly any expenses.

It was how we were raised. You take care of your family. I wasn't old-fashioned enough to think that women shouldn't work, but it was my responsibility to take care of my women. Until I had a wife and family of my own, Vik was my girl and I'd take care of her to keep my parents or brothers from dealing with that, especially when it was no problem for me. The stability of the Army paycheck was nice, and even though Tony and Angel gave me hell for being a nurse and not an infantryman "or at least a doctor" as they said, as though they didn't have totally normal jobs as a cop and a mechanic, I was proud of the living I was making.

"Vik, I'm coming up to see you soon, ok? Let's do a movie or something. We can go see that new one with Jack MacKean." We tried to get together at least monthly, and I knew she'd be first in line for the new MacKean so we might as well combine efforts.

"Ok, sounds good." Something in her voice was sad, and it stopped me.

"What's wrong?"

"It's nothing."

BS. Vik was a naturally happy person. There was usually only one thing that upset her, and it was that asswipe, Rip.

"Is Rip harassing you again?" I was immediately incensed by just saying the idiot's name.

"Why would you ask me that? You know I haven't seen him in months, and I told him not to contact me." I could picture her with arms crossed, one hip popped out in defiance.

"I know that jerk has no respect for you, and that he does what he wants. If he's bothering you or you're—"

"*Stop!* Gabriel, stop. Seriously. Stop talking about Rip and don't bring him up again. I'll talk to you soon. Thanks for the help with books." The line went dead.

That went well.

Rae

It had been a week since LTC Basto pulled me into his office to mention the SPO job. Major Toms wasn't back, but the rumor mill had somehow caught wind of the fact that I was being considered for the temporary fill-in if Toms was removed. So far I'd only received a few glares from fellow captains and one hearty congratulations from my friend Luke Waterford who'd heard about it over at Rambler battalion. We'd been in command together during the last deployment—me commanding Echo company, and him in command of Bravo. That brought about a bond that mattered, and we'd been cheering each other on ever since.

I gathered up my files and cleared all the windows in my browser. I just needed to grab some papers for tomorrow's morning meeting from the printer in the other room, and then I'd sign out and be on my way for a workout. I was so ready for the weekend, and tomorrow would be an easy Friday.

"Yeah, I heard she's up for it too," I heard a hushed voice say from around the corner, and I slowed my steps.

"You know *why* she is, right?" another voice asked. I

recognized it as Captain Talcum, a Grade-A skeeve based on the number of times I'd caught his eyes firmly glued to my chest.

"She killed her command, I know that. And I know Basto thinks she's the shit."

"I'm not gonna say anything specific, but I'll say this—I'm sure Jackson is familiar with every square inch of the underside of Basto's desk."

Ah, there it is.

The inevitable suggestion I'd traded sexual favors for any modicum of success I was having in the Army. I gritted my teeth and picked up my pace, walking past the three men trading gossip as I moved to the printer.

Dear Lord, I was sick of this. I'd been blissfully unaware of conversations like this at my first duty station. I wasn't sure how I managed it, but it was only after promoting to rank of captain and during my company command that I started hearing the suggestion I'd gotten my command in such a well-reputed unit because I gave someone a hand job, that my company had won the commander's excellence award because I'd showed the battalion commander my boobs... you name it, at this point, I'd probably heard it.

And now, here was Talcum, a man so deeply threatened by the fact that I didn't have a penis and was still somehow allowed in the building that he had to suggest I was down on my knees for Basto in order to be *considered* for a *temporary* position.

Or, more specifically—considered for that position *instead* of him.

I slid the folders in my file drawer and locked it, signed out of my computer, moved to my car, careful not to look up in case Talcum or his cronies might see I'd heard and it affected me.

Because as much as I'd like to say it didn't, it did. I hated that there was such a predictably sexist response to a woman's success. To *my* success. I'd grown used to being asked out like it was appropriate to solicit dates in the middle of briefings, used to being talked about, joked about, and objectified, even, but the perpetual need to find a sexualized reason for my professional success was infuriating.

It was certainly not coming from everyone, but those from whom it was were often loudest and most persistent.

I pulled into the gym parking lot, grabbed my bag, and walked in.

Yes, it bothered me. But it was nothing a few miles on the treadmill couldn't wipe away. Talcum wouldn't take this day from me.

~

Gabriel

I pulled into the gym parking lot with two hours until my first graveyard shift in the ER. I grabbed my gym bag, but before I reached the door, I stopped. There was Rae, bent over, hands on her knees, back rising and falling. Was she about to pass out again? I jogged to her.

"You ok?" I leaned down to catch her eye just as she stood up. Her face was bright red, the hair around her face slick with sweat.

"Hi." She breathed in again—man, she was breathing hard. "I just finished my run with sprints—got too hot in there and needed some air." She pulled a long drag of air in through her nose and squinted into the sky.

"Good. I thought maybe you were going to pass out."

"No—nope. I'm all right. Just pushed."

"What'd you do?" I adjusted the strap of my bag over my shoulder, noticed the freckles on her shoulders, then the low dip of the arm holes of her tank top that showed her bright pink sports bra and the skin stretched over the top of her ribs and obliques. I would have thought she was cold out here in the February chill if I couldn't tell she was over-heated by the flush on her skin.

"Ten, and then some sprints on and off for a mile."

"Ten miles?" I wasn't a runner. I was fit, and I definitely took pride in my body, but distance running was not my thing.

"Yeah."

"Don't you guys have unit PT in the mornings?" Since nurses all worked at different times, we had more flexibility to get workouts in when it worked for us, and as long as we could pass our PT test when the time came, the commander at the hospital didn't bother us about it.

"Yeah, we do." She tilted her head to look at me.

"Are you training for something?"

"I was thinking of doing a half marathon sometime. But I had a crap day and needed some kind of release. I find I feel less terrible if I run out my frustration than if I go fill a pastry bag at the commissary and shovel carbs in front of the TV." She pulled her lean arm across her chest and held it there, stretching one shoulder then the other.

"Makes sense. What made the day so bad?" I didn't like the idea of her having a day that made her run her guts out like she clearly just had—she was obviously fit but was still breathing fairly hard, still recovering from pushing herself.

"Ah, nothing. Just jerks. Nothing new." She grabbed a foot behind her back and stretched her left quad. "How are you? Aren't most people heading home at six o'clock on a Thursday?"

"I start graves tonight, so I got here a little early to grab a quick run. *Not* ten miles, if you're wondering."

"That's... what, seven to seven?" she asked.

"Yeah. It's not too bad, except when I try to function during the day and pretend I'm not upside-down. The next few days will be focused on keeping my supply of caffeine steady until I adjust."

"That's essential, I'm sure. Well..." she trailed off and squinted back up at the sky where the sun had disappeared over the horizon. "I hope it goes well."

"Yeah, it'll be pretty quiet until end of the month with the full moon when people start getting weird. The weirdest crap happens."

"Really? I guess I've heard that, just never thought about what it'd be like for the staff." She bent down to stretch her hamstrings, and I focused on the gym doors with all the willpower I owned.

I did not look at the little gap where her shirt rode up to reveal her lower back. I did not. "Yep. Weird stuff. I guess that's coming up, so we'll see if I end up with any good stories."

"I'll look forward to it. I'm sure you've got to get in there, so I'll see you later. Hope the shift goes well." She smiled at me and gave me a little wave. I nodded back, feeling tongue tied as I tried to figure out a way to arrange seeing her again, or get her phone number, or something, but I couldn't figure out how to do that without sounding like a come-on, despite our former clarifications.

"See you around, Rae."

CHAPTER THREE

Rae

WHAT AM I DOING HERE?

I hadn't been that nervous in years. *Years.*

Well, other than leading convoys through the streets of a small Afghan town where we knew there'd be trouble or jumping out of airplanes for my Airborne badge. But for a typical human interaction, I hadn't been this nervous— maybe ever.

I'd decided to take Gabriel some coffee. It was Friday night, and despite my hopes that it'd be an easy day, I'd ended up working until eight. Indoor soccer was canceled which would have put me home earlier, but I'd opted for something to funnel my frustration from work since I couldn't get it out on the field. After a longer workout at the gym and getting cleaned up, it was 9:30. I thought maybe Gabriel could use a pick-me-up, and since I was still on post, and the coffee shop was still open another half hour... I resisted the urge to overthink the move and just went for it.

Other than Ann, who had her own social life and was also extremely busy with work, and my friend Luke, who was never a social hang-out kind of friend, I didn't have many friends. I never had, other than Maybelline, who'd started the pageant circuit a year after I did. The friendship materialized based on the sheer number of hours we spent back stage rubbing Vaseline on our teeth to make our smiles shine, though our lives had diverged after college and I hadn't seen her in years.

Heath, my brother, was off to the Marine Corps the day he graduated from high school—that was *his* ticket out of our small town in Georgia.

No doubt, this was one reason why I fell so hard and fast for Brad. We'd been in ROTC at UGA for several years, though we didn't interact all that much. By the time we were seniors, he'd started making his interest known. I hadn't dated much—had always been too busy with dance lessons, rehearsing my routine for the talent portion, traveling for pageants, and school work in high school and then added ROTC obligations in college—so his attention, especially from this man who I thought was completely handsome, was irresistible. The fact that he understood my Army career, that he spoke the language, and that he'd be in the same boat with me in terms of lifestyle after graduation made him all the more appealing.

The night we graduated and commissioned I hugged my mom, her eyes rimmed with red, then off I went to be with Brad. We spent every waking and non-waking moment together for the week before we had to leave, and in what I will forever think of as my most impulsive moment, we got married.

We knew if we were only dating there would be no chance to be stationed together, and Brad had seemed *so* sure. His parents had been married for forty years, and his dad had always told him *you know when you know.*

My parents had been divorced since I was three. The only thing I knew was the way my mom paid the bills was with the help of my dad's child support checks and even then, sometimes she needed my pageant winnings to break even.

So, we got married at the courthouse the day he left for his basic infantry officer leader course (I was off to my course in ordnance, later to become logistics, a week later), the training everyone does in the first few months before starting real jobs in the Army, and the next day I left. I told my mom over the phone, and she couldn't even pretend to be happy for me—she'd never met Brad.

I shook off the familiar dropping sensation I felt whenever I thought of my mom's voice in that call—stiff to hide her upset and grating across the speaker in my ear as I registered her sadness. I had to learn the lesson on my own, but I wished I would have let her in on it a bit more.

Shifting the coffee cup from one hand to the other, I let the heat of it warm my cold hands. I was nervous because I was standing in the ER reception area, holding a steaming hot black coffee with individual packets of cream and sugar tucked into the back pocket of my jeans, waiting for Robert to track down Gabriel and tell him I was here.

I was trying to make friends, and I felt more than a little bit like an awkward child waiting for someone to ask her to play on the playground. But that twinge of anxiety hadn't kept me from buying the coffee, or driving here, or speaking to Robert and asking him to hunt down Gabriel, so I shook it off and squared my shoulders. I wasn't incapable or even particularly shy—this wasn't a big deal.

After four minutes (I checked my watch approximately every thirty seconds, so I knew it was four minutes), Gabriel still hadn't come. I told myself I'd give him ten minutes, and then I'd split and hope Robert never found him so he'd never know I'd stopped by to make a fool of myself.

"Hey. This is a surprise," Gabriel said as he saw me, now sitting closest to the exit, away from two kids sniffling through face masks and one woman softly crying while cradling her arm.

I stood and shoved the coffee toward him, ignoring the flutter in my belly at the sight of him in his green scrubs. "I'm sorry, I probably shouldn't have come, but I was working late and thought of how you were on day two of your new shift, and the coffee shop was still open, so I—"

"You brought me coffee?" One side of his mouth tilted up into a delighted half-smile.

"Yes?"

"Is that a question?" He bent his head a little to get closer to me. He was probably around five ten, and I was five four, so I was constantly looking up at him.

"No? I just... I'm interrupting." I was still holding the warm cup, so I stared at it instead of his face. I willed my cheeks not to turn red and betray me while internally shoving the sensation of being out of place back down to the depths of my mind.

"Not at all. This is great. I needed a caffeine break, and it just so happens I was on for a break in about ten minutes anyway, so I'll just take it a little early. Can you stay and talk?" I saw him wave to Robert and gesture to the exit nearby. Robert gave him a thumbs up. Gabriel turned to me and raised his eyebrows with a small smile.

Ugh. He's so nice. So so so nice.

"Sure. Yeah, I can stay while you take your break." I held the coffee out to him again and he took it, his fingers grazing mine as the cup changed hands. "I also have cream and sugar, if you need it."

"No, I'm good, thank you. Let's get some fresh air." He gestured with the coffee cup to the exit, and then ushered me out the doors where we were greeted by a blast of cruel, cold air. I stuffed my hands into my gloves then into my jacket pockets as we crossed the ambulance parking area to find a bench.

"This was nice of you."

I felt a dip of nervousness again. "I'm glad it worked out." I looked down at my gloved hands now in my lap and had no idea what to say next.

"Better day today?" he asked, then took a sip of coffee, tendrils of steam whispering up in front of him as he tipped the cup back and winced when the scalding coffee met his mouth. The moonlight shining on us made his eyes glittery black pools.

"Yes. Long one, but better. How's your shift going?"

"Really good so far. Moving fast—feels like I just walked in." He took another cautious sip of the coffee, then pulled the lid off and held it braced on one thigh.

"That's good." I looked at my hands in my lap again, trying to think of normal conversation topics. "So... do you like being a nurse?"

He chuckled a little and swallowed another sip of coffee. "Yes. I do. I'm still learning—I'm sure that won't ever stop. But I do love it. ER's fun too, though I won't complain when I get rotated out."

"You change departments?" I realized how little I knew about how nursing and the medical corps worked.

"Yeah they shuffle the deck. You get more well-rounded, and then if you want to continue education you have a sense of where you might want to stick. But ER can be draining so it's best to rotate those nurses. I've got about three months left and then they'll move me to ICU."

"Makes sense. What do you like best about nursing?"

He rolled his lips between his teeth so they disappeared, then gave me a small smile. "I'd say helping people, but that's a little simplistic. I like the challenge of it. I like triaging, so that's one thing I like about the ER. But I like the ability to help someone calm down and get through what they're dealing with. I like being the person who's reassuring and steady in the face of what's often terrifying for people." He looked down at me, and I realized my mouth was hanging open slightly.

He raised an eyebrow at my expression. "Does that sound selfish? I guess it is—wanting to be the person who's the savior, or at least part of the saving."

"No, it doesn't. I barely know you but it makes sense to me, that you would want that, and I know you're good at it."

His expression was serious now, and his eyes flicked back and forth between mine for a moment. I couldn't hold his eye contact. The air felt thick, and I couldn't look away from the curve of his jaw down to his neck.

What am I doing here?

Gabriel cleared his throat and shifted in his seat a bit. "Do you like... whatever it is you do?"

I flashed a smile. "I'm a logistician. And yes. I love it."

"I wouldn't have thought many people were that excited about logistics," he said with a joking tone.

"You're right. Fortunately for me, I am."

"Well that works out nicely if you want to stay in," he

said, then took another drink. He asked about which unit I was in, recent deployments, and I found myself chattering away, probably boring him. But he seemed engaged, asking question after question.

I talked about working with MEDEVAC pilots and the nursing teams in combat, and he talked about his short deployment when he was a second lieutenant.

"So, what do you do on the weekends?" He nudged me with his shoulder playfully.

"Not much. I usually do a long run on Saturdays, and then I just... hang out. I'm pretty boring, but I like being at home. Sundays I do church, grocery store, and meal prep. Real thrilling stuff, you know." Saying it out loud brought the stark sense my life was small. "Sometimes Ann forces me to be social," I added lamely.

"Nothing wrong with routine, as long as you bust out of it from time to time," he said, his smile bright even in the dim light.

We chatted until his phone lit up with a guitar strum alarm.

"That's me. I better get back in."

"Of course. Yeah." I nodded, not sure what to do with myself now.

"But, hey, do you want to go to a movie next week? I'm not working Friday and was going to take my sister—you should come if you're not busy."

"Your sister lives here?"

"Yeah, she's at Vanderbilt, so we try to get together when we can." He took one last drink of the coffee and tossed it in the nearby trash can.

"That's great. I'd love to live near my brother."

"Where's he?" Gabriel asked.

"He's deployed right now—Pacific. He's a Marine." I felt a warm glow of affection for my brother and a quick pang of missing him.

"Ah, I bet he gives you hell for going Army."

"Nah, he told me not to go Marines. Part of me wanted to just because he said not to, but in the end, I listened." I smiled back at Gabriel, remembering the stern warning *against* the Marines my brother had given me. I suspect he wanted it to apply to all branches of the service, but he didn't specify, and now he couldn't change his warning. "I have soccer on Friday, so I can't go. It sounds fun though."

"No problem, maybe some other time." He sounded casual, like it really didn't matter to him, and I felt a little foolish for feeling so disappointed. He stood.

I stood up too, and we wandered across the quiet street to the entrance of the ER. "Are you off next Saturday? Ann's coming over for drinks and food—I'm guessing a few others too. Just a small group—a little dinner party. You're welcome to join us."

"I should be off, yeah. Can I let you know for sure next week?"

"Of course. No pressure, or anything, at all." I clamped down on my tongue to keep it from saying more.

"Great. Can I have your number? Then I can text you and let you know." Again, totally casual, and somehow *can I get your number* felt far less irritating coming from him. We were friends, after all, and this ball of nervousness was because I was in strange territory thanks to putting myself out there—not for any other reason.

"Good idea," I said, and I rattled off my number. He texted me so I'd have his number too, and I gave him a bright smile as we said goodbye.

I walked back to my car slowly, thinking about what a nice person Gabriel was. I looked up at the bright half-moon, the brightest stars and satellites blinking at me from all directions and felt a little pulse of joy push through my veins.

~

The next week, I took on the SPO job. Toms was gone, Basto was cagey with details other than a quick overview of his expectations of me, which were both motivating and anxiety-inducing, and Talcum was pissed.

I did nothing but keep my head down all week. I'd sent a few texts back and forth with Gabriel and was pleased to see he was going to stop by that weekend. I regretted scheduling the small gathering of friends for that Saturday, wishing instead I could use the day for a long run and then a bonus day at the office, but I planned my week around attending the indoor soccer game on Friday night, a run Saturday, and the prep for the party Saturday night. I could still do some work from home, and I'd likely end up heading in on Sunday just to check in, even though Basto was not a proponent of working weekends.

I loved the responsibility. I hated the underwater, drinking from a fire hose sensation, but that was built in to any temporary fill-in job, let alone doing a field grade job as a company grade officer.

It didn't help that Talcum's passive aggression was edging toward outright aggression. I did whatever I could to avoid having to speak to him directly—I used email and scheduling, and he kept things tame when we were in group meetings. But when I had to seek him out after he blew off a meeting Thursday afternoon, I was surprised he didn't spit in my face after seeing his expression.

"What do you want?" Talcum barked the words at me. His dark hair was shaved close to his head, typical of soldiers in the division. His face was tan, he was fit, and as far as I knew, he was single. He was on the shorter side, but still taller than me, and bulky in a beefy way without seeming overpowering. If he hadn't been perpetually sneering, he might have been only a detail or two shy of handsome, but I'd never seen him in a scenario where I could properly evaluate that. Our relationship had been generally antagonistic from the word *go*.

"I just need your PowerPoint slide for the briefing tomorrow morning. I want to look over it so I know what I'm briefing." I made sure to keep my voice calm, pleasant. I breathed in slow, smooth breaths, kept my posture firm but not stiff, avoided crossing my arms or making any hand gestures.

Basically, I was placating him on every front, and when I thought about it, I was furious. At the same time, I knew that if I didn't, he'd only get more obnoxious.

"Yeah, well I'm not sure I'll have it done before I leave," he said, turning to walk away.

My voice took on a harder tone when I responded. "Captain Talcum, I'll need it before you leave."

He turned around with a sneer but stopped. He let his eyes linger at my chest as he said, "Yes ma'am," and only flicked his eyes up to meet mine before tossing a smarmy smirk my way and wandering off.

I rolled my head from side to side and drew in a long, slow breath as I walked back to my desk. I had no idea how long I'd be in the job, but it was a good reminder that there'd always be obstacles. Whether it was a jackanapes with an attitude or funding problems or not enough soldiers to fill positions, there'd always be problems as a leader.

This is good practice, I chanted to myself for the rest of the day.

~

Gabriel

I knocked on the door of a new-looking townhouse just off Tiny Town Road. It was a nice neighborhood and seemed family friendly though this row of townhouses was missing the bikes and plastic yard toys many of the others featured.

I was working to calm my breathing and chill. I hadn't seen Rae since she'd brought me coffee at the hospital, and it had been all I could do not to grab her hand or touch her leg or do *something* because dios mio, it had made me feel good she'd done that. Then there was that moment where I swear she was looking at me like she wanted me, her eyes sliding over my face, fixating on my neck. *Aye.*

I liked her, and even if we were only meant to be friends, I couldn't ignore my attraction to her. Well, I *could.* And I needed to.

I would.

How smoothly and painlessly that would go was still in question, and tonight would be a test of my will. She'd invited me to her house to hang out with her friends. I'd texted her to let her know I couldn't come until later in the evening, and so I was knocking on her door a good two hours after the gathering had started.

The door swung open and Ann greeted me. "Gabriel.

Come on in." She was in a black t-shirt and jeans, and I was relieved. I figured the evening was casual but wasn't sure. I'd worn a black button-up shirt and rolled the sleeves up my forearms since the night was unusually warm for February, and I was glad to see Ann wasn't in a dress or slacks.

"Yep, better late than never." I grinned back at her and followed her into the house. I noticed the lived-in feel immediately. Rae clearly spent time here, and I wasn't sure why I felt surprised that her house felt so welcoming and homey, but I was. I wanted to sit down and stay a while.

"You came!" I heard from the direction of what looked like the kitchen doorway. Rae smiled at me with her paralyzing, full-fledged smile, and someone took a meat tenderizer to my lungs.

"I told you I would," I said, shaking my head at her. She'd acknowledged I'd be late, said it was fine, all via text earlier this week. I walked toward her, enjoying the view of her in jeans and a short-sleeved off-white sweater that hung slightly off one shoulder, and she was moving to me—around the couch, skirting the coffee table, and *bam*.

She hit me with a full-body hug before I knew what she had planned, and without thinking, my arms wrapped around her and lifted her to her tip toes as I squeezed her. I tucked my face down and caught the smell of her shampoo —coconut, maybe? Fruity, fresh, and completely appealing.

I loosened my grip, prepared to release her altogether and ignore the feeling of loss I had now that she wasn't pressed up against me, but her hands settled just above my hips and she looked me over.

"You did. I just started to think you might not show. But that's ok. I'm glad you came." She smiled at me again, and that's when I realized her cheeks were flushed and her words were coming quickly—more quickly and yet disconnected than they usually did. Add to that her physical comfort with me—something that had never been part of our interactions before, and I shot a look to Ann, who was smirking at us from the loveseat.

"You doing all right?" I asked Rae.

"I'm good," she replied, and I felt her hands slide up my back and down to settle just above the waist of my pants. And that was nice, but like... maybe not a great idea if she didn't want me thinking of her hands sliding over my body and...

Stop.

"Wait, what is happening under here, Gabriel?" Her face held something like shock and I jumped back a bit.

"Um, what? What do you mean?" *Did I say that out loud?*

"You are solid under here. I know you work out but... wow. You're ripped," she said, her voice tinged with interest as her thumbs smoothed up my obliques over my shirt.

"All right, killer. Might want to reinstate the *internal* part of your internal monologue." Ann grabbed Rae around the shoulders and led her to the kitchen.

Let's keep the internal monologue out, yeah?

"She may or may not have had a double margarita on an empty stomach to kick off the evening and since she rarely drinks, is a bit of a truth fountain," Ann explained as they walked, and I followed. I didn't have time to dwell on her exploration of my torso, or the look of interest in her eye as she felt me up, which was for the best.

"Did you now? Just ready to party it up like it's your 21st?" I leaned my hips against the kitchen counter and folded my arms across my chest.

"No. I'll have you know I've had a crap week even

though it was an awesome week, and I finally had a second to tell Ann about it and don't believe her because she's a total pusher and I wouldn't have had anything but water before I ate if she hadn't been playing double-or-nothing bartender." Her face was stern and she shot Ann a dirty look at which her friend just laughed.

"Will you tell me about your week? I'm sorry it was crap-but-not-crap," I said, feeling a deep need to know what was going on now that I saw her demeanor shift.

Rae looked at Ann with a silent plea, her expressive light brown brows arched. Ann took a deep breath and explained. "The short version is this—Rae just got a promotion to the SPO, which means she's doing the job of a major as a captain. Not all her fellow *male* captains are happy about this. They've been spreading rumors, and yesterday after her soccer game she found that on her windshield." Ann nodded with her chin to the counter to my left, and I took the manila folder. I raised an eyebrow at Rae, and she nodded her consent for me to look.

Whatever I thought would be in the folder, it wasn't this. The first photo was an eight-by-ten glossy of a younger-looking Rae in a royal blue evening gown, her golden hair in an elaborate up do. *Miss Teen Georgia State*.

What?

The next photo was worse, and it had my heart sinking even as my pulse raced. The photo was her in a red bikini and high heels, posed with one bronzed leg bent, the other straight, her body canted just to the left so her small waist was stretched and showed off her flat abdomen. Her smile was sweet and though she had miles of skin exposed, looked less sexy and more... young, pure. Not sultry or sexualized, somehow (even with the heels), but comfortable in her skin and so... young. On the photo was scrawled *She looks like she'd do just about anything to win* in bold sharpie. I stared at the photo, then finally lifted my head to see Rae.

Her expression was pained. She swallowed. "So, I did pageants growing up..."

CHAPTER FOUR

Gabriel

"Claro."

"And I guess someone is trying to suggest that because I did pageants and there are photos of me in a bikini that I'm some sort of..." She shook her head and swallowed.

"A whore. They're insinuating, just shy of flat out stating, that you are a whore. This is obviously Talcum—I'd put money on it. You absolutely have to report this." Ann pursed her lips, then grabbed her beer by the neck of the bottle and gulped down the last few sips.

"You definitely have to report this," I said, searching Rae's eyes and waiting for her to say she'd already done it.

She just shook her head and looked at the ground.

Ann set her bottle down hard, the sound of the bottom clinking against countertop loud in the stillness of the kitchen. "Rae, this is unacceptable. Whoever did this is harassing you. You have to report it."

I knew she wasn't stupid, but she was clearly *not* on board with that suggestion.

Rae's arms were folded across her chest, and she tucked them in tighter as she spoke. "I know I'm being harassed, but honestly, there has rarely been a time in the last five years when I wasn't being harassed. This is new, and the SPO job has set me up to be in the spotlight in a new way, but I'm not going to go crying about it. What good does that do me? That shows the idiots doing it they can get under my skin by calling me names, and I won't have that. I won't be a victim."

Ann looked at the ceiling, then back at her friend. "What if that's exactly what they're counting on? This stuff escalates all the time. You know that—you've seen it with other soldiers. What if they are banking on you not reporting it?" Ann spoke the words right out of my mouth and based on the way they were both standing, rigid and near-fuming at each other, I knew they'd been around and around about this already. There'd be nothing I could say that Ann hadn't already tried.

"If someone makes a threat, I'll report that, of course. But here's the truth, and you know this just like I do," she looked at Ann, then back to me, "women in leadership are always maligned. Women in leadership who are even remotely successful, especially in the Army, are always questioned. It's why I work out six days a week so I can max my PT test every time. It's why I do whatever I can to look professional without looking *sexy* because God forbid my mascara offend someone or tip them off to my secret desires to drop to my knees and offer them sexual favors. It's why I've had moments when I've honestly considered having a breast reduction even though I barely fill out a C cup, and why I never dye my hair or wear anything other than ChapStick on my lips during work hours."

Was that really what it was like? Was it still so problematic to be a woman in the Army? "I had no idea," I said, not fully realizing I'd spoken aloud until the words sounded in the quiet room.

"Of course you wouldn't. You're a man. And you happen to work in one of the more women-friendly fields at that," Rae said with a gentle voice.

Gentle wasn't what I'd expected, but it was welcomed. It was true that nursing was a female-friendly field, and in many ways being a *male* nurse had its stigmas. People automatically assumed the nurse was going to be female, and I'd even had some men seem put off when I showed up to attend them. Fortunately I'd rarely faced any real problems.

"That must be true. Most of my commanders or bosses have been women—whether they were in hospital administration or at the hospital here, and even the professors for my nursing courses in school." The worst flack I caught was from my brothers who felt nursing was a woman's field, even though that really wasn't something they believed. They liked to give me hell for being a nurse and not a doctor, as though I chose nursing because I *couldn't* have been a doctor. They didn't understand the choice, and I had spent more than enough time trying to explain it to them.

"I get that you're sort of... inured to this. And I do get it —even looking like I do, I get it—and you know I have my own challenges," Ann said with a shoulder shrug as though she wasn't an attractive woman. True, she was sturdy—far more squarely built than petite Rae, and her light brown hair was cut short, unlike Rae's surprisingly long golden locks. She had a striking face highlighted by that shorter hairstyle, and she was certainly beautiful, especially when she smiled.

Ann continued. "But you can't sit there and wait for this to escalate. You cannot do that Rae. That's not strength."

Rae took a breath, all her focus on Ann. "I'm done talking about this. I told you my plan, and you have to live with that because it's *my* plan. *My* job. *My* reputation. Let this go. I promise I'll tell you if anything else happens, and if something does, I'll report it." She punctuated the "it" with a sharp "t" sound and then clamped her mouth shut. Her arms were crossed at her waist, her shoulders tight, and she gave Ann a hard look. Ann shook her head a little and turned to the sink.

"So... am I the last to arrive?" I changed the subject and at the same time finally registered there was no one else in the house. I surveyed the kitchen counters and saw the sink was clear of dishes, the counters wiped clean of all evidence there might have been a dinner party before I arrived. Apparently, everyone was long since gone.

Of course, we wouldn't have had the conversation we'd just had in front of a large group—at least I didn't think so. Rae was clearly a private person. But I hadn't thought about anything other than Rae between the hug, the hands, then the photos and the ensuing conversation.

"Yes. Most everyone left around 8:30. They all have early bedtimes just like I usually do," she said and gave me a self-conscious grin.

"Oh, right. Well, let me get out of your hair, then. I don't want to keep you—"

"No! You just got here." She stepped toward me and put a hand on my wrist where it was still crossed over my chest.

She was looking up at me with her bright blue eyes, a

little bloodshot and clearly exhausted. Her lips were a dusty pink with a pronounced cupid's bow shaping her lush top lip. Her long blonde hair hung loose down her back with a few strands draped over her shoulder and dangling down to her rib cage

It's so long.

I'd only seen it down one other time. Otherwise, it was up—up in a bun in uniform, or in a ponytail when she worked out, or in the messy pile she'd worn it in when she came to the ER that first time. Her cheeks were still pinked, but she wasn't flushed like she was earlier.

Dios mio, this woman was irrepressibly gorgeous.

"I don't want to keep you up past your bedtime," I said, trying to keep the tightness I felt in my chest out of my voice. If she'd stop touching me, maybe every cell in my body would stop trying to memorize the feeling of her skin touching mine.

"I'll stay up for you. Stay a little while, and we can talk since I know you probably stay up really late while you're on the graveyard shift." She turned to a cabinet to my left and swung it open. "Can I get you a drink? Water? Beer?"

"Water's fine, thanks." Something about her saying she'd stay up for me, thinking of my routine while I worked nights, made stomach clench.

"Did you already eat? We have some stuff left I can rustle up—"

"No, please. I'm fine. I had dinner earlier since I knew I'd be late." And I'd planned to come, see her, and then leave before I could make a fool of myself by drooling all over her. She rose to her tiptoes to reach a glass. In an effort to keep my eyes off her while she stretched up next to me, I kept my eyes glued to the floor, but they snagged on her pants curving around shapely calves... *stop*.

"I'm going to head out, Rae. I'm wiped," Ann said as she dried her hands on a dish towel. My heartbeat kicked up a tick.

"Thank you so much for helping me tonight. It was great." Rae hugged Ann, then as Rae filled my water glass, Ann grabbed her keys.

"Gabriel, good to see you," Ann said, then extended a hand to me. We shook hands and then she walked to the door.

"Ann lives right next door—her commute will be pretty short," Rae explained as she handed me a glass of water and walked back into the living room with a glass of her own. She set hers down on a coaster on the worn wood table in front of the couch and then plopped down into one of the corners. I sat down at the opposite end as the door shut behind Ann in the entryway.

"Nice. Did you guys know each other before moving in?"

"We did, actually. Met when we in-processed and then found out we'd been living next to each other for weeks but had never actually seen each other at home. Pretty crazy." Rae sipped her water and set it down. Then she leaned back against the corner of the couch, flanked by pillows, and stretched out her legs to rest on the coffee table.

I wasn't sure what to do with myself. She seemed tired —ready for bed. I felt awkward and painfully aware of everything she did as much as she seemed oblivious to me and completely at home.

Of course, that made sense. She *was* at home, and she should be, in her own home.

My thoughts had turned inane. As I shifted on the couch, crossed one leg over my knee at the ankle, I searched my mind for what I could talk to her about. All I wanted to do was convince her she needed to report that photo, but I knew she'd shut that door, and I didn't want to make her mad.

"So, the party was a success?"

"It was. It wasn't a party, but it was a success. I *never* do social things. I'm fairly socially inept because I'm more of an introvert, and that's probably partly because I actually *am* an introvert and partly because I've trained myself not to be too overtly social because I've had some misunderstandings come from that." She splayed out her hand in front of her and looked at it—her finger nails were bright blue, I noticed with a small shock. They'd been neat, filed, and bare every other time I'd seen her.

"Misunderstandings?"

"You know..." She didn't look at me.

"Do I?"

"Yeah, misunderstandings, like I'm talking to you and being friendly, and then all of a sudden you think I'm coming on to you." She didn't move her head but looked up at me through her brown lashes.

"Ah. Yes. I've experienced that more than once. In fact I seem to recall that happening between me and a former patient of mine..."

Rae gasped and the hand she'd been inspecting dropped with a thunk on the couch. Her eyes were wide. "Oh no. I totally did that to you." She was genuinely shocked at the realization, and seeing her so discombobulated by it had me chuckling softly and shaking my head.

"Yes you did, ma'am. Classic Gabriel-being-friendly-and-the-cute-blonde-captain-thinks-he's-coming-on-to-her situation. I can't help it that I'm outgoing, charismatic, and so painfully good-looking as to elicit that kind of hope from anyone I speak with."

Now her mouth was open, her body frozen as she looked at me. Her smile grew slowly and she nodded silently, then shook her head. I wished she'd speak. Then she got a gleam in her eye.

"Why yes. That's exactly it." Her voice was silken and seductive now. I swallowed and puffed out a breath. "That's exactly what it was. It was your..." she let her eyes slide over me and I felt my stomach drop. "Charisma. Your *painful* good looks." Her eyes were lit with mischief, and she bit her full bottom lip. I stifled a groan with a cough.

"Well ok, maybe I was exaggerating." I coughed again, now choking on nothing. After I coughed yet again, Rae jumped up from her seat and patted me on the back twice. She sat down next to me, her hand now on my shoulder as I took a sip of water, and then cleared my throat.

"Sorry, I didn't mean to be that dramatic," I said with chagrin.

"You ok?" she asked, her hand squeezing my shoulder and then dropping to her lap.

"Yep. I'm good."

"Well I *am* sorry for assuming you were hitting on me. I know I apologized, but I can't believe I didn't register that I'd done the same thing to you. But now you get why I'm a little stand-offish until I know someone." She exhaled and her shoulders slumped slightly. "I know I come off cold, or at least sort of... insistently polite and not much more. I'm sure some people assume I've got an attitude problem. But in my experience that's preferable to some of the alternatives, so... that's how I am." She looked down at her hands, now twisted together in her lap.

Without overthinking it, I put my hand over hers, my wrist resting on her thigh. "I think if it works for you, that's great. You're the only one who can decide what you're comfortable with, and you know what feels right to you."

"I know that. It's a choice I've made. I plan to be in a long time, and if I'm going to be, I have to do what makes sense for my career, and that doesn't always mean being the most social. It's not that I can't be, it's just that boundaries are important." She still seemed bothered by the conversation, but her fingers weren't tied up in front of her anymore.

"You planning to retire?" I asked.

"Absolutely. After I make O6."

"Really? So not just planning on twenty and done, huh? Going for the full-bird." Most officers retired as lieutenant colonels, or even majors, after twenty years. To stay in and work toward being an O6, a colonel, was not an un-lofty goal. Like anything, the longer you stayed in, the harder you had to work, the more you had to give... or so I'd gathered. It was a little different in nursing, though not altogether unlike the other branches of the Army.

"I guess more like twenty-five. Who knows. Maybe I'll be a general." Her voice held some kind of challenge in it, but I couldn't tell what it was exactly. She sat up straight and watched me through squinting eyes.

"I love it. I can totally see you as a general, and I've only seen you in uniform at the commissary—I've never seen you at work. I suspect you're kind of a badass."

Her right eyebrow raised in question, and a small smile tilted at the corners of her lips. "Why do you think that?"

"Are you kidding? First of all, I know you were doing muscle-ups when you passed out, and that you dealt with that pain with calm despite what you may think. I also know you push yourself physically every chance you get. But I also suspect that the fact that you're doing a major's job as a captain, not even a promotable captain yet, speaks to your badassery at work."

My smile grew as I watched the mixture of confusion and pride pass over her face. She looked like she wanted to speak, but I kept talking. "Also, despite your insistence that you're cold, you're a nice person. I'm sorry to break this to you but once a person does speak to you, you're kind of..." I trailed off because I was going to say *magnetic. Engrossing. Mesmerizing.*

But that could be awkward.

"I'm kind of..." she prompted.

"Well, you're nice. Very polite. You're not cold. You're warm."

Her cheeks tinged a soft pink like the thought of being warm was embarrassing to her. She was totally un-phased by my calling her a badass, and yet my telling her she wasn't coming off as cold as she thought embarrassed her.

"Well... thanks."

"Would you really want to be a general?" It was certainly no goal of mine, but my route through the years ahead in the Army would be less traditional as a nurse.

"My impression of what general officers do is limited to them spending time in DC, getting flown around in heli-copters to come visit live-fires and ranges for photo-ops, and then commanding generals of posts, which sounds less than thrilling. But I don't know. I don't think I have the pedigree for it, for one."

"Not a West Pointer, then? I would have thought maybe you had attended the Academy."

"Really? No way. Not that I wouldn't have wanted to, but I didn't have the connections for my application, and I had a decent scholarship at UGA from pageants. I did ROTC at the University of Georgia."

"I'm a Texas man myself. Are you from Georgia?"

"Yes. A little backwoods town up near Dahlonega where they do the mountain phase of Ranger school, actually."

"You don't have an accent at all though." I never would have guessed she was a southern girl. I remembered *Miss Georgia Teen* or whatever, but that hadn't registered in the context of both the shock that Rae did pageants and that she was getting harassed.

"I try not to. You don't either," she said and nodded toward me.

"True. It comes out at home, or when I talk to my mom. But a lot of times we speak Spanish anyway, so it's more of a Spanglish accent, I guess."

"Does your whole family speak Spanish?" She was sitting back on her side of the couch now, facing me with her legs curled up in front of her, her head resting to the side on the back of the couch. Her blue eyes were lit with the light from the lamp behind the couch, her golden hair soft and glowing as it snaked over her shoulder and pooled somewhere behind her legs out of sight. She looked sleepy and calm and her voice was smooth and smoky with exhaustion from her day.

"Gabriel?" My name on her lips had a surprisingly direct effect on my body, and I sat up straighter, blinking at her.

"What?"

"I asked you if your family speaks Spanish, but you spaced out on me."

Did I?

"Sorry. I was just thinking about how comfortable you look here. Obviously because it's your house, but I like it. It's warm and cozy and it feels lived-in in a nice way." I ran my hand along the back of the couch toward her and patted the back of the cushion. She was still about eight inches from me.

"Thanks. I do spend a lot of time here. Between not being super social, and feeling like I work a ton, I want to come home and stay home when I get here. Going out is nice, but I want to feel settled when I get back, you know?"

"I do. That's something my mom was always so good at. She and my dad both worked and we moved around our town a handful of times. She made us feel stable each time, even when we had to change schools because our new house was in a different district. I've heard a lot of Army families get good at that since they're moving around all the time. I hope I can do that for my kids eventually."

Rae's face darkened, but with a blink, the look was gone. "You come from a big family?" she asked.

"Pretty big, I guess. I'm the fourth son, and then Vik is my little sister, younger by seven years. My grandma lived with us for most of my childhood so there were eight of us at home most of the time."

"Yeah, that's big. It was just me and my brother, and then my mom." She eyed my hand on the back of the couch, and once I realized that was where she was looking, that same hand ached with the desire to reach out and touch her —to run my fingers through her glinting hair from the top of her head to wherever it ended.

"What about your dad?" I asked, my voice a bit rough.

"He and my mom divorced when I was three and my brother was eight. My mom had given up her plans to be a nurse, actually," she smiled at me, "so we mostly lived off child support from him, and alimony I guess. Then I got into pageants and that helped out when I won. But she never did figure out how to get back to school, and then she met her husband Jerry, who she married my sophomore year of college. He's wealthy so she just plays tennis and stuff, seems happy enough." She said all of this with an edge to her voice that sounded like disappointment.

"You wish she would have gone back to school?" I asked.

"I just hate that she had to give up her dream for my dad, and then never got back to it. I feel like she lost herself, and then when Heath and I got older, she poured every bit of attention she had into us. That gave us a lot of opportunities, but I hate that she had nothing for herself. I hate that her compromise for my father made her give up everything, and he gave up nothing." She rolled her lips between her teeth like she had to in order to stop talking.

"If that's what happened, then that *is* sad."

"I think it happens before women even realize it's happening. Seeing that, and seeing her just sort of... I don't know, surrender. Give everything up all over again once I was gone and she *could* have done something, only to become a tennis trophy wife, just..." Her shoulders were hunched and she was clutching her hands around her knees, holding them tight to her. "Sorry. I don't mean to sound so critical of her. I just know what it's like to—whatever. The point is, we were a small little family growing up."

"That's not what you were going to say—what do you mean 'you know what it's like?'" What could that mean? This was something Rae had strong feelings about based on how she railed on her mom, and then clearly felt guilty for it.

"Nothing. But I can tell you that nothing is going to keep me from my career goals." She looked at me, her blue eyes challenging mine, but I knew better than to ask anything else.

"Makes sense. Nor should anything keep you from them," I said, both to appease her and because this was a driven and ambitious woman who was deeply invested in her work. Her shoulders relaxed, and she let all but her two index fingers go, so only the two fingers were hooked together around her knees.

We sat quietly for a few minutes, just studying each other. Rae's face was unreadable, but I was discovering that was true about half the time. It was no hardship for me to look at her, so I kept at it. I wanted to know more about her—everything—but I couldn't bring myself to break the comfortable silence that had settled between us.

Rae did it for me.

"You know, you really are painfully good-looking," she said in that smoky-tired voice as her eyes swept from my hair, over my face and lips, down my neck and the rest of me. It felt like she was sliding her hand along with her gaze, and goose bumps prickled my skin.

"Is that so?" I asked, amazed my voice didn't tremble and reveal the nervous energy coursing through me.

"Yes," she said just slightly above a whisper. Then her hand came up and the pads of her fingers swept over my knuckles at the back of the couch. Her fingers traced up and down the peak and valley of each finger, leaving tingling nerve-endings in their wake.

I steadied my breathing though I could feel and see my chest rising and falling, the blood no doubt pumping furiously through the four chambers in my heart just to keep oxygen running to my brain. The sensation of her simple touch on my hand snaked its way up my arm and filtered through my body.

If I made it out of here without kissing her, I'd reward myself somehow.

A high five.

A new car.

A trip to Disney World.

Something.

She was still tracing my knuckles, then letting one finger slide up and outline each of mine.

When she bit her lip, like she was thinking of kissing me too, a small part of my willpower died and I happily buried it, then broke the shovel in half and tossed it in a nearby river. Suddenly it felt like *not* kissing her was the wrong answer. She was sending me every signal that she wanted to be kissed—wasn't she?

She ran her hands over her knees and down her shins, then gave me a gentle smile. She tucked her hair behind her ear, and I resisted the urge to look down at my chest and see if my heart really was pounding out of my rib cage. All I could hear was the rush of blood in my ears. All I could feel was the intoxicating heat that shimmered between us—a heat that appeared both because of her general existence and also because she'd started the conversation.

Was this it? Was she telling me she wanted to be more than friends?

"It's too bad." Her words cut through the pounding in my ears.

"What is?"

"That you're an Army nurse."

My heart stuttered and sank as my hackles rose. *What?* I reared back from her even though she was still sitting across the couch, no longer touching me.

"What?" Amazingly, my voice didn't sound as offended as I felt, but *where did that come from?*

"Oh, no." She shook her head at me, her face serious and eyes wide. She put a hand on my wrist—that lovely small hand—and squeezed my arm. "I don't mean that you're a nurse like being a nurse is anything but awesome. I mean that you're a nurse... in the Army."

Stunned, I watched her, looking for any sign of dishonesty. Rae had been nothing but forthright with me, and it seemed like she was being honest now, but this was a hot button for me.

Along with my brothers, my college girlfriend constantly made digs at me for choosing nursing. I got so sick of it and finally confronted her, and when she said, "No, I think it's great," I could see her lie, the false smile in her lips pressed together, her cheeks blooming red in surprise that I'd asked straight out.

"Truly, Gabriel, I think it's amazing you're a nurse, and I happen to know, at least in terms of bedside manner for difficult patients, you're an excellent one. I would never want you to think otherwise."

"Ok." My voice was rough and my cheeks heated a little in embarrassment. I had pride in my job and was so far from ashamed by what I did, but I still felt *new*. I still felt like sometimes I had to justify what I did—to my family, to soldiers in traditional units, to women I dated (or wanted to date).

"Really?"

"Yes, it's fine."

"I can tell it's not. My guess is you've had someone be a jerk about you being a nurse in the past, and I'm sorry for that. It doesn't make sense to me, and that's not how I feel. I'm sorry if my saying that made you think I don't respect your job, because I absolutely do."

She was beseeching me to believe her, her soft hand on my arm gripping me to emphasize her sincerity. Her blue eyes pleaded with me, her voice soft and filled with genuine concern.

It's too bad, indeed.

"I should go, Rae. I'm fine. But you're tired, and I should get home." I stood up and grabbed my glass.

"Ok." She followed me to the kitchen and took the glass from me, set it in the sink.

I moved toward the hallway and she followed me to the door.

"Thanks for coming."

"Thanks for letting me swing by so late." I could hear the hollow sound of my voice but was too tired to bother trying to sound like anything else.

She looked down and toed a spot on the laminate flooring of the entryway, then looked back up at me.

"Could we hug, or something?" Her hands were clasped behind her back, and her furrowed brow announced she was very much still concerned. She looked up at me tentatively, clearly shy about asking for the contact, for the resolution.

Hell, she didn't need to ask me twice. I might have been a little disgruntled, but I believed her, and I wasn't an idiot. I wasn't about to pass up that invitation.

I stepped to her and wrapped my arms around her, my hands brushing against the soft sweater fitted to her warm back, pulling her to me. Her hands slid along my ribs and pressed against my back.

She rested her head on my chest, hugging me with her whole body, and I shut my eyes. I let myself breathe in the sweet, clean scent of her shampoo. I let myself relish the moment her body relaxed against mine, and I pulled her closer.

Her body fit mine so perfectly, her head felt so good

resting against me, and her warmth and concern for me was so appealing, I knew I was doomed. With a big sigh, I pulled back before she heard my heart pounding under her ear, let my hands drop to my sides, and gave her as casual a smile as I could summon.

"I'll see you soon, Rae. Have a good weekend."

CHAPTER FIVE

Rae

I HADN'T SEEN or heard from Gabriel in six days. We'd chatted aimlessly back and forth a few times in the wake of what I had named *the awkward apology hug incident*, but then it slowed and stopped.

Six days of silence was a record for us. It was unusual, and it was a clear sign he was upset with me.

Wasn't it?

Like a genius, in order to talk myself out of launching my body across the couch and kissing him the way I'd wanted to that night—the way I wanted to basically every time I even thought about those plush, perfect, smiling lips —I reminded myself he was in the Army, on the *absolutely-no-can-do* list of people to potentially date.

But instead, I'd made the conversation horribly uncomfortable by accidentally saying it was too bad he was a nurse. Like being a nurse was some kind of issue and not just a totally amazing profession for someone to choose. I could see the hurt in his eyes and was both infuriated at myself for miscommunicating and irate with whoever had made him feel less than amazing about being a nurse in his past.

Because someone had, that was for sure.

We'd hugged, and though it was a real hug—more real than I'd anticipated, and longer, too—we'd parted on an awkward note. It was Friday, and he'd left my house before midnight on Saturday two weekends before.

I didn't realize how much I enjoyed his texts until there was a drought of them. I was desperate to hear from him but also so busy that until Friday morning, I didn't realize it *had* been that long. I was also annoyed at myself for missing his text messages so much—we weren't dating. He was my friend. I was not dependent on him for... anything.

Before I walked in to my morning meeting with LTC Basto, I sent Gabriel a text. He probably wouldn't have gone to bed yet, so maybe I'd catch him.

Me: *Hey, long lost friend. Hope your shift went well last night.*

So brilliant, I knew. But I couldn't figure out what else to say. I had nothing else to say except the desire to apologize yet again and try to clarify that I thought being a nurse was awesome, and I thought *he* was awesome, not to mention extremely attractive, but I couldn't date him. Couldn't. Wouldn't.

Would. Not.

We'd even talked about the reason why—rooted in my mother and reiterated by my marriage to Brad (though we hadn't gone there, nor did I look forward to that conversation if I did ever tell him about my award-winningly idiotic first marriage), I was no longer under the impression that compromising was possible if I wanted a career.

So I wasn't going to.

And someone like Gabriel, with his Army career ahead of him, and his Hispanic background and large family full of familial expectations, was not going to compromise *his* goals either.

Friends it was, then.

Just before I walked into my meeting, my screen lit up.

Gabriel: *Am I long lost? I knew where I was all along. Were you lost?*

I smiled and shoved the phone in my pocket.

I pulled myself out of the car and dragged into the house, dropping my gym bag full of sweaty clothes, my planner that held every piece of information I needed to remember, and my phone, to the couch, where I collapsed.

The day had been long, following a longer few weeks. My meeting with LTC Basto was good, although I was being demoted.

Well, not really, but Major Toms was coming back. In the end, that was good news. Whatever had happened was apparently over, and I could step back into my old job as an assistant to the SPO rather than *the*. I was relieved I didn't have to interact with Talcum so directly anymore—we'd have someone else facilitating meetings and generally speaking, we could avoid each other (or, I could avoid him).

I was more than pleased by the feedback I'd gotten about my job performance. It was exactly what I expected, and I felt more relief than anything, though there was some small disappointment. A part of me had hoped to keep the job long enough to actually *do* something, when in reality all I'd done was field a *ton* of emails, attend about two additional meetings a day, and get dirty looks from Talcum when he thought I wasn't noticing.

That guy.

He was a mercenary kind of man, and I knew it because I'd heard how he'd thrown a supposed friend under the bus during their platoon leader time years back, and that pattern had continued. He was doing well for himself, and somehow he was generally well-liked from what I could see, but he certainly couldn't share victories or celebrate other people for doing well. It was counter to the community feel that I liked best about the Army, and yet I'd come to expect it from him.

But now? Now he was starting to give me the creeps. If he was the person who put that folder on my car, then he was digging pretty deep into my personal life. It wasn't like I was ashamed of my pageant time—I'd defend the merits of pageants 'til I was blue in the face and had done exactly that a time or two in college—but it took some work to find that information. Paired with the dirty looks and the fact that I'd heard him making comments about me two more times since the episode weeks ago when he suggested I was on my knees for LTC Basto, things were not looking good.

My taking Toms' job seemed to have increased his frustration. The tension rolling off him at any given time was repellent to me, and so I continued the trend of avoiding him whenever possible.

At PT that past Monday, I thought he was going to scream. Truly, I thought he might yell in my face. Lieutenant Sala was in charge of PT for the battalion staff that day, and he'd planned sprints and walking lunges. It was brutal.

But I happened to love running, did it often, and made a point to push myself. I pushed, and pushed, and pushed, just to the point I might puke, and ultimately beat Talcum every time. It was luck he was on the bulkier side or he likely would have been able to beat me, but he wasn't quick, and I smoked him.

More than once.

His face was candy apple red by the time the last round ended. We'd done them in groups of six at a time, and I'd won every group I'd been in except the one Lt. Sala himself was in. The fact that Talcum couldn't beat me had gotten under his skin.

"She's smaller. It's easier when you're small," he said, then spat to the side, still walking off the exertion with his hands on his hips.

"That, or she's faster than you, sir," Sala said good naturedly, then pointedly walked to check on Sergeant Erhalt when he saw the fury on Talcum's face.

I wasn't aware a person's entire head could turn red, but now I could confirm. I bent and wiped my face on my PT shirt, then straightened and took a breath, twisting at the waist to loosen up. When I scanned the area, I saw Talcum, his head a ripe tomato, giving me the angriest look I'd ever seen.

It wasn't a shock he was competitive, but it didn't make sense—I'd done nothing to him, and no one was directly comparing us except MAJ Toms, and LTC Basto, and that was only for professional assessments. This meant nothing.

Or, it meant nothing to me.

I debated reporting him since he seemed to be growing more pointedly disgruntled but could only see that going south, and fast. It'd be a headache for everyone, and most of all me. Now that I wasn't his boss, I was less concerned.

He'd had a chip on his shoulder about that, and now that was a non-issue. Case closed.

I closed my eyes for a moment and breathed deep. I could smell the clean linen-scented candle that sat in the entryway from here. I wasn't usually big on artificial fragrances, but I loved something fresh when I walked through the door.

I hadn't texted Gabriel back because after my meeting, I was in a rush to get things prepped to hand back over to Major Toms. I'd left work and gone straight to my soccer game and finally made it home.

As though he knew I was thinking about him, my phone lit up on my chest.

Gabriel: *So you text me about being lost, but when I respond, you're nowhere to be found. What is this madness? I've gone to bed and am now about to head to work and nothing from you. Are you, in fact, lost?*

Me: *Simmer down there, nurse Gabriel. I just had a stupid-long day and am currently reconsidering my weekend plans so I can appropriately hibernate tomorrow.*

Gabriel: *She lives!*

Gabriel: *Sorry about the long day though. Not ideal.*

Me: *Such is the glamorous life I lead.*

Gabriel: *Don't hibernate.*

Me: *I'm not going to. I'm going to trek to Trader Joe's and then I'm meeting Ann for dinner.*

Gabriel: *I've never understood the fascination with Trader Joe's.*

Me: *Blasphemy.*

Gabriel: *No, just truth. That's what you'll get from me, Captain.*

Me: *You just haven't found the right person to take you yet. You need an expert.*

Gabriel: *Ah, the height of arrogance. I'm not sure I can enjoy something like that. You think you're the right person?*

Me: *I will make it painless for you, I promise. You might even enjoy it.*

Gabriel: ...

Me: ?

Gabriel: *Are we still talking about Trader Joe's?*

This was how it always went with him. We'd chat a bit, make jokes, and end in some kind of innuendo. He had no problem joking with me, and it was usually in the context that I was seducing him when really I was thinking about things like eating take out food or going to the grocery store.

Still, I kind of loved it.

I'd never had that kind of relationship with a man—a friendship with a little flirting that was fun. Just *fun* and made me laugh.

In the end, we made plans to have dinner on Sunday before he started his shift. Despite the little explosion of nerves I had before I walked into my favorite Mexican place, we had fun. It was friendly and light, and there wasn't any weirdness.

Well, maybe there was a little, in that I felt a little pang in my belly anytime he let loose one of his boisterous laughs, or when he slipped into rapid-fire Spanish speaking to the waiter or the owner. But I buried that, way down deep, and enjoyed the friend I had in him.

We messaged each other constantly after that, the unmentioned rift between us fully repaired with the dinner on neutral territory, even though he claimed to be offended by my choice of Mexican restaurant. In the small area around Fort Campbell, there were probably twenty different Mexican restaurants, each with its own twist on the Tennessean version of Mexican food. Gabriel and I had different favorite places and spent a good quarter of our dinner squabbling about how I could like El Bajio when it was clearly inferior to his favorite.

It sounded stupid when I reflected later, but I'd enjoyed it—the simplicity of the joking. Maybe it was because the only jokes I'd heard at work lately were muffled behind hands at someone's expense or just rumors.

By the next Friday's end, I was lying on my couch again, feeling the weight of another week having passed in a flash, though this time with notably less weighty stress since I wasn't doing someone else's job.

Gabriel: *Come to Nashville with me tomorrow. I'm taking Vik out for her 21st and I need another grown up there to oversee the kids.*

Me: *Hmm...*

Gabriel: *They need someone to keep them out of trouble.*

Me: *You're making this sound* super *fun.*

Gabriel: *Vik's fine, and her friends aren't bad. Plus she told me to bring you, and since I like to keep the women in my life happy, I told her I'd ask.*

My smile faltered at this. *Women in his life?* That didn't sit right. Yes, he was talking about his sister, but I suddenly got the sense that maybe there *were* women in his life. The mere thought of him taking someone out made my neck itch.

Me: *Lots of women in your life, then? Busy man.*

I wasn't jealous, but it sounded so... flippant. Was he out dating women left and right? He was certainly good looking enough. Stable job, practical car, the whole gorgeous Latino man thing... he'd likely been beating them away with sticks.

Or... not.

I felt foolish. We weren't dating, but I felt naïve or silly for not having a dating life of my own—for not having even an interest in dating anyone.

And yet, I also knew my own mind. I knew *why* I didn't date much, and why I wasn't dating him, as appealing as he sometimes seemed.

Gabriel: *Yes, always busy. They're a demanding group.*

Ok, this had gotten weird. Gabriel didn't strike me as a player, or even one to talk about his conquests. Let's not worry about the fact that I was starting to feel genuinely irritated by the conversation.

Me: *Perhaps you should take one of them—two birds, one stone?*

The little ellipsis popped up to show he was typing, and I tossed my phone down and walked to the kitchen to reheat some chicken to put on my salad for dinner. I saw the screen light up and walked back to it after pressing *start* on the microwave.

Gabriel: *Somehow I doubt Vik would appreciate my mom and grandma being at her 21st.*

I let out a begrudging laugh and found myself smiling as I typed back.

Me: *Have you asked? She is the baby of the family—it might be a parental right to attend such an event.*

Gabriel: *Well good thing for Vik, they're in Texas. Plus I'm not sure I want them there either—Mom can get a little wild when tequila's involved.*

Me: *Really?*

Gabriel: *She can drink most men under the table, as long as it's tequila.*

Me: *Tequila is my drink of choice too, but I'll make a note to never challenge your mom to a drink-off.*

Gabriel: *Wise choice. Someday my older brothers will*

learn this. I learned by observing long before I made my own challenge.

Me: *Wise man. So, where are we going?*

~

I did hibernate, at least for me, and woke up after twelve solid hours of sleep. I'd been working long hours and not sleeping well, and the fact that I had less responsibility, and hopefully less interaction with bitter coworkers, was clearly a relief on more than one level. I took a long run, and then laid around watching *Modern Family* on Netflix until it was time to get ready.

Gabriel was picking me up at five so we could drive down together, meet his sister, have dinner, and then head to the club.

Heading to the club. Not on my usual agenda for the weekend, but I did enjoy a night out, and I felt like celebrating—a job well done as interim SPO, the end of a long week, and hopefully the end to Talcum's passive-aggressive hallway chit chat, among other things.

I was sure we'd go to a honkytonk bar that called for boots and jeans, but when I asked Gabriel, he said we were going to a place with salsa night and that Vik and her friends would likely wear dresses. I got the impression he was warning me, like I might not have a dress, or that I'd feel out of place if I showed up in jeans and sneakers. I realized he hadn't seen me in much else—only workout clothes, or jeans and various shirts, and then in uniform.

He must have forgotten I spent the majority of my high school years wearing evening gowns and high heels on stage in front of hundreds of people. Or maybe he had no idea— the photos he'd seen didn't hint at just how much time I'd spent doing pageants, how many hours of dance lessons and rehearsals, and interviewing I'd done. He had no idea I'd placed in the top three of every pageant I ever entered, and that in many ways I felt just as comfortable in high heels as I did my combat boots.

Ok. No. That was a total lie. Combat boots were about a thousand percent more comfortable than even the most comfortable pair of heels, but still. I could rock some stilettos when needed, and I planned to do that tonight.

Maybe there was some part of me that wanted Gabriel to see me as more than a friend. After the texts yesterday, I felt that unwelcomed irritation at the mention of other women climbing my ribs. I felt unsettled.

He'd made clear he wasn't interested in me in the same way I was maybe becoming interested in him—I was too blonde, or *white*, and I couldn't blame him for wanting to please his family and marry someone his family would approve of. And again, he wasn't an option, and we were just friends, so it didn't matter.

But the fact that he'd warned me about his sister wearing a dress, trying to clue me in without saying something specific about how I would probably want to too, had me wanting to prove something. He'd seen me at my worst in the ER, all heaving and sweaty after my run weeks ago, and then out of it and tipsy after the party was over and my lips were chapped from dehydration and drinking too much.

I wanted to look *really* good. I wanted him to *know* I could look good. I wanted to *feel* good. I rarely went on dates (read: never), and when I did, they were typically casual coffee dates that rarely led to a second date. I didn't remember the last time I'd gotten dressed up.

So tonight, I did. I curled my long hair in loose waves

and pulled the sides back so my neck was exposed and my hair spilled down my back. I wore a black dress with a wide, low V-neck and cap sleeves that just barely covered my shoulders. It fit my body and was fitted right down to my thighs, landing just above my knee. There was a band of sheer black material about an inch and a half wide that wrapped around my waist and two around my thighs giving it a more provocative feel without actually revealing anything except my upper abs and some leg. Despite the form-fitting element, I knew I could be comfortable if anyone wanted to hit the dance floor and even though the see-through bands around my legs were sheer, I could still comfortably sit without feeling like I was putting on a show.

I wore high-heeled black sandals that had straps that crossed at my ankle and buckled at mid-calf. Now that I was dressed up, and even wore eyeliner and shadow and mascara—something I rarely did anymore—I was ready. I heard the doorbell ring as I glossed my lips and grabbed my small, bright red clutch and my phone.

I swung the door open, feeling a little breathless, and whatever breath I had left whooshed out of me when I saw Gabriel. He was standing there in black slacks and a dark green button-up shirt with the first two buttons open, which highlighted his gorgeous brown neck and just a hint of his chest. His hair was styled and looked conveniently careless and glossy black.

But his face? His face looked almost offended.

"Uhhh... You ok?" I think the "uh" sounded like more of a groan, both because he looked particularly attractive and I felt a dread crawl up the back of my calves and tuck into my lower back. Why was he looking at me with that... horrified look?

He just kept staring. His brow was wrinkled, his thick

eyebrows practically glued together in the middle thanks to the sharp look of consternation. His lips (still gorgeous) were slightly parted, like he wanted to speak, but wouldn't, or couldn't. One hand hung by his side, the other one was lowered slightly from his knock on the door but was halted.

He was frozen. His eyes flitted around my body, taking me in—heels, hips, chest, shoulders, neck, lips, ears, hair, and finally my eyes.

He looked genuinely and deeply disturbed, and he still wasn't speaking.

"Gabriel?"

Nothing. His eyes kept searching me, and I ran my hands over my belly to settle myself. He was completely dazed. I stepped forward, tilting my head up to snag his eyes. I set my hand on his forearm, which was surprisingly warm.

He jerked, blinked a few times, and his focus came to my eyes.

"What's wrong?"

"Wrong?" His Adam's apple bobbed as he swallowed.

"Yes. Wrong. You look like someone murdered your cat." I couldn't hide my smile from growing, though I tried. Was he really this confused by me in a dress?

"No cats. I, uh... I don't like cats, much." He sounded winded and thrown.

"Oh, no? Well we'll address that later. For now, can you tell me what's wrong?" I was smiling full-fledged now as his eyes darted over me, taking me in again.

He cleared his throat, licked his lips, and looked down at his feet for a few seconds. Then he leveled me with his gaze. "You are absolutely and painfully beautiful, Rae. I feel physically winded when I look at you."

Uhhhhh.

That was not what I'd expected him to say. Maybe he'd fumble a little bit, trip over a word or two, and that'd be that. Maybe he'd comment on never seeing me in a dress before. But this?

This was awful.

He was looking at me with a kind of hopeful reverence combined with a confusing dose of hunger I couldn't shelve. I couldn't tuck it away to think about later—it was confronting. In my face.

I forced a laugh and snatched my hand back from his arm. "Thanks. You look great, too."

"I... you... really. I am reconsidering the desire to go with you tonight." He still looked troubled, and my stomach sank to my toes.

"Why?" My fingers twisted together with my clutch, and I held my breath.

"This is going to be hell," Gabriel said, and then leaned in to kiss my cheek.

It felt like he was moving in slow motion. As his smooth jaw brushed against mine, his soft lips kissed the hollow of my cheek and lingered there. I breathed in and my eyes fluttered closed for just a second as I savored the rich scent of his cologne, the faint tinge of mint chasing after him as he moved away.

"So glad you're excited," I said as I shut my door.

"It's not me I'm worried about. I'm going to be beating the men away with sticks," he said, scowling at me as we walked down the short path to his car.

"I'm not your sister, Gabriel. You don't have to beat them away for me. I'm actually pretty adept at that," I said, trying to get a rise out of him.

"Trust me, I know," he mumbled as he thumped down into his seat and pulled the door shut.

I tucked my clutch next to me and surveyed his car. It was clean, clutter free, but definitely well-worn.

"Are you on beat-them-away-with-sticks duty for Victoria? If you and she share genes, I'm guessing that's a chore," I said, trying to lighten the mood.

He flashed his eyebrows at me, and then smirked. "You think?"

CHAPTER SIX

Gabriel

I DON'T KNOW why it was such a surprise to see her in a dress, but it was.

Holy hell, was it.

I was feeling excited to spend time with my friend after spending almost a week without contact and reminding myself that we *were* just friends, and that was all we'd ever be. She'd made that clear *again* last time we were together (granted, it was on the heels of a confusingly charged moment during which I thought she might kiss me, but whatever. Point taken).

So I'd made a point to look good but had been focusing on my sister's night—made reservations at a restaurant for all of us, then got things arranged at the club. I wasn't a big club guy but Vik loved to dance, and *loved* to salsa, so this was her requested party.

But when I opened the door to Rae in that dress, a

confusing mix of emotions swirled around me, and I couldn't think of anything to say except *why*. I hadn't actually said it, thank God, but all I could think was *why is this woman torturing me?*

Once I made it to the car I shook that off—her clothing choices weren't about *me*, she hadn't gotten dressed up for *me*, and me thinking that made me an arrogant jerk.

We were about halfway to Nashville and I was doing my best to keep my eyes on the road and not get distracted by her bare knees, which rested against each other right next to my gear shift.

If I'd ever wanted to touch something more, I didn't remember what it was. Her skin was light but still slightly tan—I guess from running outside in the fairer months. It looked smooth and firm, and I could imagine myself running my hand down her shin—

"Don't you think?" Rae's voice cut through my daydream.

Probably for the best, that.

"Think about what? Sorry I was so focused on the road..."

"I was saying I think the early twenties are great years, but it's a time when most people do stupid stuff." She was sitting in her seat at an angle so her legs were closest to the center console, and she was leaning back, part on her seat, part on the door, so she could see me fully. She did this whenever we sat side-by-side somewhere, and I wasn't sure I liked that she could always see my reaction to her so clearly.

"Right. Yeah, definitely. I guess so. Although I was a pretty boring kid in college. I studied hard, passed all my classes, didn't party. I'm a first generation college kid and was the first one in my family to actually graduate—felt like there was a lot at stake for me." My hands gripped the wheel tighter.

"That's impressive. I bet your parents were so proud."

"They were. Everyone was pretty great about it. My brother Marco went to school but left before his senior year to play in Spain." My parents had been so proud of him for going, and even though I knew it bothered them that he didn't finish school, they were proud to have a professional athlete in the family."

"Play?"

"Soccer."

"Wait. Your brother plays professional soccer in Spain?" Rae sat up a bit and wiggled in her seat.

I swallowed a pebble of dread. "Yep."

It wasn't that I wasn't proud of Marco, but he and I weren't close—he wasn't close with any of us anymore, and none of us knew why, though my parents seemed to understand his absence from our lives in a way the rest of us definitely didn't.

"Is your brother Marco Marquez?"

"You know who he is?" Usually people were intrigued by the fun fact that I had a brother who played pro soccer, but it just wasn't something Americans typically knew a lot about. Me included.

"Yes I do. He played for AC Madrid for years, right?"

"Yes. I don't know where he is now—he got traded a few times and I don't remember."

"He played on the US National team in the last World Cup. He—he's good." The admiration in her voice had me gritting my teeth.

"Yeah, I guess he is."

"No, he's like—he's awesome." Rae didn't get flustered. She'd passed out twice and her level of cool was just shy of polar, but here she was talking about my oldest brother —*talking*—and she was tripping over herself like a freaking fangirl.

Hijole.

"Yep. Pretty cool." I could hear the edge in my voice. So what if it made me a jerk that I was jealous for her amazement and didn't want her drooling over Marco when she wouldn't give me a second glance.

"Wow. *Wow.* You are not happy about me knowing who he is, are you?"

"What? No. That's—it's cool. Usually people have no idea." *She totally called me out.*

I felt her inspecting me but kept my eyes on the road as she chuckled at me. "I've always been into soccer. I thought about trying to play in college but couldn't get enough scholarship money and ended up focusing on ROTC to pay my way instead."

"Makes sense. You play on an intermural team on post, right?"

"Yeah. Indoor this time of year—the outdoor league starts in April or May, usually. It can get pretty cut throat, but it's fun. Gets some of my pent-up aggression out." She winked at me when I glanced at her.

"You have pent-up aggression? You seem so calm." I felt myself relax into my seat, felt my grip loosen on the steering wheel, and I took a deep breath. We were done with the adulation of Marco and back into normal conversational realms that didn't make me want to punch my own brother in the ear for no good reason.

Rae laughed quietly to herself, and I could see her shaking her head out of the corner of my eye. "Well, if you ever want to see it, you'll probably have to meet me on the field, or run with me. You won't see it otherwise."

"Good to know."

The rest of the drive went quickly and we arrived at Vik's apartment building right on time. Before we left the car, I stopped Rae with a hand on her wrist.

I didn't want to have this conversation, but I needed to just get it over with and avoid any awkwardness inside. "So Vik may or may not think we're dating."

She jerked back so slightly, I might not have seen it if I hadn't been looking right at her. "Why does she think that?"

"She told me to bring my girlfriend." *Shit.* This was a terrible idea.

"Gabriel. We've talked about this—"

"I know. Trust me, I know. Message received, and I get it. But Vik is worried about me. As much as I take care of her, she wants to take care of me. I mentioned meeting you a while back and that may have given her the impression I'm dating you since we've hung out a few times and she's always pestering me about dating." I ran a hand through my hair, then back the other way to keep it from looking too disheveled.

What an idiot.

"Ok..." she said, looking more uncomfortable than I think I'd ever seen her. She swallowed hard, then asked, "And what do you want me to do with that information?"

"Just... ignore it?" It was a long shot, but I didn't want her to feel like I'd kept something from her by not telling her, especially if Vik said something to her.

"Uh... ok." Her voice was small and had an edge to it.

"I'm sorry Rae. I had sort of planned not to worry about it—just convinced myself Vik would be occupied by her friends, but she's been texting me all day about meeting you, and I knew she'd end up saying something about it. I don't want you to think that anything is happening here other than me just trying to appease my little sister by not clarifying. She has had a rough few months, and I just wanted to take something off of her list of worries—or at least not outright shoot her down." As much as I was interested in Rae, I understood I was not on her list of eligible bachelors—she'd made that more than clear.

"Ok. I'll just...not say anything if she asks me directly, I guess? I just..." She trailed off and my heart thumped in my chest waiting for what was next. Would this be too much?

"You just—what?"

"I just have to think of a good way to get pay back for this, that's all." She looked up at me with a playful grin and I exhaled loudly.

"Oh thank God. I thought you were going to kill me." I ran my hands through my hair again.

"Am I that shrewish? You think I'd murder you for allowing your sister to think we're dating? I guess now I know what you think of me." She opened the door and stepped out of the car at the same time I did.

"Not at all. Just, you've been very clear with where we stand, so I didn't want you to think I didn't get that. At the same time, I love the crap out of my sister and don't want her worrying about me." I stuffed the keys in my pocket and watched as she walked toward me.

She came around the side of the car and stopped on the sidewalk next to me, her little clutch slung over one wrist. "Come here," she said, her eyes intent, looking up at my hair. "Your hair is crazy—let me fix it."

I stepped forward and bent down so she could reach it. One hand rose up, and I felt her fingers tugging and smoothing my hair for a few seconds. It occurred to me what an intimate moment this was—definitely the closest contact we'd had other than a hug, and very much something a woman would do for her man.

I liked it.

A lot.

I watched her face as she fixed my hair, her blue eyes focused securely above my forehead. I caught a waft of her perfume, or shampoo, or whatever it was…coconut, citrus, mint.

"Ok, you're presentable again." Her lips twisted into a small smile, and she gave me a light pat on the cheek.

"Thank you."

"So how should I act? I don't want to do anything to discourage her—should we discuss living arrangements? Pet names we call each other?" She turned to walk toward the building, and I followed.

"Not necessary. We've been dating a few months, as far as Vik assumes. Fairly new, nothing super intense, so she won't be expecting me to declare my eternal love and devotion to you and present you a key to my house."

"Good to know. I'll set my expectations accordingly."

"As for pet names, that's up to you. I'm not sure what nickname I'd give you, but I'll think about it." I made an exaggerated thinking face, stroking my chin. She laughed.

"I'll do the same, baby." She quirked an eyebrow at me.

Baby out of Rae's perfect mouth was a spell—some kind of witchcraft. She clearly heard the strangled sound I made because she grabbed my bicep as we walked and said, "Ok, not a fan of baby. Honey?" She gave me a mischievous grin, and I felt relief mixed with anticipation.

I hadn't been sure how she'd respond to all of this, but she was taking it better than I would have thought. She was making it a game, and that definitely meant we'd have more fun.

"Hmm," I said, waiting to see what else she'd come up with.

"Babe?" she asked.

"Eh," I said.

"Lover?"

Si, gracias.

"Does anyone actually call someone else that? Like, as a name?" I asked to cover the fact that it would not be a hardship to be this woman's lover.

"I have no idea."

We got to the door and went inside to wait for the elevator. We stood close now but not touching.

"What'd you call your last boyfriend?" I asked and saw her tense, her back straight, and the arm swinging her clutch stilled.

"Uhh... well..." she stuttered, not looking at me.

"Your pet name for your last guy was that embarrassing?" I tried to make a joke of it, but she didn't look up.

"Not so much boyfriend as husband," she said, finally looking up at me as she dropped this bomb in my lap just as the elevator dinged open.

"You were married?"

"Yes."

"But you're not *still* married, right?"

"What? No! Of course not."

"So you're..."

"Divorced." The word hung between us as the elevator doors shut.

"How long?"

"Remember when I said earlier that the early twenties are the time for big mistakes? My biggest mistake to date happened on May Fourteenth of my twenty-second year and ended about fifteen months later." She gave me a regretful smile.

"I can't believe I didn't know this about you," I said and put a hand on the elevator door to hold it open as she walked past me into Vik's hallway.

"We haven't talked about your relationship history either. Not ground we've covered yet. Not necessarily ground we need to cover as friends." She said this gently, like she was trying not to let me down again, and I guessed in context, that was only fair.

"Ok, fair enough. But we're not done with this. Now I've got to know what happened."

"I'll tell you. I'm not ashamed of it." She was looking me in the eye, not flinching, and I could tell she wasn't happy about mentioning it, but she meant what she said—she would tell me, if I asked.

Vik's door flew open, and she rushed out and practically jumped into my arms. "Goobs! I'm so glad you're here."

Rae

Gabriel's sister called him *Goobs,* and I couldn't have been happier about it. What a perfect follow-on to our discussion about pet names and a way to get away from the awful discussion of my marriage.

Ugh. I had no problem with him knowing, but it wasn't exactly something I was proud of either. With that said, in a way it was helpful. It'd be good to tell him what happened, and what I'd learned from it, and why my relationship with Brad was one of the driving forces for not dating anyone in the military ever again.

I believed he knew we were just friends. I also believed he didn't want his sister to worry about him, and based on the way she launched herself into his arms and tried to squeeze the life out of him, her face just beaming when she saw him, they were close. It was adorable.

But it would be good to remind ourselves, especially after a night of pretending to be dating for his sister's sake, or at least *not* acting like we weren't, or whatever, that that wasn't going to happen.

Gabriel introduced me to Victoria and her friends Ashley and Marie. Victoria watched me closely and when she showed me to the bathroom, she stopped me before I went in.

"You're really pretty," she said, her hand on my arm.

"Thank you. You are too."

She smiled at that and smoothed down her long black hair. "Thanks." She glanced over her bare, bronze shoulder to see Gabriel chatting with her friends, and then her face sobered completely. "But know this—if you hurt my brother, I will cut you." She squeezed my arm and gave me a saccharine smile, then stepped away as I stepped into the bathroom.

That was intense.

But I couldn't blame her. Gabriel seemed to be her primary support system, and I knew what a younger sister's love for her brother felt like. Sometimes I wished Heath and I were closer, both in age and location. Even with the distance of years and miles, I felt fiercely protective of him.

I stepped out of the bathroom a few minutes later to find the girls chatting in the living room and Gabriel out on the balcony.

"He wanted to talk to you before we walk over to the

restaurant. The reservation's in ten. It's just a few blocks away," Victoria said and motioned to the sliding glass doors.

"Thanks," I said with a smile.

I closed the doors behind me and stepped up behind him, placing my hand gingerly on Gabriel's back. "Hey," I said.

He was leaning his forearms on the bannister and looking down, but he straightened at my touch and turned to me. He brought his hands to my shoulders, and then pulled me toward him. He dipped his head, and I felt the soft scratch of his chin against my cheek bone, then the flutter of his lips against my ear.

"I don't want you to be uncomfortable." His voice was low but sure. I kept my breath steady even as I felt my heart rate kick up.

"I'm fine," I said, my body flush with his now. Despite the chilly evening air, I was surrounded by warmth.

"I don't want you freak you out, but if we were dating, I wouldn't be shy about being close to you. That's different than the dynamic we've had, obviously," he said, his breath hot in my ear. I gripped his biceps—one of his hands held my forearm, the other pulled me close with a hand at my lower back. My heart was beating wildly.

"I'll be fine. It'll be fine." I cleared my throat and stepped back just a bit, giving him a smile and fully aware of the eyes watching us through the door.

We were seated at a hip bistro a few blocks from Victoria's and I was glad I could walk in heels or I'd have been done for at block two. It was only four blocks, but that long in super-high heels when you're not a master at them can fell even the most graceful and Barbie-footed of us all.

Gabriel slid into the booth after me and we sat across from Victoria and her two girlfriends. Gabriel made a big show of Victoria ordering her first legal drink, and when the drinks arrived, he toasted her.

"To my beloved sister, who is always challenging, creating, and blasting through the best defenses. May your twenty-first year be your best, and may you know that you are loved and valued, just as you are." We all raised our glasses, and though Victoria's eyes didn't shine or give away any emotion, I saw her swallow and clear her throat in the wake of his toast.

"Love you Goob," she said quietly and gave him a sweet smile.

"Love you too Vik."

Halfway through dinner, I was overheating. Gabriel was sitting next to me, and we'd finished our food but hadn't gotten dessert yet. He had his arm slung behind me in the booth, and his hand was lightly brushing against my arm.

Back and forth.

Back and forth.

Back and freaking forth, his fingers grazed over my skin so lightly.

It shouldn't have held my attention. It shouldn't have distracted me. But oh boy, did it.

Every once in a while he'd lean in and say something in a hushed voice just for me. It wasn't usually anything all that special.

How was your salmon? Do you want more wine? Did you save room for dessert?

These words spilled into my mind with a brush of his lips on the sensitive cartilage of my ear, and somehow even though they were nothing special, my mind whirled around them and I lost focus on whatever Victoria was saying.

For her part, Victoria was watching closely. Her eye would catch his fingers smoothing down my arm, or she'd watch as he whispered something to me. I'd been quiet, though I tended to be that way anyway, and she and her girlfriends were chatting loudly, putting on a bit of a show. They seemed happy and carefree, and a small part of me envied them having someone like Gabriel to be with them and delight in them in a non-predatory way.

Heath had left for the Marines the day after he graduated high school. From then on, it'd just been me and my mom, and college was a largely solitary series of classes, shifts at work, and ROTC duties. Sometimes I got postcards from Heath when he was deployed, and about every six months one of us called the other. But we weren't close—not anything like this.

All told, dinner was delicious and we were all loosening up. We walked back to the car and Gabriel shuttled everyone to the club downtown. The sky was fully dark by the time we entered, so the low red glow of the lights seemed less intense coming from outside.

Gabriel walked us past a crowd of people waiting for seats and whispered to the hostess who then took us to our reserved seat. He hadn't touched me much to this point, other than the grazing my arm with his fingers, but the minute we walked into the club, his arm was around my waist, his large, warm hand splayed along my side in a kind of possessive grip that told anyone watching I was with *him*.

Apparently this portion of the evening, we weren't just looking for ambiguity. There was certainty in his contact.

If someone had asked me to say words at that moment,

my mind would have showed up as an old-school salt and pepper TV station.

Our table was low to the ground, the circular booth equally low. It made no sense considering women were dressed in their short cocktail dresses and there was almost no way to sit comfortably against the deep back of the booth without showing far too much thigh, but maybe that was the point.

"We're getting drinks!" Victoria yelled, then disappeared into the mass of bodies.

"You all right?" Gabriel leaned in to me and spoke loudly over the music.

I smiled at him and nodded. A few moments later the girls came back, each with a drink in hand. As they sipped and chatted, I could see their energy building.

"I'll get us drinks," Gabriel said, squeezing my shoulder as he stood. I watched him walking away, admiring his fluid movement through the crowd, his pleasing posture, his excellent neck.

"It seems like my brother likes you," Victoria said as she leaned to set her drink down, her smile sweet. I smiled back at her, hoping that would suffice as a response. "I just hope you feel the same." Her smile was gone now, and there it was again. Not as intense as it had been at the apartment, but she was in there—his baby sister, trying to protect him.

"He's great," I said and meant it. He was great. That I could say with surety, with conviction.

"Yeah," she said, but gave me the side eye. I could see her lean toward her friends and purse her lips. I imagined her rolling her eyes but I didn't look to see.

The screen of her phone lit up and she laughed at Ashley, then glanced down. Her smile faded immediately and then she shoved her phone in her small purse, but a moment later she was back to smiling and chatting with her girls.

Gabriel was back with drinks, and he sat down and narrowed his eyes at me.

"What?" I asked, taking my glass from him.

"What'd she say to you?"

"How do you know she said something to me?"

"I could see her saying something from the bar—saw you say something back. What'd she say?" His face was dipped close to mine so no one else could hear, especially with the loud music pulsing around us.

"She said she could tell you like me, and that she hoped I liked you too. She seemed unsure about me," I summarized.

His eyes surveyed me, lingering on my lips before he spoke again. "She'll come around." Then he dipped his face toward mine and placed a kiss at the corner of my mouth—mostly on my cheek, but oh.

Oh.

It was close enough to make me want to turn toward him, to capture his lips with mine, to discover whether they were as soft and ready as they looked. He pulled back slowly—slow enough I could still feel his breath at my jaw, the brush of his lips leaving a tingling trail as he caught my eye and didn't look away.

I inhaled deeply, working to steady my pulse. I swallowed and finally broke eye contact.

"Let's dance," he said and grabbed my hand. Before I could respond, or make sure Victoria would stay and watch our drinks, or think about what I'd done with my clutch, he was stepping into my space, one hand at my shoulder blade, the other hand gripping my own out to the side.

The band's song shifted moments after we took the

floor, surrounded by other couples all twirling around with varying degrees of finesse. My stomach was in knots from Gabriel's closeness, and now he was moving me around the floor like we danced together all the time. My body responded to his without having to think.

We started with the traditional dance frame—arms to the side and taut, my hand on his shoulder and his on my back. But moments after Ed Sheeran's "Shape of You" began, his hand slid to my waist, then gripped my hip as we moved, then slid across my collar bone as he stood behind me.

"So... you can dance," I croaked after that affecting move.

He moved us around, flung me out, and tugged my fingers so I twirled back in. Just the slightest cue from him and I was moving.

When we were face to face again, he smirked. It was the most arrogance I'd seen out of him.

"Yes. And so can you," he said, his voice rich next to my ear as we mirrored each other's movements.

Our hips moved together, our bodies close, and I was becoming more and more aware of Gabriel as a physical presence. It'd been hard enough to ignore up to this point, but his comfort with his own body, and now his confidence in essentially commanding my own was... unexpected.

Problematic.

He dipped me low, then hauled me back up in one swift move, and the song stopped. We both breathed heavily, and I laughed to relieve some of the pressure building in my mind, my body, everything.

"One more?" he asked and immediately started moving me around again as another song, an even faster one, began.

CHAPTER SEVEN

Rae

After this night, I wouldn't have been surprised if Gabriel told me he was a spy. Or at least a retired professional ballroom dancer. He could dance like *whoa*.

After we sat down and guzzled water, then waved the girls off to dance, he explained Victoria had wanted to ballroom dance professionally for a long time and had danced in high school. He'd always ended up being her practice partner because there were very few male dancers at her school.

"And you? How'd you learn to dance?" He'd seemed incredibly pleased by my ability to follow, and after the first song, we danced several more when he was sure I could keep up.

"I took dance lessons for years as a kid—it was something my mom never got to do so when I expressed interest, she was all over it. Then once I started pageants, it was beneficial to keep going so my talent could improve as I grew. It was also surprisingly helpful with my footwork in soccer."

"So pageants were a pretty big part of your life." He took a sip of his water and leaned close to hear my response.

"Yeah, they were. I did my first one in seventh grade. I did my last one my freshman year of college, though that was the only one I'd done in a year. But before college, I did several a year."

"I'm impressed."

"So Victoria doesn't still dance? Because she's... wow. I can't believe her." We'd watched her dance, and whenever she had an even remotely capable partner, she owned the dance floor. Her hair whipped around accentuating her movements, her feet moved quickly, her body bending, swirling, snapping up to emphasize a musical point.

"She does, actually. She does a ballroom dance *team* if you can believe it. But it's a hobby, not a real focus of hers, I don't think." He scrunched his nose in distaste, but I couldn't tell why.

"You don't like that she dances?"

"No, I love that she still does. But when she was in school, she had some trouble with a dance instructor. He was only a few years older—came on to her, they started dating, and it was toxic. I don't know how she kept up her grades, but it's one reason she's here and not in Texas."

"I'm sorry. It sounds like it's good she got a fresh start here."

"Yes, it's a good thing."

~

Gabriel

Rae and I spent the rest of the night watching Vik and her friends tear up the dance floor and occasionally make fools of themselves. Fortunately I didn't have to threaten anyone, and by the time we poured the girls into my car it was almost 2 a.m.

"Thank you so much Goobs. I seriously love you," Vik said as she leaned her head on my shoulder.

"Glad you had fun."

"You should bring Rae down for dinner next weekend. She passed my initial approval tests, but now I need to actually pay attention."

"Oh yeah? You get to approve, huh?" I glanced over at Rae who was grinning down at her lap.

"Yep. Little sister. I have final say. She better come with her A game if she wants you."

I parked the car and we watched the girls wobble and skip into the building to escape the now frigid night air. It was late, and I pulled away before we got the text that they were safely inside the apartment.

"Will you grab that and see what Vik said?" I handed Rae my phone without letting my eyes leave the road. "Pin is 1976."

"It says 'ok,'" Rae said and set down the phone as I kept driving, but I felt a prickle of unease race up my arm.

"Can you ask if she's sure? Just say 'you sure' and let's see. That... *ok* is a very atypical response for Vik on a night like tonight."

The only sounds in the car were the road and the distant sound of the radio turned almost all the way down.

"She typed 'such a great time. I'm wiped. Call me tomorrow.'"

"Ok, good."

"Are you worried about something? We can go back," Rae said, eyeing me from her seat.

I blew out a breath and pulled my wallet out of my back pocket so I didn't have to sit on it for the whole ride home. "No, sounds like she's fine. I guess I'm a paranoid big brother."

"That's not such a bad thing. You're sweet with her." I could hear the smile in Rae's voice and I smiled in response.

"I can't help it. We're seven years apart but a lot of times I feel like I raised her. I didn't, obviously, but we were close. Part of me is glad she's so close by."

"Just part of you?" I heard her shift farther against the passenger door and knew she was taking up her spot where she could see me more fully.

"The part of me that likes to see her, likes to know she's doing well, and is proud of her for going to a great school, yes. The part of me that knows that a big reason she left Texas was because of a creep... not that part of me."

"Ah, that makes sense. I'm sorry."

"She's doing so well, so there's nothing to regret now." I could hear the shadow in my voice, the clear twinge of regret that obviously still lingered.

"Well, I'm glad she has you. And it sounds like we did a decent job of the night—she didn't call BS on us, at least."

"True. You apparently passed the first test. I had no idea there was such a thing, but there you have it. I'm not at all surprised." Rae chuckled next to me, and I thought what a rare and light sound it was.

"I like her. She loves you so much—it's sweet."

"She's great." I shifted in my seat and settled in a bit more. The drive to Clarksville was only about an hour, but the roads were very dark in places and I couldn't enjoy glancing over at Rae in the darkness anyway. "You up for talking to me to keep me awake, or do you want to sleep?"

"I'll keep you awake. What do you want me to talk about?" Her voice was rich and tired sounding, both from the late hour and the loud-talking we'd done in the club, no doubt.

"I'm definitely going to need to hear about your ex-husband at some point. I understand if now is not the time."

"I'll tell you whatever you want to know."

"Really? Ok. Start from the beginning. How'd you meet? What'd you like about him? How long before he asked you to marry him?" It was possible I was coming across as over-eager, but I couldn't help it. The thought of her marriage had been swirling in my mind all night, and I couldn't talk to her about it while at the club because the atmosphere wasn't exactly conducive to conversation. But now, I wanted to know everything.

"His name was Brad. We met in ROTC at UGA. We weren't even friends the first few years, but senior year we interacted more, and in the last few weeks of school, he asked me out. I hadn't dated much... or, at all, and he was sweet and interesting. Plus he spoke the Army language, and he understood wanting to serve. It felt too good to be true." She stopped then and sighed a little. I couldn't decipher exactly what kind of sigh. Regretful? Resigned?

"So... was it?" My voice was quiet in the small space.

"Indeed it was. We got married before we left for BOLC at different posts. We were co-located at our first duty station, but he was assigned to a unit already deployed so he left almost right away. He got back nine months later and was ready to start a family. Something about the deployment gave him a sense of urgency. I was open to it and we... we tried a bit, but then I was getting close to deploying so I wanted to stop. He wanted me to go ahead with it so I didn't deploy. In the end I didn't, or, uh, couldn't get pregnant, I'm not sure which, and then I deployed."

My heart clenched in my chest at the sound of her voice. It wasn't so much defeat as it was disappointment and sadness, and it sliced me open.

"He divorced you because you didn't get pregnant?" I couldn't keep the disbelief out of my voice.

"No. During the deployment we kept talking, and he kept bringing up how the deployment was derailing our family plans. He'd mention how if I wasn't in the Army, I wouldn't be so stressed, I would probably get pregnant more easily, and if not, then I'd be more free to get infertility treatments or whatever came next. I found myself thinking about it, starting to think that me being in the Army was the problem."

I didn't know what to say. It was hard to imagine Rae ever doubting her future in the Army.

"The combination of the deployment being a rough one, and feeling like maybe I was making a huge mistake in being there—maybe sacrificing my marriage, my future children, everything—had me in a miserable place. But at some point I said something to a friend, and he looked at me like I was crazy—in the nicest way possible. Having someone cast doubt on all the guilt I was feeling gave me clarity."

"I'm guessing Brad didn't appreciate your clarity." I disliked this guy. I was in no danger of meeting him—I didn't even know his last name. But... I didn't like him.

"He did not. I thought we could focus on having kids when I got home, and he seemed appeased by that at first. Then when I talked about maternity leave and how we'd work out childcare once I went back to work, he lost it. He expected me to get out when my initial obligation was done and never look back."

"Was that ever something you talked about while you were dating?"

"No. In fact, I told him how I'd started ROTC with the plan to pay for school, but the further into the program I got, the more excited about the prospect of serving, of the career over the long haul, I got. We'd talked about being dual military and how hard that seemed but how worth it."

A calm quiet settled around us, and I could tell she was remembering the dissolution of her marriage. I wanted to comfort her in some way but conversely felt deeply grateful she was telling me about it at all.

"The worst part was that I started thinking I should get out. I started thinking I should just fold up shop and stay home, barefoot and pregnant like he seemed to want me. And then, at some point, I thought of my mom."

"And her wanting to be a nurse?"

"Yes. I was heading down the same path—compromising everything I believed in and knew I was called to for a man. And in the end, not just *a* man, but my husband, who didn't seem to understand me at all."

"That must have been incredibly lonely," I said.

I heard her exhale. "It was. It was heartbreaking. But part of the heartbreak was realizing I'd married him without knowing him. We'd had so little time together—really only five months between his deployment and mine. We didn't know anything about each other, and if we had, we wouldn't have married."

"Sounds like you have a good perspective on it," I offered.

"I do. And it taught me a lot."

I felt the tension build in my chest at her words, and

then it hit me. "So that's the reason you won't date a soldier? Because your first marriage failed?"

"Yes and no. It's not so much that it failed as I saw how weak I could be. I also know how much it takes to be in the Army, and how most soldiers, especially the kind of men I tend to be attracted to, are ambitious and want careers. Women are almost always the ones to get out in dual military situations when kids come around. I want to retire. I don't want to compromise, and I don't want my potential spouse to feel like he's sacrificing something so huge. So... I'll marry a civilian, or maybe I won't marry. I don't know."

I opened my mouth to speak but snapped it shut again. Finally I found the words I was searching for, and I spoke them, even though I felt like someone set a two-hundred-pound barbell on my chest. "Sounds like you learned a lot. That's important. And now you have your rule firmly in place."

Rae

After our conversation about my failed marriage, we drove in silence except for a few short exchanges. When Gabriel pulled up in front of my house, I felt a pang of disappointment that the night had ended so focused on me and my past and the biggest reason I couldn't date a soldier—at least, that's what I thought had me feeling my heart pressed into my back.

I opened the car door and stepped out, then pulled the hem of my dress back down since it had ridden up during the drive. It was just after three am, and I took a moment to breathe in the chilly air and take in the bright stars winking down at me.

"I'm sorry it's so late," Gabriel said from just a foot or two away.

"Don't be. I figured it'd be a late night. I can sleep in and relax and I'll be fine before the work week starts." I ran my hands over my bare arms and we walked slowly up my walkway.

"Thank you for coming, and for being uh... a good sport." His voice was rough with the late hour.

I shivered and stepped up on my porch, then turned to face him. "You're welcome. I enjoyed it. Your sister is lucky to have a brother like you," I said with a small smile.

He nodded and folded his lips between his teeth. His eyes were shadowed in the night's darkness and my porch light did nothing to reveal his thoughts. He started to reach out to me—maybe to touch my arm, or grab my hand, or something—but pulled back and tucked his hand in his pocket. "I'll talk to you soon. Get some sleep."

The week was shuffling along, and Gabriel was responsive to texts, if not overly friendly. He wasn't shrinking back, repelled by my sad sack of a story about my failed marriage or my once-more-with-feeling clarification that I couldn't date him. Of course it was an ironic conversation after our evening dancing, laughing, and flirting, but we had the excuse that it was all for Victoria's sake and we both clung to it.

Fine. I admit it. I like him.

After he'd left me I'd fallen asleep almost immediately, but I woke six hours later feeling sore and sad and intensely scared he'd back away from our friendship. I knew he liked me, at least to some degree more than platonically, though I wasn't arrogant enough to think he was secretly pining for me. We had crazy chemistry, but that didn't mean much beyond a shared attraction.

But it wasn't a conventional friendship—not really. Because as much as I wanted to think of him as just cute nurse Gabriel, my friend, I found myself thinking about kind nurse Gabriel who was compassionate and warm and a crazy good dancer. I'd space out looking at my computer screen thinking about dark-skinned, warm-handed, perfect-smiling Gabriel who was an adorable older brother, an engaged friend, and was likely an incredibly hands-on and attentive boyfriend—and then I'd shake myself and clench my jaw and remind myself yet again he was off limits.

On Wednesday, Major Toms startled me from one of my now-frequent mental rabbit trails about Gabriel while making copies at the battalion building.

"Captain Jackson, I appreciate you stepping in for me. I know it was an unusual situation." His tone left no room for me to ask questions, though I wouldn't have anyway. He laced his large hands together and stood stalk-straight.

"Certainly sir. I learned a lot, even in just a few short days."

"I'm sure. You did well, especially for being thrown into the fire like that, with little warning. I didn't expect—" his voice caught and I saw the rims of his blue eyes redden. He took a deep breath and pursed his lips.

The look on his face was all raw pain and emotion, and without thinking, I reached out and put a hand on his arm and squeezed for reassurance. He acknowledged my movement with a nod and cleared his throat.

"Anyway, I appreciate it." He nodded again and left me

staring after him with the copies in hand and questions in my mind.

What happened?

It was a strange interaction, but I appreciated him making the effort to thank me. He probably hated himself for tearing up, and frankly, I would have hated myself too. I had no idea what happened, but the sudden nature of his absence had brought up questions and of course, rumors.

They'd faded when he returned not long after he left, and I'd made a point not to let myself hear them. I didn't have time or energy to let rumors influence the way I worked, so I shut myself off to them. That wasn't altogether difficult considering I wasn't close with anyone in the battalion and most of the rumors hadn't skipped the fence to other battalions before they were quashed by his return.

Whatever it was, I hoped he and his family were ok. He had always treated me fairly, never made me feel anything but like a junior officer in his battalion.

Gabriel

Me: *Vik cancelled dinner tonight. I'd still like to go check on her, but then we can hit Trader Joe's and eat at my place after?*

Rae: *Is she ok? Sounds good. I have my list for TJ ready.*

Rae and I were planning to meet up with Vik for an early dinner before we went to Trader Joe's. That was just her wanting to go to Trader Joe's and stock up while we were already in Nashville, but I was game for her to try to talk me into liking the place. I was game for anything she wanted, really, even when I knew how pathetic that was.

I'd been looking forward to seeing her, spending time with her in the car, and even seeing her interact with Vik, who'd hopefully be a bit less prickly with her this visit.

"I'm going to blow your mind, Marquez," she'd said, like that was a threat, when I told her yet again I wasn't impressed with her beloved Trader Joe's.

Please do.

Vik cancelled dinner though, so now I had an entire afternoon and evening with just me and my friend Rae. We'd swing by Vik's to check on her and see if she needed anything—I was a nurse after all—and then be off to do our own thing.

Rae and I had parted on the odd note of reviewing all the reasons she was motivated not to get involved with someone in the military. I'd been completely clear about that when we parted, and had hated the way her ex-husband had treated her, and that I wasn't in a position to talk her out of her conviction about not dating *me*.

Dios mio, how I wished I could think of a way to remove myself from the *absolutely no freaking way* category.

But then, over the course of the week, I reverted back to wanting to be with her. Be with her, and *be with* her, and everything in between. And I became determined. I'd play the long game and let our friendship deepen—I'd be patient and understanding and at some point, our chemistry and the magnetic pull that always flared between us when we were in each other's vicinity would defeat the stark determination to avoid me as more than a friend.

Perfect plan.

I kept calm as she hopped into my car, her hair braided down her back. I didn't stare at the pleasing bright blue colored V-neck shirt she wore that made her eyes look like sapphires, nor did I let my eyes linger on the way her worn-in jeans hugged her hips.

I just smiled at her. "Good to see you," I said, all golden retriever friendliness.

"Likewise." Her small smile seemed completely at ease, and I felt a deep contentment with just having her sitting next to me in the car. I shook my head at myself as she looked out the window—I was getting sappy about having her in my proximity and it wasn't a good look.

We knocked on Vik's door at five o'clock. It took her a moment to answer.

"Did you tell her we were coming?" Rae asked.

"No. I'm sure she would have told me not to bother, that she'd be fine. But I just want to make sure it's just a cold and not something worse. Flu season can stick around this time of year, even after it's super cold."

Just then, the door swung open, and my lungs turned to lead.

Vik stood in sweatpants and a t-shirt, her hair piled high on her head in a black knot. Her eyes were dark and puffy—she'd been crying. Her face was red, all but the black and blue slash against her left cheek.

CHAPTER EIGHT

Rae

Gabriel's voice shot out. "What the—"

"I know it looks bad, but I've dealt with it, G. I don't want you freaking—" Victoria held out a hand to him as Gabriel's entire demeanor shifted, expanded.

"What is going on, Vik? You said you were sick. You didn't tell me you were sitting here with a smashed-up face because that sack of shit is stalking you again. *Don't* try to deny it—I had a feeling that idiot was messing with you again, and I can see all the proof I need." Gabriel ran his hands through his hair and pulled on the ends so it stood up in all directions. He'd brushed past Victoria as soon as he saw her, and I followed him in and closed the door but stayed near the exit.

"I wasn't going to drag you back into this, and I've dealt with it."

"Like hell you weren't. What do you think you're going to do?"

"Call the cops, just like I did." She crossed her arms over her chest, and her hip popped out in defiance. Her jaw was set as she looked at her brother.

"So they've arrested him?"

Victoria huffed and looked at him. "No. He was gone when I came to—"

Gabriel swore violently and let go a string of Spanish I had no hope of following. He pulled out his phone, gestured angrily at Victoria, and then slammed out the door to the balcony, leaving me with his sister, who was still breathing heavily, trying to control her response to his tirade.

I took a step into the room and waited quietly. My heart was pounding wildly in the wake of Gabriel's harsh words, his anger, and mostly, his very real fear. I could feel it rolling off of him, springing from his hunched shoulders.

"Have you iced it?" I asked quietly.

"I have, but the ice melted. I probably should again." She moved to the kitchen without looking at me

"Let me get it for you. Go sit and rest." Victoria stopped and took a deep breath, then walked to the couch without a word.

I found the baggy of water and emptied it, filled it with ice, and grabbed a towel with a smiling cactus on it.

I sat by her and handed her the ice. "Is your head hurting? Do you think you should go get checked out?" I was sure she didn't want me trying to take care of her since we hardly knew each other, but I was concerned that whoever had attacked her had knocked her out.

"The cop who came asked me that too. I'm ok. When he calms down, Gabe will check me over. If he thinks I should go in, I will." She held the bag of ice nestled in the towel to her cheek. Then she turned her eyes to me. "You may have gathered this isn't the first time this has happened."

Her eyes looked endlessly sad then and full of so many questions and thoughts, I lost my breath. All I could do was reach out to her, place a hand on her knee.

"I'm sorry. So sorry Victoria."

I looked out to see Gabriel gesturing wildly with his left hand and his phone to his ear on his right. He turned and was clearly shouting into the phone.

"He'll calm down. He's probably talking to my brother." Victoria sunk back into the couch.

~

Gabriel

I smashed my finger against the phone as I hung up with Angel, resisting the urge to throw it against the brick wall separating Vik's balcony from her neighbor's. Angel was a cop in our hometown and was supposed to keep an eye on Rip. He'd failed, had no idea, and I'd ripped him a new one.

I felt the rage fizzle out as I hung up and took a deep breath, breathing in the cool evening air and trying to blow out the fear that gripped my heart like a steel cage. I ran my fingers through my hair again and turned to survey the scene inside. My heart stuttered and stopped altogether.

Rae had her hand around my sister's neck, holding her gently at the back of her neck. Her face was inches from Vik's, and she was speaking. Vik's lips were smashed together, clearly in an effort not to cry—she hated to cry and wouldn't want to do it now, not in front of me or Rae. She nodded once, twice, then lunged forward and hugged Rae tightly, practically pulling Rae into her lap. Vik let Rae go just as suddenly, just as I walked through the sliding glass doors.

"I talked to Angel. He had no idea Rip was out of town," I said, hoping to get insight on what I'd just seen.

"He's gone. I don't think he'll be back. The restraining order obviously didn't stop him, but I think he scared himself. I don't think he meant to knock me out." Vik's voice was small, but steady.

"Don't defend him, Vik. It turns my stomach."

"I'm not defending him. I hate him. I never want to see him again. But I don't think he actually wants to kill me. I think the idiot thinks he loves me, and he hit me so hard he knocked me out. Now you've told Angel, and I did call the police, and they are on the lookout for him too." She was trying to reassure me, like I was the one who'd just been beaten and bruised.

And it hit me. I'd done nothing to comfort *her*. I'd yelled at her, stormed into her apartment, then stormed out again to yell at Angel.

I rushed to her and sat by her on the couch, then wrapped my arms around her shoulders and pulled her head to my chest. "Gracias a Dios, Hita, I'm so glad you're ok. I'm sorry I yelled at you. I'm so sorry this happened." I spoke into her hair as she wrapped her arms around my middle and squeezed, then released me. She wouldn't let me hold her long, but I had to take what I could get and feel she was ok.

"I'm ok Goob. I promise." Her using the nickname she'd given me as a toddler was a good sign.

I watched her as she pulled back and settled the ice against her cheek. "I want to check your pupils," I said as I grabbed her wrist to count her pulse. I felt Rae stand and heard her move to the kitchen, but I was in nurse mode now, making sure my *hita* was ok. Sometimes I felt like I was her father, even though I was only seven years older. But the protective feeling I got when I saw her like this, the fear that swelled in me when I thought about how vulnerable she was with him here, was like chalk in my throat.

"Vik, did he—hurt you anywhere else?"

Vik grabbed my hand. "No, no. He didn't. Just the cheek, and I hit my shoulder blade when he shoved me inside. I fell against the wall trying to get to my phone." She was looking me straight in the eye, making sure I could see she was telling the truth. I knew she wouldn't lie to me about that. Not again.

Rae silently set two glasses of water on the table, set a hand on my shoulder and squeezed lightly before disappearing again.

~

Hours later, we emerged from Vik's apartment.

"I'll drive," Rae said.

I didn't have it in me to argue, but I wouldn't have anyway. I was spent. Shifting from fear-fueled rage, to concern and care, back to more rage, and then landing on a bone-deep sadness had me exhausted.

There was no doubt Rae was exhausted too—she'd been quiet, but present all evening in small ways—refilling water, refreshing Vik's ice pack, ordering pizza and serving it on plates with napkins at the couch before we even registered a knock at the door. She'd been amazing.

"Thank you," I said as I slumped in the passenger seat. She gave me a small smile and steered us in the direction of Clarksville.

"I promise I'll go with you to Trader Joe's some other time," I offered weakly.

"I'm not worried," she said, not taking her eyes from the road.

When we pulled into her townhome's driveway, I shook off the sleep that had pulled me under for the last half hour or so of the drive. I hadn't meant to fall asleep, but there was no avoiding it, evidently.

Rae parked and got out, then came around to open my door and handed me the keys as I exited the car.

"Thank you again," I said in a sleep-roughened voice.

She looked at me with her brow wrinkled for a moment and then stepped into my space. She slipped her arms around my waist and pressed into me, hugging me tightly. She didn't let go, not for a long time, and neither did I. I felt a mixture of relief and total heartbreak. I couldn't think of Vik's face without seeing the bruise, and then other more gruesome images from the last few years played without permission.

Eventually, Rae's grip loosened. She stepped back and gripped my wrists. "I'm so sorry about Victoria."

"Thank you. Thanks for everything you did tonight."

"Go home. Sleep as long as you can. Text me when you wake up, please." She squeezed my forearms lightly, then dropped her hands.

"Ok. Yes ma'am. I'll text you tomorrow."

Rae

It was technically my rest day, and after a late night and bad sleep, I needed to rest. So I couldn't funnel my concern for Victoria and Gabriel into a run like I wanted.

I was worried about Victoria.

I was worried about Gabriel.

I couldn't get his face out of my head. He'd been so angry, so fearful, so passionate as he stomped around her apartment. Then he was so painfully sweet as he checked her bruised cheek, looked her over, questioned her gently, but insistently.

Problematic.

I was past the point of liking Gabriel. I'd passed it weeks ago. He was thoughtful and funny and charismatic. He was interesting and passionate and gorgeous. He had a scar on his chin that, for whatever reason, I found completely adorable.

He was forbidden.

And yet, I'd found myself thinking of him in all the forbidden ways. I'd heard myself ask *why not?* I felt myself opening to the possibility of him, considering breaking my rule that didn't factor in someone like *him.*

Gabriel texted around three to say he was finally awake and asked if I had dinner plans. We decided on his favorite Mexican place—a different one than mine of course—and met there a little over an hour before his shift. They were notoriously fast with the food and the check.

I was already inside and sitting when I saw him approaching. I stood and held out my arms signaling for him to hug me. Instead of leaning over the table like I expected, he walked around the table and stepped into my space.

Right into my space.

The toes of his black work shoes bumped the toes of my tennis shoes. His eyes were coal as he leaned down and wrapped his arms around my shoulders. I felt his lips graze my temple, my cheek, just to the left of my mouth.

Little champagne bubbles floated through my mind at the feel of his hands, lips, breath. I leaned back and opened my mouth to speak, but before I did, his hand fisted in my ponytail, he angled my head back, and covered my lips with his glorious mouth.

I was an orderly person. I was methodical. I was successful because I didn't give up. I wasn't ever the smartest or best, but I was always the hardest worker. I was consistent. Things I did followed procedures and processes long-established by my peers and mentors. I and those around me followed the rules. I was not someone who enjoyed surprises.

But *this?*

This didn't follow the rules. It wasn't expected.

This was hard not to like.

If I made a sound, I didn't remember. Before I could think, or kiss him back, he'd pulled away. He'd kissed me. More than a peck, less than... well, less than was necessary. Less than was essential.

Less than I want.

"What are your Easter plans?" His voice was rich and steady.

What?

"Rae, what are your Easter plans?" he asked again as he sat in the seat opposite me. He grabbed a menu and opened it without looking at it. He sat casually, like his choice to kiss my face, my mouth, wasn't something new and perplexing in a not-unwelcome way.

I swallowed and lowered myself into the hard wooden chair. "Well... my friend Maybelline and her husband are coming Friday for the night, and I think we'll do brunch that day around noon instead of Sunday. Ann's coming over too. She's bringing a date." My voice sounded different—distant, maybe. Probably because I felt like I was having an out of body experience.

Little spirit Rae was floating above me, all shimmery and elated, watching corporeal Rae sit stock-still and try to breathe and keep her mouth from falling open. Or keep from lunging across the table and shaking the man in front of her and asking him what he'd done.

Or asking him to do it again.

"Oh, yeah? I haven't met Maybelline, have I?" he asked, as casual as you please. He knew good and well he'd never met Maybelline—I wasn't sure I'd even mentioned her to him. He'd only met Ann, who was certainly my only real friend in Clarksville who I saw with any regularity.

Well, besides Gabriel.

"No, you haven't."

"I'd like to," he said, closing his menu, his eyes not leaving mine.

I glanced down at my menu, trying to make sense of the trifold. I knew what I wanted—had known since the moment I walked in. I shut the menu and set it down.

The waiter appeared and Gabriel nodded to me, again as casual as if he hadn't just tilted the globe of our friendship on its axis with lip-to-lip contact.

"I'll have chicken fajitas, extra guacamole." I smiled at the waiter, then watched Gabriel. I could have recited his order since he'd ordered the same thing the last time we had Mexican, and we'd talked more than once about what we order at our chosen favorites.

"Tacos al pastor, extra salsa, no lettuce, gracias," he said and handed the menu to the waiter, who disappeared as fast as he'd arrived.

"So what time are you guys eating?" Gabriel asked with a pleasant smile I found completely irritating.

"I'm sorry, are you planning on addressing what just happened?" I asked, an edge in my voice. I clasped my hands in my lap to avoid gripping the table. I was generally capable of appearing calm, even when I wasn't, and even though I felt like a butterfly garden had exploded in my chest, I didn't want him to know it. Especially with that smug little smile like he *did* know exactly what was happening in my mind.

"We ordered dinner at the best Mexican restaurant in the city, and now we're talking about your Easter plans, which I'm not-so-subtly trying to gain an invite to." He smiled that charming, blazing, maddening smile to punctuate his willful ignorance.

"Before that." I crossed my arms in front of me on the table and leaned on them to peg him with my skeptical glare.

"Oh, *that*." He drummed his fingers in front of him, his smile never wavering.

"Yes, *that*."

"No. I'm not going to address that," he said and leaned back in his chair. He draped one arm over the chair next to him, and his t-shirt stretched over his chest. I did my best not to notice this detail, but failed.

"Yes. Yes, you are. Why did you do that?" I heard the pitch in my voice rising. My heart hadn't slowed down its tripping pace, and I took a breath as I waited for his response.

He peered at me a moment—yes, he peered. He squinted his eyes and then leaned forward.

"I greeted you. Thoroughly."

Um...

"I don't—"

"Here we go folks. Buen provencho!" The waiter shoved our scalding plates in front of us, refilled our waters, and then was off again.

We both sipped our water, and I poked at a few pieces of chicken on the sizzling platter in front of me, hoping Gabriel would clarify what he meant by kissing me. Before I prompted him, he spoke.

"Thank you for your help yesterday." I wasn't prepared for the shift in topic, or his somber tone.

"Of course. I'm glad I could help." I smiled at him, trying to show it wasn't a hardship. "I'm so sorry for her."

"Me too." His voice was hard, and I could see the muscles in his jaw flex as he took a breath.

"Did you talk to her today?" I asked.

"Yes. She's sore, but no headache, which is good." He took a bite of food, and his eyes fluttered closed for a moment before popping back open. "I told you, Don Julio's is the best."

"False."

He sat up straight and took another bite, then groaned loudly in exaggerated enjoyment. "Definitely the best," he said, then licked his fork.

I did not notice the fork licking. No, I did not.

"El Bajio is the best. You even admitted their salsa is better the first time we went." I took a bite of my fajita. It *was* good, but not as good as my favorite.

"I think you're missing some taste buds." He took another bite of his meal and raised an eyebrow at me.

"I have a perfect tongue, thank you very much," I said with a saccharine smile.

Gabriel made a sound, then coughed. And coughed.

"You ok?" I asked, not holding back from laughing at him.

He coughed a bit more, then drank some water. His face had turned a little red, and he took deep breaths as he recovered. "Yes," he croaked. "I'll make it. Prognosis is good."

"Good. So what are you doing for Easter weekend?" Of course I was going to invite him—I'd already planned on it.

"I have to work nights all weekend, so I'll head in for seven to seven. But I'd be willing to wake up early for brunch, should I be invited to such an event."

"Oh, you would? Wow, that's generous of you. What about Victoria?"

"She's heading home. She'll be back there for a bit in the summer when I'm there for leave, but with what happened, I think she wants to be home," he explained. He scooted food around on his plate until he'd piled up his last bite. We were both fast eaters, likely because in the Army you quickly developed the ability to inhale food when you have the chance during training and even while deployed depending on the job. We'd never lingered over dinner because there was always something coming after—him going to work, or me falling asleep in my soup after a tiring day behind me.

"Isn't the guy there, though?"

"I don't know if he is, honestly. But I'm positive she won't be going anywhere alone at any point. Usually she'd get frustrated about that, but this visit, I doubt it. Plus she'll have homework, and she loves just lying around the house until the family arrives, and then she'll be cooking and she loves the cascarones." He took the final bite, then leaned back and rubbed his flat belly.

I raised an eyebrow in question at the unfamiliar word.

"Cascarones are traditionally dyed or painted eggs filled

with confetti that you crack over someone's head. It's really fun, and my abuelita always sends me a dozen if I don't make it back for Easter." His eyes were lit with excitement and I got a fleeting glimpse of Gabriel as a kid, smashing confettied eggs in his sister's hair.

"That's awesome, and I'm glad Victoria will be there for that. So you'll be all alone for the weekend?"

"Isn't that sad? Most of my friends are working too or don't do much to celebrate." He gave me a sad little look with his eyebrows arched expectantly. He was about the least pathetic-looking man I'd ever met, but he did the puppy dog eyes very well.

I shook my head and set down my fork. I wiped my mouth, then tilted my head and sweetly asked, "Gabriel, would you like to come to my house for Easter brunch on Friday?"

He looked around and put a hand to his chest like, "Who, me?" Then he hit me with that killer smile again. "Do you have room? I wouldn't want to impose."

I laughed and shook my head again. "Yes. I will make room for you, especially now that I've heard your sob story about being alone."

"Oh, so this is a pity invite?" he asked and grabbed the check the waiter had set down. He pulled out a few bills from his wallet and set them down. I moved to take a look at the check and he pulled the little tray back with a half shake of his head.

Ok. Buying me dinner. Also new.

"Absolutely, it is."

"Well, in that case, I'm not sure I can make it..."

"Fine. I was always going to invite you. I just hadn't gotten there, even though it's less than a week away." As I said it, I realized with a trill of nerves I was right—it was coming up. Maybelline would be in my house with her husband in a few days. They'd arrive early Friday and take off Saturday morning. I hadn't seen her in six years and hadn't spent time with her since college and her wedding.

And mine.

"I'll happily accept and be there. Tell me what to bring." He looked at me with raised eyebrows, wordlessly asking if I was ready. I grabbed my purse and walked to him where he stood waiting for me to go ahead.

"Do you cook? Or, I know you cook, but do you have a family recipe you love? Ann's doing the ham, and I'll do a potato casserole and quiche. I'll have fruit and salad too. I think Maybelline is bringing pie—I have to ask her."

Then I felt it. His hand on my back, sure and strong and my stomach flipped. I swallowed back the audible acknowledgment of his touching me again because me saying *Oh, I really like that* would make things awkward.

But what was happening? Gabriel was friendly, and obviously we liked each other, but it was like he'd made a decision about something but hadn't told me. I knew I had to ask him and was about to as soon as we got out of the restaurant.

He held the door for me with one arm and I walked through, then stood to the side while another couple followed me out, and then Gabriel emerged.

"I'll think about it. I'll bring cascarones and some wine." He reached out to usher me to my car, that same warm hand on my lower back.

It wasn't that I didn't like it. I did. And I enjoyed being with him so much—in fact, I often felt annoyed with myself by just how much I enjoyed being with him because I shouldn't want to be around anyone that much, should I? I was an independent woman and one who'd learned the ugly lesson of what love, or presumed love, could do to her.

I knew better than to let myself soften up to Gabriel, and yet it'd happened. The only thing keeping my heart safe from him was my repeated acknowledgment that we were friends and the physical barrier placed between us by that friendship.

Gabriel had brought his sledgehammer today and evidently wanted to use it on said barrier.

He stopped by the side of my car door and I turned to look at him, ready to lighten my heavy thoughts with a friendly goodbye.

When I turned to him, my mind stalled out. His eyes were on mine, on my face, on my lips, and the look in them was one of intensity and hunger.

"I—"

His voice was low and clear. "I don't want to talk anymore, Rae."

CHAPTER NINE

Rae

"What?" Even though my mind couldn't understand what was happening, my heart and body reacted. My blood was leaping in my veins, heat crawling up from my toes and lighting every nerve in its wake.

Though I would have said it was impossible, his face became even more focused, his whole body looming in front of me in the most confusingly appealing way, like the atoms that composed him were calling to mine.

Instead of speaking again, he stepped to me, slid one arm around my waist and pulled me into his space. There was nothing between us now but our clothes, and I thought maybe they'd be incinerated by the heat radiating off him, off me. His eyes bore into mine as he ran a finger along my cheek, then slid his hand behind my head, cupping the nape of my neck.

Then he didn't move—not except his chest, which rose

and fell against mine, his breathing heavier than normal. His eyes searched mine, back and forth. He inched his head closer to me, his mouth making its way toward mine.

My heart busted out of normal heart rate range and was racing far faster than it did after sprints. I felt the need to bend over, catch my breath, but I couldn't, or wouldn't, since being crushed up against Gabriel was the sole focus in my mind.

He bent down farther and I knew, finally, he was going to kiss me again. I tilted my chin so my lips were centimeters away from his. I was ready, but not so much that I could be the one to initiate—not so much that I could be the one to break every carefully crafted rule and plan I'd made. It had to be him.

But he didn't move.

He just looked at me, torturing me.

Maybe that's his plan. He wants you to know what you're missing.

"Yes or no?" came his rough whisper against my lips.

Yes.

Yes!

YES!!!

"Yes," I said, and our lips touched.

Before my eyes fluttered shut, I saw his quick smile, and then his mouth met mine. Slow at first, like he was giving me a chance to get used to him, to make sure I meant what I'd said. Then when I wrapped my arms around his neck and pulled him impossibly closer, he deepened the kiss and devoured me.

I kissed him back for all I was worth, savoring the sensation I'd been thinking about for months now. His lips were plush and a little cool in the April air. With one hand on my back and one hand tight in my hair, he held me to him, only our mouths moving.

If I'd ever been kissed before, it was a pebble. It was a grain of sand in the small collection of intimate experiences I'd had in my life.

Kissing Gabriel was Pike's Peak. It was Kilimanjaro. It was insurmountable, unavoidable, unforgettable, uncontainable. All the uns.

Too soon, because any amount of time would have been too soon for me at that point, the wake of our first real kiss, he broke away. He looked at me with something soft and knowing, one corner of his mouth kicking up into a self-assured smile.

"Ask me why I did that," he said.

I was still breathing heavily from the kiss, still recovering from what felt like a life-altering moment. I folded my arms across my chest, not sure what else to do with them now that he'd stepped back from me.

"Uh, why did you do that?" I asked, my voice faint and unsure.

"Because I wanted to. And you wanted me to. And so I did," he said, a challenge in his voice.

I should have been astounded, but the far more astounding event had just occurred. His confidence was surprising, and maybe new, though it wasn't like he was a retiring flower. No, Gabriel was confident in himself and what he wanted.

"Ok," I said, still not sure where he was going with this.

"We have things to discuss. I'll be over on Thursday night so we can get things worked out before your friends arrive Friday. I can help you prep or whatever you need."

"Ok," I repeated, unused to being the one getting told what was going to happen. In life, in relationships... I was usually the one calling the shots. I'd basically been doing that in our friendship, or so I'd thought.

~

Gabriel

She kissed me back.

She kissed me back.

Gracias a Dios, she kissed me back.

I'd been thinking about her all night after I drove home from dropping her off at her house. I didn't sleep but a few hours since I was too busy worrying about Vik and thinking about Rae. I finally passed out around six in the morning and let myself sleep until I woke in the early afternoon since I knew I had to work that night.

She'd asked me to check in and tell her how I was, and I did. We made plans for dinner, and somehow I kept my cool as I walked in and kissed her lips like it was my right. Like she was mine and that was how I always greeted her.

But I kept it short, controlled, and she didn't throw me off. I managed to quell her curiosity about why I'd kissed her lips and not just her cheek, but I knew we'd have to talk about it.

But mostly in our relationship to that point, we'd talked. Or we'd found ourselves in impossible situations—dealing with the aftermath of someone harassing her or discovering Vik at her apartment the night before. And each time, we'd talk some more, grow closer. And I'd discover one more thing I liked or admired about her.

Like how she was strong, and she respected her friends' perspectives, but she wasn't necessarily going to heed them if she didn't feel they were right. Or how she wasn't scared to interact with Vik when she was upset and hurting. I didn't know what she'd said that made Victoria hug her, but whatever it was, it was impressive. Then she'd proceeded to simply care for us while I checked out Victoria and distracted her.

She did nothing to insinuate herself into the moment except to *care* for us. Maybe it was because I'd been raised in a family where the language my grandmother and mother spoke was that of acts of service to show their love. Maybe it was because I was a nurse and found value for myself in meeting peoples' needs so I took particular notice when others did or didn't do the same.

Or maybe I'd been foolish enough to underestimate Rae and assume she wasn't particularly nurturing—I'd bought her claim that she was cold when every time we interacted I found her to be nothing but elemental fire.

I kept picturing her hugging Vik, just enveloping her, offering her comfort and support. She'd only met her one time, and yet there she was sitting down in the madness instead of excusing herself and going for a walk, or calling a cab, or asking if she could take my car back to Clarksville.

I couldn't even think of her concern for me. I didn't think it was pity—at this point I'd felt the chemistry between us enough times. And it wasn't that I didn't hear her when she said she didn't want to date someone in the Army—I did. But, and yes I did realize this was the height of arrogance, I was different.

I wasn't an infantryman or an armor officer. I was a nurse. I had flexibility and freedom both in and out of the Army that no other man she'd even thought of had. And I wasn't hell bent on twenty years in, if it came to it. I'd likely make more money as a civilian, depending on where I lived.

Sitting there comforting Vik, and frankly myself, I kept

thinking how hard it was to find someone good. Someone you matched with and liked and wanted to be with who also felt the same way *and* treated you well.

But for me, at least so far, that was Rae. I couldn't be more attracted to her—literally, it was impossible to be more attracted to a person than I was to her, physically and in every other way.

I enjoyed her. I looked forward to her—anything I could get. Talking with her. Texting with her. I even enjoyed just thinking about where she might be—at work, at the gym, at a soccer game, with Ann. It was practically pathetic, except that I had started suspecting she felt the same way, even with her continued reminders about being just friends.

It wasn't something I took lightly. I knew it was a risk, and that I could have very well created an irreparable rift between us by kissing her, by pushing her. But I'd had to try because everything in me told me I wasn't going to *talk* her into dating me. I wasn't going to convince someone who'd spent half a decade set against dating a fellow Army officer I was different. I had to show her, and that started by me taking a chance.

And all the angels in heaven said *hallelujah* because it paid off.

I was still nervous about what she'd say when we talked. We hadn't texted. I figured the radio silence was each of us giving the other personal space, and likely we both recognized we didn't want to have any kind of real conversation over text, especially when I'd told her I'd come see her on Thursday.

Well, it was Thursday, and I had the night off, and I couldn't wait to see her. I felt anticipation and a pinch of trepidation as I approached her now-familiar door. I was praying she hadn't talked herself out of something other than friendship in the days since we saw each other. It'd only been four days.

Four days couldn't ruin everything, could they?

She opened the door a moment after I rang the doorbell, and before I could fully appreciate her worn-in jeans and snug t-shirt, she stepped to me, wrapped her arms around my neck, and pulled my mouth to hers.

That went well.

Her fingers stroked the back of my head, running through the short hair there, and I stifled a groan as I kissed her back and paced us a few steps over her threshold through the doorway. I groped for the door and finally grabbed it and swung it shut without ever breaking contact with Rae's perfect, pliant lips.

She pulled back when the door slammed shut a little harder than I meant to shut it, but you couldn't blame me. Being greeted that way wasn't something I'd even let myself think about.

Ok, fine, maybe I'd *thought* about it. But I hadn't expected it.

I smiled as I took in her swollen lips, her flushed cheeks, her dazed eyes. My heartbeat thudded in my chest as I had the intense urge to crush her to me again and not let go.

But I didn't do that. Because we did have to talk.

With words.

Because that was what friends who weren't going to just be friends anymore did if they didn't want their relationship to implode.

"Hi," she said, a shy smile playing on that gorgeous mouth.

"Good to see you too," I said and let loose my rather satisfied smile.

"I can see you're very proud of yourself," she said, though she was beaming back at me just as brightly.

"Why shouldn't I be? I ring your doorbell and you greet me like that? This is how I know there is a God, and that I've done something very good to please Him." She laughed as I cupped her jaw and ran my thumb over her cheekbone, then let go and backed away. I was in danger of kissing her again, and I wasn't sure she'd stop me.

Not the worst idea you've ever had.

"Well, I've had some time to think..." she said as she walked into the living room and sat on the couch.

"Do we need to work on food for tomorrow?" I asked as I sat next to her. I didn't leave her room—I sat *right* next to her and put my hand behind her so she was caged in by the arm of the couch and my body.

I wasn't trying to corner her, I just wanted to make sure there wasn't distance between us. My biggest concern about what would happen tonight was that she'd back away and try to step back into the friendzone.

I wanted the friendzone with Rae like I wanted a craniotomy.

She raised an eyebrow at me as she scooted to the side of the couch an inch to give herself space, and then grabbed my hand and laced her fingers through mine. My pulse thumped in my wrist, my neck, all through me at her warm palm lined up with mine, her fingers folded over the back of my hand.

Bueno.

"I figured we should talk sooner than later since it's all I can think about, if that's ok with you? We can deal with the food prep later."

My heart hadn't calmed down, and it was roaring now, too anxious to hear what she'd say.

Logically, I knew she wouldn't have kissed me upon opening the door if she wasn't interested in more. That just wasn't her style. But I still wasn't sure what would happen.

"Ok," I agreed.

We sat there silently, her small hand in my larger one resting on her thigh, and looked at each other. I'd expected her to say her piece, but she didn't move or speak.

"I feel like since you started all this, you should go first," she said with a small smile and squeezed my hand.

"What do you want me to say?" I asked, chuckling at the look of frustration wrinkling her brow as soon as I said it.

"I want to know what you want. What you're thinking." She extracted her hand from mine and folded her hands together, then shifted so her back was to the arm of the couch and her knees were folded up between us. I adjusted so I was angled toward her and let my thumb run across the top of her bent knee.

I felt a burst of nerves and breathed out sharply, embracing the moment and very open invitation. I looked into her bright blue eyes rimmed with dark lashes and went for it. "You. I want you. I want us to be more than friends—for us to be together."

Her mouth opened, then shut, like she wasn't sure what to say. "Wow." Her voice was disbelieving, or shocked, maybe. Another wave of anxiety washed through me.

"Bad wow?" My voice sounded strangled, and I cleared my throat as I watched her thinking. I could actually see her mind racing but had no idea what was going on there.

"No, not bad wow. I just didn't expect you to be so direct, I guess." She gave me a small smile I found immensely encouraging.

"I'm past the point of pretending I only want to be your friend. I thought I made that clear on Sunday."

"Oh, you definitely did. And I appreciate your clarity on the matter." She suppressed a grin, and I could swear I saw a little color pink her cheeks. She was delectable even when I felt myself dangling over the side of a cliff.

One more concern I knew we had to deal with. "And listen, I know you outrank me—"

She waved her hand, then said, "We're not in the same chain of command. It's not... it's fine."

"Ok. I'm glad. So, your turn."

"I'm..."

And now, the moment of truth.

"Amenable." Then she gave me a look I couldn't decipher, but I thought was a good thing. Amenable.

That was a good thing, right?

"Amenable? Like, you are agreeable to the idea of being with me?" Dios, what a ridiculous thing to say out loud. I ran a hand through my hair and tried not to roll my eyes at myself.

"I am," she said with one firm nod. She looked determined. Maybe like she was talking herself into it.

"Really? You sure?" Why I was trying to talk her out of her agreeing with me, I didn't know. I wasn't—not really—but she'd been so set against us dating I wasn't sure how to proceed. While I'd planned to kiss her, to push her to this point, I hadn't actually planned on what would happen next.

Probably because I never expected her to go with it.

She gave me a confused look with a tilt of her head and a small smile. "You having doubts? Sounds like you're trying to talk me out of dating you now."

I sat up straighter, not surprised she'd called me out.

"Absolutely not. I wouldn't do such a thing. If I'm honest, I didn't expect you to do anything other than let me down easy," I said with chagrin.

She leaned back and folded her arms across her chest and squinted at me like she was trying to see through what I'd said. "I don't buy it."

"What?"

"I don't believe you thought I'd reject you."

"Why wouldn't I think that? You've told me repeatedly you wouldn't date me. I have no reason to expect you'd do anything but reject me." I didn't need to argue this point with her, but I also couldn't let her have this one. She couldn't believe it'd been an easy call for me to march up to her and kiss her, could she? I'd felt like the bull with all the balls after that, and she hadn't even said a word to me.

"Something must have made you think I'd say yes, or you wouldn't have kissed me. You're smart, and you're respectful, and if you'd thought you'd be harming me or you, you wouldn't have done it." She unfolded her arms and leaned her head against one she propped on the back of the couch as she waited for me to respond.

"I was obviously hopeful. We've talked enough for me to know we have a lot in common outside the Army, and we enjoy each other's company. We have insane chemistry—that helped. But I had to hope maybe you felt a little something more for me the way I do for you, and I knew it wasn't something we'd come to by talking about it *first*." I watched her face, completely absorbed in her smooth, pink cheeks, her soft lips, her blue eyes.

"Ok." She said it in a way that felt final, and I was sure my face conveyed my confusion.

"Ok?"

"Yep." She unfolded her legs and stood up. "Let's do the

food prep. I'll be up early getting the house ready, and I haven't seen Maybelline in years so I'm a little nervous about having her here. I probably won't sleep well. Anyway, I don't have much to do—just need to prep the quiche and the vegetables for the salad." She was already in the kitchen, pulling out a cutting board and knife, grabbing celery from the fridge, skinning an onion...

And there I sat, unable to process what had just happened.

Had we gotten anywhere? I reviewed our conversation.

I said I wanted her—to be together.

She said wow.

I asked if that was bad.

She said I was direct and that surprised her.

I said I was clear on what I wanted.

She said that was a good thing.

I asked her what she thought.

She said she was *amenable*.

And then we got onto the subject of how I made the move. But we hadn't actually established where that left us. Were we dating? Was she into me too? Did she want to date me too? Or she was just, what? Flattered?

Rae wasn't the kind of woman to jump up and down and toss glitter when I asked her out. But I now recognized that she'd not said anything definitive. Was that purposeful? Was she being evasive or indecisive, or whatever this was, to spare my feelings?

A tepid wave of misery washed over me as I realized that was what this was. This was her being purposefully vague so I didn't have to feel embarrassed and she didn't have to outright reject me.

She'd been kind. Maybe she was even interested in me,

or in some kind of friends with benefits situation, but she hadn't been clear about what happened now.

That was the whole point of me coming here, and now I was sitting there like a slug on the couch, not sure how to get out of there with any dignity left. But I would.

I stood, and nodded to myself, psyching myself up for helping her with the food and then getting the hell out.

I washed my hands in the kitchen sink, then sidled up next to her, maintaining a level of outward ease I absolutely did not possess.

"What can I do?" I asked.

"Wash and cut the vegetables? You can use that cutting board." She gestured to a board to the left of the sink with her elbow and looked up to give me a quick smile as she chopped through half an onion. Her knife hovered over the translucent pile when she saw my face. "What's wrong?"

"Oh, nothing. I want you to temper your expectations, ok? Remember my cooking skills are average," I joked.

"No. Tell me. What's wrong?" She put the knife down and wiped her hands on the towel she'd tucked into the waist of her jeans. I didn't know why but I liked that about her—she did things in a way that wasn't fancy, but that made sense. She needed a towel? There it was. No cutesy apron—just a clean blue and white checked kitchen towel.

"I'm good," I said with as much confidence as I could, then moved back to the sink to rinse celery and carrots.

She was quiet and I could feel her watching me as I rinsed a pepper, zucchini, tomatoes, green onions under biting-cold water. I picked out a small handful of tomatoes from the bottom of the container that were wrinkled or rotten, focusing all of my energy and mind on the task.

Except the small part of me—well ok, not entirely small, but probably less than half, or maybe just slightly, *slightly* more than half—that was attuned to her. That part of me was on edge because I hadn't heard her knife continue chopping in the last few minutes, and I could feel her eyes on me.

I refused to turn. I refused to say I had no idea what was happening to us despite the conversation we'd just had that seemed to clear things up but had, in fact, only served to confuse me. I refused to acknowledge I was pretty sure she was blowing me off. Eventually, the crunch of the celery giving way under her chef's knife started again, and I let out a silent breath.

For the next half hour we moved around each other in the kitchen. I could tell she wanted to ask me what I was thinking—maybe only a little more than I wanted to ask her the same thing—but I wouldn't, and she didn't. The only time we spoke was when she gave me instructions or I asked where something I needed was. It was a strange and stark contrast to the earlier warmth and closeness.

At the same time, it wasn't. It was another reminder of how well we cooperated—she explained things quickly and clearly, and I could take her direction and go. We moved around each other in her small kitchen with ease. All it did was cause me a small pang of regret.

The vegetables were roasting in the oven while I scrubbed cutting boards and rinsed prep bowls. Rae came back into the kitchen after a quick trip to switch some laundry she had going and set her kitchen towel on the counter. She leaned a hip on the counter and watched as I set a bowl in the drying rack and wiped my hands on the towel that hung from the oven handle.

When I looked up at her, I saw she was studying me. I gave her a small smile.

"Now will you tell me?" she asked.

"I—" I started but couldn't figure out what to say. I couldn't keep pretending everything was fine or that I was hunky dory, but I wasn't about to whine.

She stepped to me and grabbed my hand. My stomach dropped at the contact, and I gritted my teeth against the warmth snaking through me at just that small gesture. She pulled me to her, close. She tilted her chin up and didn't break eye contact as she took my other hand. I willed my pulse to slow, but like the jerk it was, it didn't listen.

"What is happening in that head?" she asked, her quiet, smooth voice a small form of torture.

"I don't know what's happening," I admitted, though I was sure she could hear the discomfort in my voice. She squeezed my hands, then dropped them. She leaned back on the counter, then hopped up and sat on the edge. She stretched out her legs and used her heels to pull me closer to her.

I nearly swallowed my tongue. I stepped forward, my hips cradled between her legs, her hands reaching for the sides of my t-shirt to hold me in place.

CHAPTER TEN

Gabriel

WELL THIS IS INTERESTING.

I set my hands on the counter on either side of her thighs and looked into her very determined eyes, which were now closer to eye level.

"You don't know what's happening between us?" she asked, pulling me a little closer.

I shook my head slowly, instinctively leaning in. Blood rushed in my ears as I waited for... something.

"Ask me, then. Don't stay quiet. We've never been like that with each other, have we? We've always been honest."

"Yeah, we have." *Unless you count all of the inappropriate thoughts I've had to silence. Or all the times I agreed to be your friend while feeling so many unfriendly things.*

"So ask me what you want to know. I'm not trying to be mysterious," she said with a small grin.

"Well... where do we stand?" My voice was low and I

hated how unsure I sounded and felt. I was generally confident, but Rae threw me off balance. I felt like I was constantly course-correcting around her, constantly working to figure out how to show her enough of who I was without being so vulnerable she'd crush me.

Because I knew, from the moment we'd held our cease-fire and agreed to be friends, that she could crush me.

"You're the one standing. And right now, you're between my thighs," she said and pursed her lips together to stifle a laugh. Then she let it loose, a light and buoyant sound, as she pulled my shoulders to her and hugged me. She let go and took a big breath.

"But really, do you think I stand around with all my male friends like this? Do you think I kiss them?"

"I don't know..."

"You do. Unless you're going to believe the rumors about me, then you do know, Gabriel. You know me better than almost anyone. I don't let people into my life easily, and you're in here."

"Ok." It was good to hear—the thought of her sitting like this with anyone else made me want to hurl, and the thought of her kissing someone else threatened to turn my vision to blood.

"So you said you want me," she started, her voice a little husky and a lot appealing. "You want us to be together." Her eyes searched mine.

"I do."

"Ok then. We're together."

My heart thudded in my chest. Was it that easy?

"Really? Just like that?"

"Yes."

"I just had to ask?"

"You didn't ask, but yes." She smiled at me and pulled me closer so our faces were just six inches apart.

"How are you agreeing to this when you have been rejecting me since we met?"

"I've been trying to figure that out. I don't have a good answer for you except despite my best efforts, you matter to me. I want to be around you. And I am a little attracted to you." She held up her index finger and thumb an inch apart.

"Wow, that much, huh?"

She nodded.

"So you're breaking your rule for me?" I asked.

"I guess so. Against my better judgment, I guess so." I saw a flicker of unease cross her face. I traced her eyebrow with my finger, chasing away that look.

"You know I'd never hurt you, right?"

"I know you'd never mean to, yes," she said with a sad smile.

She was killing me. *Killing me.*

"So I can take you on dates?"

"You kind of already did that the other day, but yes," she said, a real smile that reached her eyes on her beautiful face now.

"And I can kiss you again?"

Her gaze was intense and I saw her chest rise and fall, then she pulled me in for a quick, focus-shattering kiss. "You've already done that too, but also yes."

"Gracias a Dios," I said to the ceiling and she laughed at me.

"But I'm not big into PDA, ok? And definitely not—"

"Rae, you know I wouldn't ever touch you in a professional setting. I'm not an idiot."

"I know. I just—this is uncharted territory for me, and it's not like I know what I'm doing. I haven't dated someone since Brad, and we were barely on the same post together. Plus we were married. I know you're not in my chain of command but if we're going to do this, I can't be worrying about what people are saying." She gave me an embarrassed look.

"I get it. There's nothing wrong with us dating, but you're protecting yourself. I don't want you to stop doing that. Though I'm glad you're not going to keep protecting yourself from me," I said, leaning in to kiss her lightly.

"And—" She started, then clamped her mouth shut.

"And?"

"Are we—uh, would we be—am I your..."

"I don't want to date anyone else. I haven't dated anyone since I met you, nor have I wanted to. And it may make me a jackass, but I'm pretty sure I'm not mature enough to handle you dating someone else." It was honest. A mild version of the truth, since if she was dating someone else I would have a tantrum followed by locking myself in my house so I didn't punch whoever it was in the face.

She gave me one of her blazing smiles. "Well you are dating an older woman. How do you feel about that?" she asked with mock seriousness.

"I feel fantastic about it."

She rolled her eyes at me. "You're too cocky. I'm going to regret this."

"No, not cocky—confident. I know who I am. I know what I want. I know for a fact a less confident man would get lost with you because you're the same way." I leaned in and whispered against the shell of her ear. "Eventually, I'll know what you want, and you'll appreciate my confidence in that, too." I pressed a kiss behind the curve of her ear.

Her hands gripped my forearms and I felt her shiver. Right as I was about to take some time figuring out just what she liked, the oven beeped and she jerked back. She blinked and looked to the left and right of me, then huffed out a small breath.

"You're a dangerous man..." she said quietly as she hopped down from the counter. I watched her and appreciated the view of her moving in her kitchen, the tension that hung over me earlier now replaced with a far more pleasurable kind.

"So what time are we eating tomorrow?"

"I asked Ann to come around noon. We'll eat soon after, unless you can't be here that early?" She set the vegetables down and hung the pot holder back on its hook on the wall behind the oven.

"That's fine. I'll plan to bring my stuff and leave for work from here at 6:30, if you don't mind." I reached for her hand and wrapped it in mine. She followed as I moved to her front door.

"Works for me. Thank you for your help."

"My pleasure," I said, pulling her into a hug. "I wish I could pretend I didn't know how tired you are, but I can tell you're exhausted, and I know tomorrow is going to be a long day hosting your friends. So I'm going to say goodnight and leave, even though I am, at this moment, still trying to convince myself not to ask you if I can stay."

She leaned up on her toes and kissed me lightly once, twice, three times. She stayed like that, pressed against me, then whispered against my lips. "You're not invited."

Of course. I barked a laugh as I pulled back from her. "I shouldn't have made it sound like I thought I was, but thanks for keeping me in line."

"See you tomorrow," she said with a smile that made me feel a little dreamy when I could appreciate it was just for me.

"Tomorrow."

~

Rae

I tossed and turned all night.

This wasn't a surprise since all I could think about was Gabriel and how soon I'd see him again. Would it be awkward? I didn't think so since we'd talked through some pretty awkward things in the course of our relationship so far.

But, it might be. He took my comment about him not being invited to stay with good humor, but at some point, we'd need to have *the talk*. The yeah-I'm-not-having-sex-with-you talk. *That would go well,* based on his very physical approach to the twenty minutes we'd actually acknowledged being *together*.

On the other hand, he did know me. And he even knew, at least somewhere in his mind if he hadn't forgotten, that I hadn't been sexually active in six years, or since I'd been with Brad. So he couldn't be all that surprised, could he?

I knew him. I knew he wasn't going to freak out on me. I didn't think.

The truth was, while I knew a lot about Gabriel in some ways—he was a devoted brother, a great nurse, a thoughtful man, a lover of tacos al pastor—I didn't actually know a lot about him in the boyfriend capacity.

Ugh. My stomach sunk at the thought. *What am I doing?*

I'd planned to stay far away from this, but the fact that I wanted to be with him was unavoidable. And the other fact

—that we were basically dating without the physical side of things—was too.

But I couldn't answer the questions that kept popping up. *Where can this lead? What are you expecting out of this? How long until you recognize what an idiot you're being?*

I spent the night working to silence those voices, those naysaying jerks. I'd spent a lot of my life telling those voices to shut up, but they were hard to ignore after so long. *He'll get tired of you as soon as you won't sleep with him. If you stay with him, he'll want to have kids, and you'll have to give up everything. Look at you, you're already compromising what you said you wanted for him.*

Yeah, those voices. I couldn't do anything but tune them out because I didn't have answers. We hadn't talked about that, but we also didn't need to—not yet. And as much of a planner as I was (because that was literally the main part of my job—*planning*), I didn't want to self-sabotage this.

I knew Gabriel was special. I could see that from the first time we talked and agreed to be friends. I felt it every time I was with him—he made the people around him feel special, and he made them better.

When I wasn't thinking about Gabriel, I'd try to lull myself into thinking about less emotionally demanding things like when to put in the quiche and whether I ever bought nicer napkins. Then I'd think about seeing Maybelline and that'd set my mind racing again.

I wasn't exactly nervous to see her. We talked on the phone or messaged each other every few months, so it wasn't like she didn't know anything about my life. She'd even sent me a few packages and letters while I was in Afghanistan this last time.

The problem was she and I had the same beginning, and so far, very different ends.

Well, fine, not *ends*, but our lives had been parallel. We'd been in pageants together for seven years—she showed up on the circuit about a year after I did, and we were fast friends. We were competitive, but not cutthroat, and we clicked in a way I hadn't with so many others. She sang opera for her talent, even when she was young, while I danced.

We both went to the University of Georgia, but she stuck with pageants and I begged off for ROTC. We both got married the week after graduation to someone we'd met in school.

And that's where the similarities ended. She was still blissfully married to Daniel, and I'd divorced before most couples had even settled in to folding each other's socks. She'd always wanted to be a mom, and she was one. She had a six-year-old and was pregnant and due with her second child in about two months. Her parents were keeping her daughter so she and her husband could have a minute to themselves before the new baby came—and they were spending their first night with me, of all places. They were then heading to Nashville for the remainder of their holiday, and though I was sad to miss meeting their oldest, I was relieved I wouldn't be wrangling a kid.

Maybelline had always wanted to be a wife and a mom. I hadn't always had the vision to want a life in the Army, but I always had ambition to do something more.

Something more. I knew how it sounded. But that was how it felt, probably because I saw my mom as giving up her something more for my dad, and then for me and Heath, and then for Jerry. It wasn't that I thought being a wife or mom was easy.

I didn't think that.

Maybe I even recognized it was harder—maybe that's

what scared me so much. I didn't know. But what I knew was I was made to be in the Army—about that I had no doubt. I wondered how much Maybelline and I would have to talk about.

I wondered, too, what she'd think of Gabriel.

I rolled out of bed at 0600 and got in a chilly run before I showered and started the prep work. I'd set the table last night, but I left vacuuming and dusting and all of that until this morning. I made the potato casserole like my grandmother made. It was something I ate exactly once a year and was something that sent me flying back to my happiest moments in childhood at first bite.

I did everything else I could think of, double checked my guestroom and bathrooms, added more water to the small vase of flowers I put in the guestroom and finally heard the knock.

Before I could let the nerves climb up my throat, I threw open the door and found a rotund and adorable Maybelline on the other side.

"Rayanne Elise Jackson you are more gorgeous than you ever have been, and I'm gonna slap you for it!" she scream-shrieked as she brushed through the door and barreled into me. I hugged her back, tight, and felt a rush of joy I hadn't expected melt over me.

"You should do pregnancy pageants, May—you're actually glowing." I took in her platinum blonde hair that was darker at the roots, her light yellow sweater that off-set her tree-bark eyes, and her skirt, or maybe it was a dress, that was a deep purple and clung to her perfectly curving belly.

"Shut it. I don't even want to think about getting judged with this booty," she said, holding me at arm's length by the shoulders.

"Hey, Rae," Daniel, Maybelline's quiet husband, peeked over her shoulder as she held me out.

"May, let me greet your husband," I said and squeezed her elbows. She dropped her arms and moved past me so I could give Daniel a quick side-hug. He'd always been quiet and calm to Maybelline's loud and bold. I hadn't spent too much time with them, but each interaction we'd had over the years had told me he treated her well and loved her with a singular kind of exuberance he didn't seem to show for anything else—at least that I'd noticed.

I led them into the living room, and Daniel excused himself to the guestroom to freshen up and settle their bag.

"This is a nice place, sweetie. I hope you have good neighbors with 'em being so close like this," she said and sat on the edge of the couch. "Mind stuffing a few pillows behind me?"

I stuffed two throw pillows behind her, and she leaned back and sighed. "I'm going to tell you this and know you won't take it wrong. I could not be more excited not to be pregnant. I cannot wait to pop this baby out and have my uterus return to its regularly scheduled programming. This pregnancy has been great, but I got big, then pregnant big, and now I'm *real pregnant* big, and I've still got more to go."

I'd forgotten how much I loved just listening to her talk. She'd talked incessantly back stage, even when we were told to hush. Her voice was high and sweet, and her accent was far more prevalent than mine was—likely due to her lack of shame when it came to her small-town heritage. She had nothing to hide.

Neither did I, but I did it all the same. One less thing to draw attention to myself.

"I bet you're so ready. I'm so glad it's going well, though," I said gently, sure she wouldn't want to talk about the two pregnancies after her first and before this one that hadn't gone well at all and that had ended in utter heartbreak.

She grabbed my hand and pulled me down next to her on the couch. "Me too, sweetie."

We talked a few minutes about how their travel had gone—they'd broken up the trip with several stops so her back didn't hurt her too much, and she was relieved that Jessie, their daughter, hadn't been at all upset to see them go when they dropped her off at her grandparents' house. I puttered around the kitchen and living room on and off, and we continued talking.

"So who all is coming today? What should I know?"

"My neighbor and fellow Army officer Ann Richards is coming with a date—at least, I think she's just a date and not a girlfriend yet, but I may be out of touch on that because we haven't gotten caught up in a while. And, uh, my friend Gabriel is coming." For some reason I didn't elaborate, but I saw May's eyes cut right to me.

"Friend?"

"Well, more than friend." The moment *more* was out of my mouth she was grinning like the Cheshire cat.

"I knew it. I could tell you were happy, or happier, or something. I just knew there was someone. Tell me more," she demanded from her throne of pillows on the couch.

"He's... well, we actually met when I went to the ER a few months ago and then just kept running into each other and became friends."

"Why were you at the—"

"Nothing serious. He's a nurse, and he helped me." I felt a little color creep into my cheeks, and I took a sip of the water sitting on the table in front of me.

"Ok. And so you're dating now?"

"As of last night, yes."

"Last night?"

"Yes… it's pretty new."

"Well, yeah, just a little. And so, he works in town or something?" she asked.

"He works on base, at the Army hospital," I said quietly. I watched as Maybelline's eyes narrowed.

"He's in the Army?" She knew about my swearing off Army men. I'd never said much about it other than that I would never date anyone in the military again.

"Yes. He's a first lieutenant—he's a little younger than me."

"Wow. Younger *and* in the military. This guy must be something," she said with a whistle and a raised eyebrow. She'd always been extremely expressive.

I smiled to myself despite feeling under the lens of her questioning. "He is."

"And when should I expect my invitation?"

"Invitation?"

"To your wedding. So he can become Mr. Rayanne Jackson?"

"Oh, no. That's not—we're just dating. I mean, we're exclusive, but I'm not—we're not—" The doorbell saved me. Or, maybe it didn't, since it was either Ann, who'd chat away with Maybelline and tell her anything she wanted to know about Gabriel and me, or Gabriel, who would make me have to work harder to form complete sentences when he got close to me, which he'd definitely do (and which I was looking forward to him doing, but was still distracting).

"Give me a sec and I'll grab the door," I said as I hopped up, nervous energy now shooting through me. I grabbed the door and let out a breath—hard to tell whether it was relief or frustration—at seeing Ann. "Hey friend. Great to see you." She held a sheet pan in both hands covered with a kitchen towel, and I knew what I'd find beneath.

"Is Gabriel here yet? I didn't think I saw his car," Ann said as she followed me to the kitchen and set the tray down. I'd never been one for biscuits instead of rolls, and didn't eat a lot of bread anyway, but I may or may not have invited her for her biscuits alone.

"I think he'll be here any minute," I said as I noticed the clock. 11:53—he wasn't late. He said he'd be here. I had no reason to doubt him.

But I'd gotten crazy nervous and didn't know why.

Well, that was a lie. I did know. I wasn't sure how it would go, all of us together. I hadn't even had a conversation with Ann to let her know, or a conversation with May's husband since they arrived. It had the makings of awkwardness, squared.

And then, the doorbell rang. I felt my heart jump like a little cartoon character at the thought that it might be Gabriel. *What's he going to say? What's he going to do? What will he be wearing?*

Good grief, I had it bad.

I opened the door, hoping Maybelline and Ann were acceptably occupied by introducing themselves, which I'd failed to do since I'd been mentally preoccupied with thoughts of my missing guest.

"Hi, lovely," he said as soon as I opened the door.

"Hi..." and that's as far as I got because I'd almost said *honey*. I'd almost actually given him the pet name I'd joked about, and I felt a flush of embarrassment even though he couldn't possibly know what I'd almost said.

"Were you going to say something else?" he asked as he stepped inside and I closed the door.

"What? No."

"Yes you were."

"I was *not*."

"You were," he insisted, and even though I found it maddening, it also somehow spoke to me—his insistence, and pushiness, was unavoidably appealing.

"I was not. What would I call you, anyway?" I asked.

"You can call me whatever you want, carita." Just the word, one word, and my heart was jumping, blood pumping, cheeks flushing.

This was not normally me. Even when I liked a guy, I was pretty tame. It wasn't that I was without passion, but I'd trained myself to be circumspect about such things, and it'd stuck. It was hard to let go, in any sense of the word.

Gabriel brought that out of me.

He leaned in and kissed my cheek but lingered there, and it was... too much—the warmth of his breath at my jaw, the heat of his hand on my arm, the scent of his cologne so light I couldn't quite separate it from the smell of the food in the house.

"Did you sleep ok?" I asked as I pulled back from him, glancing into the living room to see that May and Ann were absolutely watching our exchange.

"Once I got settled, yes. I did. Did you?" He set a grocery bag and a small basket full of beautiful colored eggs on the kitchen island and moved to the sink to wash his hands.

"Uh, yeah. I did. Eventually. For... a bit." He arched a brow at me like he suspected something—maybe he even knew I was thinking of him. "Oh don't assume I was awake because I was thinking about you because, well, just... don't assume that."

I couldn't lie to him. I had been awake because of him. But I didn't want him to get too confident here. As much as

I liked him, I didn't want to be at a disadvantage and him having any idea how *much* I liked him was a disadvantage.

"Well, carita, I can tell you that while I didn't have trouble sleeping, I had very compelling dreams." He ran his hand from my shoulder to my hand and then raised that same eyebrow at me.

I tried not to audibly sputter.

"Oh?" Because what else could I say?

"Mmm," was all he said, like it was an acceptable word and not a sound he made as he was remembering some illicit encounter we'd had in his dream world.

"All right, that's about all I can take of this nonsense. I guess you two have had a DTR and made it official?" Ann's question came from the living room where she looked exasperated, and May looked delighted.

"Uh, yes. We did," I said, and though I didn't mean to, I glanced at Gabriel and beamed at him. I bit my lip because how else could I contain the bubbling elation I felt at Ann's crusty comment?

"Claro, we did." His face was lit from within, I would swear it. He seemed genuinely pleased, and that did something to me—it changed my internal chemistry, or something similarly severe, because I had to physically brace myself against the counter to keep from attacking him and showing him *just how much* I liked him.

"Good. 'Bout time. You two were ridiculous," Ann grumped, and it was then I noticed she seemed... miserable.

"Congratulations," May said and then hoisted herself off the couch belly first. She came and shook Gabriel's hand and they chatted a moment, me once again failing to introduce my friends. But I was moving to Ann, seeing her eyes redden and shoot to the floor as I reached her.

"What's up?"

"Nothing." She clamped her mouth shut and her whole body shut down. All openness and friendliness was *gone*.

"When's your woman coming?" With this she winced, and I knew something was very wrong.

I grabbed her arm. "Tell me."

"It's fine. I'm fine."

"Stop. Tell me, Ann."

I watched her swallow, clench her jaw, and then look at me with an impassive glare. "She's not sure if she wants to be exclusive. So she's not coming." She stopped, her voice catching. I knew she wouldn't cry, probably only because I'd never seen it happen. I grabbed her wrist and waited for her to meet my eye.

"I'm sorry. I'm so sorry," I said and pulled her to me. I hugged her, which wasn't something we did often since neither of us were particularly physically effusive people. She had to bend to do it, but she did, squeezing me tight and accepting the comfort for a moment before she stepped back.

"Thanks. I'll be fine." She cleared her throat and gave me a flat smile.

"You will. I have no doubt." I ushered her to the kitchen, and Gabriel was pouring her a mimosa. He handed it to her and gave her a pat on the back.

"You look great, Ann," he said.

"You too, nurse Gabriel. You clean up nice," Ann offered weakly.

"Well listen, I'm starving, and as the only one currently nurturing another human life, I'd like to request we eat in the next ten minutes. I'll just run grab Daniel," May said and off she went up the stairs.

"Let me go get the ham. It's resting but should be ready to carve. I'll be back in a sec," Ann said. She gulped down her drink, set her glass on the counter, and walked directly to the door.

Gabriel and I watched her go. I kept my eyes on the door, feeling the thick wretchedness that comes when a dear friend is hurting. If I saw Dr. Jordan again I'd be biting my tongue.

"Hey," Gabriel said softly, turning me to him with just his voice.

I looked at him for a moment, finally absorbing his presence there in my kitchen, the first time since we'd decided to officially date. Strange that it'd only been a little more than twelve hours when it felt like weeks since I'd seen him.

It felt odd, but not bad.

He wore black slacks and a light blue button up shirt. His hair was styled artfully, and it looked fantastic. He pulled me in for a hug, then leaned away. "We match."

I felt the vise in my chest ease a bit at the sight of his amused smile. "Did you know I was wearing a blue dress? I hear color-coordinating is all the rage these days with couples."

His face exploded in a smile. "Mm, couples. Yes. That's what we are, huh?"

"We did talk, and I thought—" I started, feeling the drop of the thought that I might have been totally wrong about how our conversation ended last night.

"Yes, we did. And you're right. We are. I just didn't realize we were at outfit-coordination level yet. But now I know, so it's a good thing I lucked out and wore a shirt that matched this delectable dress." He twirled me around and the skirt flared out. It wasn't anything fancy—a robin's egg blue dress with sleeves to my elbow that fitted close on top and flared out around my waist. I wore saddle brown sandals despite the day being chilly and my hair was in a low, stylized knot. I liked having my hair down when I wasn't working out or in uniform, but I wanted my hair pulled back and out of the way for serving food.

"Now you know," I said, and before I could pull him in to kiss him, I heard the front door creak open and jumped away. "Better not be too... enthusiastic," I said with a frown.

"Understood," he said, and I could see he did as he rushed to close the door behind Ann.

CHAPTER ELEVEN

Gabriel

Brunch was perfect. The weird little conglomeration of Rae's friends at her tiny table was perfect. I couldn't have thought of a better illustration for this woman if I tried.

She claimed she wasn't warm, that she was guarded, that she held herself close. And she did. But then she reeled people in, and she kept them, it seemed. Once you were in, you were *in*.

I hoped I was *in* in. As I sat there next to Rae watching her react to a story Maybelline was telling about their daughter, her eyes shining and her mouth wide with a delighted smile, I wanted it so bad I could have choked on the wanting.

As the day went on and I caught Daniel with his arm around Maybelline's chair, or saw him lean to whisper something in her ear, I felt it again. When Rae grabbed my hand and squeezed it after I talked about my family, like she was glad I'd share my life with her friends, I had to compose myself so I didn't fall at her feet and beg her to marry me.

Because that was what was happening to me. My idiot little brain had taken her *yes* to dating me and it had bolted. There was no stopping it. When I'd talked to Vik this morning, she could hear something was different. She asked me if I was going to propose to Rae. She thought I'd been dating her for months now, so that didn't seem so far off base.

The ridiculous thing was, instead of getting freaked out that she'd even ask, I felt that idea dig its claws in and take hold of me. As I showered, got dressed, brushed my teeth, packed up my clothes for my shift, my mind was on a runaway train. I was seeing little brown-haired, blue-eyed babies running around Rae's feet. I could see spending the afternoon with Maybelline would force me even further in that direction.

"So what about you, Rae? Will you dive in again?" Maybelline asked, a curious glint in her eye.

I hadn't heard the beginning of the conversation. Rae had set her hand on my leg—*my leg*—and my thoughts had been occupied with that contact for the last several minutes. My quad muscle would be in danger of atrophying because there was nothing in the world that could make me move that muscle if it might cause her to move her hand.

"Uh, yeah, no. I don't, uh... I don't foresee that," Rae answered, her voice shaky.

"No?" Maybelline pressed. She set her napkin down on her plate and took a sip of water, her eyes not leaving Rae's. I could see Rae clinching her jaw, and Daniel studied the napkin in his lap like his career depended on it. Ann was busily tapping on her phone and avoiding the conversation too.

What did I miss?

Rae cleared her throat. "No."

"And you, Gabriel?" May asked just as Rae sat up in her chair and gave her a hard look.

"Sorry, I must have missed what we were talking about," I said, my smile and tone easy.

"Marriage. Do you think you'll get married sometime?"

Oh.

Oh.

I don't foresee that. That's what Rae had said. And suddenly, my pleasantly full belly felt like I'd been forced to drink a gallon of barium sulfide at a chug. I'd been punched in the gut by this chipper, pregnant former beauty queen.

"Ahh," I managed, though it might have sounded more like I was in pain and less like I was discovering the conversation topic. "Uh, yeah. Marriage is... marriage is important to me." I licked my lips, wiped my chin with my napkin, arranged my utensils on my plate, scratched at a drop of jam that had congealed on the table cloth next to my plate. Anything to avoid looking at Rae.

Her hand was notably still on my leg. It was so still, I would have sworn she was carved out of clay and not an actual person, except that she wasn't malleable at all—she sat rigid and silent next to me.

Aye.

"Hey, I'm going to have to leave before dessert," Ann mercifully interrupted.

"What's wrong?" Rae asked and pulled her hand from my leg.

"Nothing, actually. Or, I hope not. Alisha's coming over to talk..." she trailed off as she stood and took her plate.

"Oh. Oh!" Rae hopped up too and grabbed the plate from Ann's hand. "Just go, and then... you know, feel free to come back for pie, if you want. Or not." She smiled brightly at Ann, and Ann seemed to be suppressing her own smile. She grabbed Rae's hand and squeezed it and off she went.

"Well let's clean up and then eat pie." Maybelline shouted this, like the idea was the best thing she'd ever thought of and she hadn't just brought up some major points of contention for me and Rae in the course of a three-minute casual conversation-turned-grilling.

"Yes, let's. But let's do your eggs, too, ok? The..." I could hear it in Rae's voice, but I knew she wouldn't let me see the conversation bothered her. I'd figure out how to talk to her, and we'd confront it. We would.

"Cascarones. Yeah, we'll do them." As we moved into the kitchen and plates clinked against the counter and food was scraped into the disposal in the sink, I refused to let my good mood falter.

After a round of pie and a few minutes of chatting in the living room, I passed around the basket full of cascarones, the sight of delicate, colorful eggs Abuelita had sent launching a pang of joy and homesickness through me. Once everyone had one, we broke them over each other's heads. Rainbow-colored confetti poured out in a cheery spill from each egg. We all laughed, because you can't not laugh when you're covered in rainbow confetti and you've cracked one over someone else's head. Rae's smile was real and wide and it made my pulse race to watch her laugh and break another egg over May's head. It helped my heart resist the pull toward sadness.

May declared she needed a nap, and Daniel followed her upstairs. This left me with Rae, who was sitting in a chair on the opposite side of the room. We hadn't had a minute alone since the marriage conversation, and I felt the strain return as the confetti settled around us. I knew she did too. But was this something to talk about?

What I did know was that a long shift was coming, I was already tired because the truth was, I hadn't slept much, and I was alone with my woman for the first time since she'd decided she'd be *my* woman.

At least for now, an ugly voice in my head reminded.

"Come sit by me," I said quietly, just over the low roar of the dishwasher.

She looked at me a moment, then moved to sit next to me. She sat about a foot away from me, but before I could protest, she grabbed the hand from the back of the couch, wrapped it around her neck and across her chest, and leaned back against me, her head on my pec.

"Hello there," I said to the top of her head.

"This ok?" she asked with a tilt of her head. Her eyes were bright, but tired.

"Of course. I want you near me any time you want to be." *Lame. Totally lame, man.* My inner monologue was not helping my confidence.

"I'm so tired. I hope you did sleep because I can't imagine how you'll stay up and work all night," she said, then rotated so she was nestled between my arm and side, her legs now resting on the couch.

"I didn't, actually, but it happens. I'll make it," I said, a small flutter of dread flapping its way through my gut.

"But you can't just sit and zone out at your computer. You have to actually *help* people. You have to make decisions and give medicines and... I don't know, triage." One arm slid over my ribs and a hand slowly smoothed up and down my side. I tightened my abs to resist jerking away.

She sat up, her eyes wide. "Are you ticklish?" She asked it like it was the best news she'd ever received.

"Absolutely *not*," I said in a mock-stern voice. Her

whole face was lit up with the revelation, and it was hard stay straight.

"I'm going to store this information away for strategic use," she mused, then slowly leaned back down and rested her arm across my stomach again.

"Always plotting against me, are you?"

"Just making sure my dossier is gaining the important info."

"I should know the same about you. Are you ticklish?"

"*No.*" Her voice was a little too loud, her body a little too tense.

"Ah, si, you are. But you're probably one of those people who end up giving black eyes in mindless self-defense because of just how ticklish you are," I surmised. I could just see it. My cousin Carla was like that—she'd given my uncle a black eye when she was ten because he was tickling her and she was kicking and flailing so hard. She felt awful, but no one had dared tickle her since.

"You'll never know," she said, her voice calm and sure.

"Why not? What if I decide to test out my theory?" I gave her a small eyebrow raise.

I felt her push up, one hand on the couch next to me, one hand flat on my chest. She leaned over so she was looking me right in the eye, her blues giving me a dangerous glare. "You're a smart man, Gabriel. I know you're smarter than that, at least."

I returned her glare for a moment until I couldn't take it and broke the falsely frosty stare down with a laugh. She laughed too, and her face pulling into a wide, simple smile stopped me.

She saw me sober, my smile waning as she searched my face for clues. "What?" she prompted.

"You're so beautiful, you know that?" It wasn't a question.

In response she closed the gap between us and touched her lips lightly to mine, then pressed in with more pressure. Before I could deepen the kiss, she pulled away and put her head on my chest. My lungs filled slowly and I let out a sigh. I ran my fingertips over the arm that rested against me.

"I'm worn out," she said quietly.

"Everything was great today, carita."

"Thank you. Thanks for your help, and for coming."

"I'm pretty sure I had to beg to get an invitation. I wouldn't have missed it."

I could see the apple of her cheek rise in a smile even though she wasn't facing me. She took a deep breath, and I felt her relax against me even more. "I could fall asleep right here," she said, just above a whisper.

"Then do."

~

Rae

The problem with dating someone who works nights when you work days is you never see them. Gabriel left later that day to get to his shift, and May and Daniel went out to dinner. I felt worn down in an unexpected way, and they agreed they'd love a date night, so off they went. I slept deeply that night despite my two-hour nap on the couch with Gabriel that afternoon. When I woke, I saw I had a few messages from him from when he got off work.

It was a simple thing, but it set me at ease to know he'd been thinking of me at the end of his work day. I wouldn't see him again until midweek, most likely, because I was busy with May and Daniel, and then he had work in the evenings. I knew I'd get tired of all the free time, but so far I'd been entertaining and I knew some down time would be welcomed.

On Saturday morning, May and Daniel must have gotten up early for a walk, but I was awake by the time they came back, offering them coffee and eggs and some of Ann's leftover, still amazing biscuits.

"You're so sweet. And yes. I'll have biscuits with all the fixings." May was energized from her walk and was practically jolting around the kitchen collecting silverware and coffee mugs and a glass of water for herself.

We chatted about the baby's nursery, how their oldest was doing in school, and then May got down to business. I knew it would come but wasn't sure when she'd broach the subject.

"So you don't believe in marriage, but your adorable, gorgeous boyfriend does," she said, her eyebrows raised to accentuate the obvious drama of the situation.

"*Gorgeous* huh?" Daniel asked with a smirk.

"You can admit honey—he's beautiful. Rae's beautiful. They'll make beautiful babies someday, if Rae'll let him." She pursed her lips at me like all that was standing in the way of me pushing out a little chubby-cheeked Gabriel baby was my admission that I didn't think I'd get married again.

"He believes in marriage, but that doesn't mean he'd marry *me*."

"I'm not sure if you were here for the same meal I was..." she started.

"True, he does seem to orbit you," Daniel added with an amused smile.

"You are the sun to his planet, my dear. And I know you studiously avoided observing his response to the news that you have no plans to marry, but he looked like he'd been told Santa's a fake." She took a large bite of the biscuit sandwich she'd created with the eggs and bacon and some raspberry jelly all smashed in the middle. She closed her eyes and let out a breath as she chewed. Then started talking, her words slightly muted by the biscuit still in her mouth. "He'd ask tomorrow if he thought you'd say yes."

I shook my head at her theatrics. "You are *insane* my friend. I know he likes me a lot, that he's attracted to me—I won't deny that, nor do I want to. But he's Catholic, and I'm not. He knows I won't marry someone in the Army *if* I ever got married. And he can't possibly be thinking about that already—we've been officially dating for less than forty-eight hours." *Of course he knows that,* I thought after I'd said it. *He has to, right?*

"I think you better make sure he *does* know those things," she cautioned before devouring the rest of her sandwich.

"I know we'll have that conversation soon thanks to your extremely subtle conversation cues yesterday. I don't need the pressure of that in my life right now. I've talked myself out on a ledge just in convincing myself to date him, and I'm certain he knows that." I sat back in my chair, my food growing cold. I didn't have an appetite anymore and my head was pounding.

"Do you really think you'll stay single the rest of your life? Don't you want to marry? I know Brad was... I know it didn't work out. But Rae, you're not even thirty—that's a lot of life left." Her eyes were sympathetic, maybe even pitying.

"I don't know. I don't want to be alone—I understand that on some level. But I won't give up my career for someone else's. I won't have someone look at me with the disappointment he did when I can't..." I looked at the rounded swell of her belly and watched as she reached for my hand and put her other on her belly.

"Oh, sweetie. I know. I could slap that man for the way he dealt with that. You don't know what'll happen going forward." Her eyes were so kind and her hand was soft and warm.

I bet she's a great mother.

"I know. I know that. We never got to the point of figuring out why it wasn't working because we were confronted with the fact that it wouldn't work between *us*." I didn't feel sadness over Brad anymore, but the uncertainty of my future, of what kind of family I'd have someday, if ever, settled on my chest like steel beams. I kept busy, stayed fit, and focused on my career because they were the only things I could do something about—the only things I could control.

Daniel had excused himself, aware enough to know May and I needed a few moments to ourselves.

"Are you happy, May? Are you glad you're married and your options are limited?" She frowned at me, so I hurried to clarify. "I mean, that you have to constantly consider him, and factor him in. And with his job, I know you don't have to work, but do you wish you did? Do you wish you got to choose more?"

"I did choose. I chose the day I married him. You know I never had career ambitions—I was in college for my MRS degree and when I snagged Daniel I knew he was it for me. I've always wanted to stay home with my kids."

I nodded, not looking at her, part of me wishing I felt the same way.

"It's not easy—don't think that. I still have days where I feel underappreciated, undercompensated, and ineffectual. I envy the woman across the street whose kids go to daycare while she works in an office. But I know she envies me the ability to stay home. There are no clean lines, no shortage of guilt and dissatisfaction if you sit down in it." She scraped the crumbs on the table into her hand and sprinkled them back onto the plate.

"What I can tell you is that if you've found a person who is your *partner*, it's worth it. There is no end to the compromises you'll make. But there's also no end to the compromises *he* will make. And when you find that man, the one who meets you in the middle in a way Brad didn't and never would have, you'll be thinking differently about marriage—I know it." She grabbed my wrist and I looked at her. "Don't lock that part of yourself away. And don't keep it from Gabriel if it gets to that point. Promise me you won't."

I huffed out a breath. Could I make that promise? "I don't know if I can."

"I know the idea of needing someone like that, of trusting someone... it's terrifying. But you're one of the bravest women I know, Rae," she said, her smile warm and encouraging.

"I promise I'll at least try. That I won't rule it out, if I find the right person," I conceded.

She gave a decisive nod, and then stood with her plate, which I immediately took from her. I could tell she had something else to say by the tug of a smile on her lips. "What?"

"I was just going to say that *Mr. Gabriel Jackson* sounds good. Just putting it out there."

I chuckled at her enthusiasm, not allowing myself to wallow in the tidal wave of mixed emotions she'd caused.

May left me to the kitchen while she and Daniel

packed, and then, before I was ready, Daniel was out in the driveway packing their car.

"I can't believe you guys are leaving already. I'm so glad you get to explore Nashville, but I'm sad to see you go," I admitted.

"You seem surprised by that," May said, always one to tell it like it was.

"I wasn't sure how it'd be. We haven't talked on the phone all that often, and I feel like our lives are so different. You're married, second kid on the way, and I'm here in a totally different world." I stuffed my hands in the pockets of my jogging pants and scuffed my foot on the floor of my entryway. My body felt heavy, my bones tired, my heart sad.

"I know. Our lives are pretty different, except that we're both smart women trying to figure out what we want and what our place in the world is in one area or another. You'll figure this out Rae, as long as you don't get too stubborn and refuse to listen to yourself." She pulled me into a hug, and I smiled at the feel of her belly between us, such an alien and glowing sensation.

"Enjoy Nashville, and call me if you need anything. I know you have your plans settled but, just—"

"We'll call. And I'll call you in a few weeks to catch up." She kissed my cheek and when she pulled away I saw the tears in her eyes. "You have to answer."

"I can promise you that—I will." I cleared my throat, unwilling to get wrapped up in the emotion of the moment. Sometimes when I thought about how much I'd missed her, and how far apart our lives felt most of the time, it made me ache in the hollow of my chest.

"Bye for now, Rayanne."

I waved them off and then returned to the house. I

pulled their sheets from the guest bed and found the towels already in the laundry room. I tidied up the guest bathroom and changed into my running shoes.

I felt foggy. My mind was swimming in murky water, and I needed to clear my head. I made it five miles before I let myself head home and rest. Maybe it was because I hadn't run more than a mile or two since the weekend before, but this workout felt like death. It wasn't uncommon for a longer workout to feel bad after not staying on schedule, but normally five miles was nothing—at least not while I was training for a race and not pushing the pace.

I couldn't shake May's insistence that the *right* person would make a difference. In my heart, I knew that was true. It wasn't that I thought marriage was a place where women's ambitions and dreams and perky breasts went to die. I knew there was happiness in marriage—I'd felt a few fleeting moments of that myself, even with Brad. But it'd mostly been hard. Hard. *Hard.*

Toward the end, everything about interacting with him broke my heart—I felt like a nagging pest, I felt exhausted and unfocused at work, and I felt disappointment in myself. I couldn't get pregnant and then I felt relieved when I couldn't. Then I walked around with guilt piled so high I couldn't see through it to realize Brad and I never should have been together. He wouldn't entertain going to counseling, and once I realized he expected me to quit working the minute I got pregnant, I didn't feel I could move forward with IVF. That was the deal breaker, the heartbreaker.

But was it?

I got home and showered, hardly able to pull my arms up and scrub my hair. I thought about my heart and knew I hadn't felt for Brad enough—I liked him, and he was handsome, and I wanted someone. *He was there.*

I managed to towel off and put on sweat pants and a t-shirt, force down a banana and some water, and then lay down on the couch. I felt myself spiraling, physically and mentally.

The worst part of the divorce was the shame I felt for ever having married him, and then for not seeing what he wanted. Had I missed that he'd expect me to stay home? Had I ignored it, or expected him to change? I didn't think so, and really, we might not have ever talked about it.

We'd been single-minded in our interest for each other, and we'd made it official *so quickly* because the timelines of our training would have kept us apart for years if we hadn't. It wasn't an uncommon series of events for military marriages, but it was the wrong one for us.

And now? Now as I lay there on the couch, my head pounding from exhaustion and the worst headache I'd had in ages, I knew Gabriel was different. It was why I'd resisted him initially and why I felt myself pushing against any more serious talk. Dating, kissing, chatting—that was fun. That was easy, or so I could fool myself into believing.

But marriage? Marriage to a man I'd only known a few months—I'd done that. Never mind the fact that he wanted kids, and he'd already hinted at his personal values being at odds with mine in terms of his future wife working. Sure, he hadn't said that in so many words, but he'd made the point about providing for Victoria, how that brought him joy, and how he would do that for his family.

So that wasn't where we were headed, and if I'd broken my rules enough to allow myself to date him, I would stop there. I wouldn't allow myself to get wrapped up in him, get to the point of giving everything I'd worked for up, because he was *not* the man who was about to compromise for me.

He was caring and thoughtful and kind and beautiful but he was stubborn too, just like me.

The thought of disappointing Gabriel—of having to explain to him that I didn't want to stay home or leave the Army no matter how much I'd love our future children, was paralyzing. And worse, the thought of him making me feel... less than. Like less of a woman for wanting to work, like less of a mother for leaving her kids, like less of *anything*.

No. May might think it was worth the risk, and maybe she was right. But for me, I wasn't ready. I couldn't face it, not yet, and not with him.

CHAPTER TWELVE

Rae

I woke up to a distant banging sound, then the frantic ringing of a doorbell.

My doorbell?

I sat up slowly, my head full of cotton and my mouth a desert. I had to stop at sitting upright and ground myself, blinking dry eyes into seeing again. I stood on shaky legs and knew without a doubt I was very, very sick.

The bang sounded again—a knock on my door.

I padded gingerly to the front of the house, each movement causing my body to ache, my head to press down on my neck like an anvil.

"Carita, are you ok?" Gabriel asked, grabbing my arms and inspecting my face.

"I'm sick," I said, the words like gasoline in my dry throat.

"Claro, but why didn't you tell me? I haven't heard from

you since before May left." He closed the door and shuttled me into the living room, easing me down on the couch where I'd just been.

"What? What time is it?" I looked to my wrist but my watch was missing.

"It's eight am on Sunday morning. I got off an hour ago and when I still hadn't heard from you, I decided to just come check on you, make sure you were ok."

"I'm sorry. I went for a run after May and Daniel left and then passed out on the couch." I took in his scrubs, the long-sleeved knit shirt underneath, and the hair on his head, no longer styled, but mussed like he'd been pulling at it.

"What time was that?" He gently pushed me back against the couch, and I let my head fall against the cushion. "Stay there, I'm getting you water."

I forced myself up. "I think it was around three. Let me go brush my teeth and stuff, then I'll come back down. I can't believe I slept that long."

"Do you need help on the stairs?" he asked from the kitchen.

"I'm ok, I think," I said as I made my way up.

A few minutes later I came down, the necessities taken care of, but feeling no better. I flopped down on the couch, and Gabriel came to tuck me in with the blanket on the back.

"I'm certain you have a temperature. Take this," he set two pills in one hand, "and then I want you to chug as much of this water as you can. You can rest while I make you some soup, and then you should eat a little something." He sat down on the couch next to me and put a warm hand on the back of my neck, my head cradled between his index finger and thumb. He eased me up into a sitting position, and I took the pills with the water he supplied right when I needed it.

He watched me swallow the pills, then lowered me back down. He kissed the top of my head and disappeared into the kitchen. I could hear him banging around, and despite how terrible I felt, a warmth unrelated to my fever settled in my chest.

I dozed on the couch until Gabriel brought me some soup he must have found in my pantry. He helped me sit up and would likely have spoon fed me if I hadn't given him a look that said I could do it myself.

"You must be exhausted after working all night. You should go home." My voice was a wisp, but I was gaining strength after the water and a few calories.

"I'll be fine," he said, skimming his hand from the crown of my head down through my hair, a small smile on his lips. He kept stroking my hair, and soon I couldn't keep my eyes open.

"I'll be here when you wake, carita."

"You should go home and rest."

Gabriel

You should go home and rest.

Like that was going to happen. Did she not remember I was a nurse? That I was a caretaker by trade and also a compulsive fix-it personality? Oh, and then, the whole thing where I'd been inching my way to being in love with her since the day I met her in the ER?

Yeah, no. I'll be right here.

I didn't say it, but she'd see soon enough. I did run home

and grab a change of clothes and my stuff for work that night, plus my toothbrush and other essentials. When I got back, she hadn't moved, but when I touched her, I could tell her temperature was up. I pulled off the blanket and roused her, making her move from the curled up ball she was in and having her spread out on the couch. Her head was in my lap and I placed a cool washcloth on her neck to help lower her temperature.

She looked up at me like I was torturing her, her bright blue eyes glittering and rimmed with red from the fever. Her face was flushed, her lips dry, and her hair wild around her as I looked down at her.

"Got to bring your temp down, baby," I said, running a thumb along her cheek.

Her brow furrowed. "I don't have a thermometer."

"I can go get one. Go back to sleep here without the blanket, and I'll run to the store, ok?"

I was gone for ten minutes, maybe, but when I came back she'd crawled back into a ball with the blanket wrapped around her. "I'm freezing."

I ran the thermometer over her forehead and stopped at her temple. *Aye.*

"One hundred three point four—that's very high. We need to cool you down, all right?"

Her eyes fluttered. "Heath hallucinates when he gets a fever," she said as I helped her stand, my arm wrapped tight around her waist.

"Yeah? That must have been a fun discovery. Has he had that as an adult?" I asked as we mounted the stairs one at a time.

"I don't know." She stopped, one hand clinging to the railing, one to me. She turned those blue eyes on me, and the look there nearly knocked the wind out of me. Her reddened eyes watered as she said, "I don't talk to him hardly ever. I have no idea what he's doing or how he is. He has no idea about me—he doesn't even know you exist." Her voice was a quiet sob, and alarm shot through me. I'd never seen her emotional like this, and though I didn't fault her for it, it was more a clue to how bad she was feeling.

"Let's get you in a cool shower," I said, urging her to lead the way at the top of the stairs. We were through the bedroom and standing in front of her shower before I fully registered that I'd just walked through her bedroom, past a queen bed piled high with a fluffy stark white comforter and pillows, and was standing in her master bathroom.

I moved to the tap, turned the water to lukewarm, and kept my hand there to make sure it didn't heat. When I turned back to her, she'd removed her t-shirt and stood there in a white bra and her slouchy gray sweatpants, her posture speaking her illness. My eyes took her in, one hand against the wall, the long hair I'd braided to keep out of her way over a shoulder. She looked at me with exactly zero enthusiasm or shyness, and no sense that I was, even when I knew she was sick, desperately fighting the urge to let my eyes run over her nearly naked torso.

I swallowed hard and flipped into nurse mode. "Do you need help getting in?"

"I'm ok," she said, her voice low and shaky, but no hint of awkwardness there.

"I'll be right out here. Keep the water cool and stay in at least five minutes. Just yell if you need anything." I didn't look back as I closed the door, sure she'd keep undressing and sure I didn't want *that* to be the first time I had the pleasure, the privilege, the satisfaction of seeing her undress.

How many people I'd seen naked in the years of nursing, I couldn't have told you. It wasn't a sexual experience, ever. But being in her bathroom, in her bedroom, and also having her be *mine* in some small way, stripped away the barriers, the layers of protocol and protection like scrubs, gloves, and the sterile hospital smell. There, at work, it was just bodies—the first time I'd seen her, for that matter, I'd seen her as another body in pain, needing assessment. A very fit, very attractive body, I'd allowed myself to register after the fact, but still a patient.

With that said, I could tell she was miserable. I wanted to hold her, but she needed to cool down. I lasted eight minutes before I peeked my head in, hand over my eyes. "You ok in there?"

"I'm all right. I'm trying to stay as long as I can so I only have to do this once." Her voice rasped from behind the curtain.

"Ok. Just another few, though. Don't overdo it," I said lamely.

I leaned against her dresser, staring at the bright white bed, my eyes not seeing. I didn't think I needed to take her to an emergency clinic unless her temp wouldn't come down, and I'd be shocked if after this ten minutes in the cool shower she wasn't almost over it. Plus the meds I gave her should help, and she had a little something in her stomach now. She'd be ok. I'd make her drink more water, and then put her to bed in her bedroom so she could rest.

The door opened, and out came Rae, wrapped in a towel with her wet hair down her back. "My clothes are out here."

"I'll go get you some water. When you're dressed, get in bed," I said and fled downstairs. Her color was down—she looked pale and weak but fortunately no longer so flushed. By the time I was back upstairs she was in bed, and surrounded by her pillows, she looked tiny. She looked like sick Goldilocks in the too-big bed.

"Drink at least half of this before you sleep again, all right?" I handed her the glass and she took it obediently and gulped down a little more than half. She handed it back to me, and then watched, waiting for instructions.

"Now, carita, you should sleep some more." I put a hand on her wrist and let my thumb swoop over her delicate, cool skin. "You need anything else?"

She let out a small sigh, and her blue eyes watched me for a moment. "You?"

"Me?" Something about that one word, the simplicity of it—stunned me.

"Can you stay? Just a while?"

Did she think I'd refuse her?

Like I would ever tell you no.

"Of course. I wouldn't leave."

"If you're not scared of germs, you can sleep there," she said, pointing to the other side of the bed. "I changed the sheets today—or, I guess yesterday—when I did the guestroom."

"All right. Do you mind if I change? Maybe shower? I'll use the guest bathroom, if that's ok." I squeezed her wrist where it rested and then moved to the door.

"Do whatever makes you comfortable."

After a quick shower and changing into my sweats and t-shirt, I moved as quietly as I could back into her room. In almost any other circumstance I wouldn't have gotten into that bed for any reason, but this circumstance, where Rae had asked me—*Rae had asked me*—I absolutely would. Plus, I'd kissed her two days ago, so if I was going to get what she had, the odds were good that ship had sailed.

I pulled back the covers and let the clean smell of her

detergent surround me as I got in and sank down into the soft bed. I looked to Rae in the late morning light and saw she was watching me.

"Thank you," she whispered.

"De nada, carita."

I called in sick that night and stayed with Rae. I was tired and worn down but no fever. She, however, had started throwing up and was violently sick for hours that afternoon, until finally, it seemed like whatever was going on was taking a break. I'd seen a few people come in with similar issues on my last few nights in the ER—high fevers, then throwing up. The only thing to be done was keep them hydrated and watch the fevers.

So that was what I'd been doing. Rae was miserable, though an incredibly good patient in that she did exactly what I told her without question. But she'd been sick enough, and I'd been sleepless enough, that I didn't want to leave her. I didn't want to interrupt Ann's evening by asking her to come by and watch Rae, though she'd texted several times to check in after I let her know Rae was so sick, and I was sure she would have come if I'd asked.

I woke early on Monday morning since I was used to being awake all night. I'd been tired enough, and we'd only slept in fits and starts, but she'd passed out around one am and hadn't woken up. I sat propped up in her bed, which was how I'd slept. Her head was on a pillow in my lap, one hand tucked into her chest, one arm stretched over my legs. I had no plans to move.

Watching as her chest rose and fell, I wondered if I could touch her forehead without waking her. As I debated, she stirred, and I decided against it. It wasn't worth her waking again—she needed sleep.

I looked around her comfortable room, noting the neat, lived-in feel. She had a confidence about her style that was appealing, both for her person and for her home. I ghosted a hand over the length of her braid, now snaking down her back—we'd washed and re-braided her hair more than once since I'd found her the morning before. I thought about the worst of the night—the part that should have had me begging to go home, to not have to take care of one more person since it was all I did for twelve hours every night.

"I'm so sorry," she said, looking up from where she was curled around the base of the toilet.

"You can't help this. Don't apologize." I set a cool wash-cloth on her neck and gave her a tissue for her face.

"This is so awful. I'm so sorry," she said again, closing her eyes against the glare of the bathroom.

"Baby, please, don't apologize. I'm glad I'm here. Trust me—I don't want to be anywhere else." I sat down with my back against the tub across from her. I didn't want to crowd her, but I wanted to be right next to her if she needed help.

She opened her eyes to look at me then, staring over at me with her head against the cool tile floor. "I trust you."

And she must have because I'd held her hair, rubbed her back, and at one point wiped her face. I'd started laundry and made her food. I'd done more than I ever did for patients in the hospital.

While I was a natural caretaker, I had a low tolerance for taking care of people outside of work unless it was family. The fact that I cared for people four or five days a week as part of my job made me less inclined to help at times like these—I had to take time to refuel so I *could* care about the people who came through the ER door with everything from life-threatening knife wounds to a tough case of the sniffles.

But the worst part about taking care of Rae wasn't that I had to take care of her during my time to sleep, or that she might be getting me sick while I was helping her. It was seeing her in pain—seeing her so mild and meek she didn't question anything I said.

"Gabriel?" Her soft voice reached me from the pillow in my lap.

"How do you feel?"

"It's always worst in the mornings, right? Let me see if I can go shower and then maybe eat something." She sat up slowly, tentative, and then moved to her bathroom. She'd already spoken more words in a row than she had since I'd arrived, so I was hopeful.

Rae

Tuesday morning was a slap in the face, and I thanked God that Monday had been a day off before I ever got sick. I was better—the virus, or whatever it was, had hit hard for about forty-eight hours and then subsided. But I still felt like a time-lapsed version of myself as I dumped my bag and keys on my desk at the office.

My boots felt too tight, the laces looped around my shins somehow cutting into my skin despite the layer of padded boot between lace and leg. My belt felt too tight, despite the fact I hadn't eaten anything solid other than a banana after my run Saturday. My eyes felt a little too big for my head, and every part of me felt wrung-out. I was still working on hydrating and hadn't yet worked up to drinking caffeine again, choosing instead to baby my stomach and avoid any potential repeats of the weekend's events.

The weekend.

What could I say about it other than it had been terrible, yet full of some of the sweetest moments of my life to date? I hadn't had the mental clarity to sort through it, and each minute Gabriel cared for me, I vowed to store away in the vault of memories-to-keep-forever and inspect when I could wrap my brain around what had happened.

This morning was most definitely not that time. I signed into my computer, feeling like it was only minutes since I'd been here last despite the long weekend feeling longer for my sickness.

I sifted through emails, and then more emails. Who were these people working over the long weekend? More than a few were from Major Toms, so he'd clearly been playing catch up. Major Flint had sent a few too—he was executive officer of the Rambler Battalion, and I didn't think he ever took a day off. He didn't have a family or a life outside of the battalion, and it appeared he had no desire for one.

Talcum arrived late morning and mumbled under his breath as he passed my desk. I had no desire to tangle with him today. I kept working and by lunch was on top of my email and on to dealing with operational orders and other things on my list.

I went to the fridge to get my lunch, and as I was microwaving the oatmeal I'd made—I'd wanted something filling but easy on the stomach—I heard low voices in the hall.

"Heard it's been going on for a while."

"Really? Who told you that?"

"I'm not going to say. But it's on good authority. It's why he was gone last month."

The voices faded to an unintelligible murmur as the rumormongers wandered down the hall. Did they not have any respect for Major Toms? People had been speculating about what happened when he was gone and I'd taken his place, and they hadn't stopped when he came back. There was apparently new fuel to that old fire.

I didn't want to hear the rumors, and I prayed there was nothing suspect going on. It was always disappointing to find someone you respected didn't have the integrity you thought.

Based on the interaction I'd had with him, I knew *something* was going on, but I wouldn't have assumed it was something *wrong*.

By five, I was completely exhausted. There weren't any major deadlines coming up since most people were slow to get back into the week after even the smallest break, so my work load wasn't super heavy. I still had a long list of to dos after the long weekend, but I felt just fine leaving on the early end.

I'd left my phone at the bottom of my bag, and when I got home I was sorry to see I'd missed several messages from Gabriel asking how I was feeling. He'd left me the night before to go to work and I could tell he was unhappy to leave, but he didn't feel like he could call in sick another night. I told him to go.

Gabriel: *Are you ok?*

Then a half hour later: *Please let me know how you're doing today.*

Then an hour later: *I'm going to assume that you're not lying dead in a ditch somewhere.*

Finally, hours later, about a half hour before I got home:

I'm also going to assume that you have not checked into the hospital in the hours I was at home asleep. I'll find you if you're there, and I'll be pissed—fair warning.

I wrote back right away, telling him I was ok, and that I was sorry I missed his messages. Minutes later, my phone was buzzing with his call.

"I promise you, I'm fine," I said as I unpacked my empty lunch container and water bottle.

"I'm not trying to crowd you, but I apparently can't stop worrying about you." He sounded exasperated—with himself or me, I wasn't sure.

"I didn't mean to worry you."

"I know. You were working—that's a good thing, as long as you felt ok."

I moved to pack a lunch for the next day and find something I could eat—probably canned soup for one more day before I'd try something more substantial. I had no appetite.

"I did. I'm worn out now. I'll probably just go to bed early, and I bet I'll feel back to normal tomorrow," I said as I opened the can and dumped it into a small pot on the stove.

"Good. I'm glad," he said.

"What about you? Did I make you sick?" I felt a rush of embarrassment at the thought of all the ways he could have been exposed to the virus—all the ways he'd taken care of me so fully.

"No, so far, so good."

And that was it. Then we hung there in an unusual silence as I moved around the kitchen, clanking bowl against bowl as I took one from the stack in the cabinet.

"Is everything... ok?" I asked, aware that the weekend's events might have changed something. He'd reassured me over and over he wanted to be there, and I'd believed him, but maybe it'd been the febrile stupor I'd been shrouded in for more than half the time he was there.

"Si, carita. Everything's fine."

"I don't want things to be weird now that you've seen me throw up like three—"

"—So many times." I could hear the smile in his voice, and the tension in my chest eased a little.

"I know it couldn't have been pleasant. And I appreciate it. I'm sorry I was so out of it, and I should have just let you go home—"

"Rae, baby, you've got to stop apologizing for getting sick. That's not something you control. You couldn't have made me leave because I didn't *want* to leave you. It killed me to leave last night to go to work, and you were doing much better. Believe me when I tell you I was right where I wanted to be, and no amount of puke or febrile babble could scare me away."

"Febrile babble?" *Oh please, let me not have said anything embarrassing.*

"You had some incoherent thoughts, we'll just say that. But from what you told me about your brother, I got off easy," he said, his voice kind.

"Great. You'll have to tell me what I said at some point. Maybe when I'm totally better and have my sense of humor back." I stirred the soup in the pot and dipped a pinky in to test the heat. It was warm, but not hot—good enough for now.

"Deal. For now, tell me, before I have to head into work, when I can see you. I'm off Wednesday and Thursday, and then on again for a few."

"How much longer are you on nights?" I poured the soup into a large mug and thought about how much I'd like to have him there. I'd just seen him yesterday, but I felt a dull ache at the thought of always being without him at night. I shook that off, feeling annoyed with my sentimental whining and attributed it to getting over the sickness.

"I'm back on days in July." He sounded tired, his voice abnormally gruff. He'd stayed up with me for most of Sunday, much of that night, and then most of Monday, so he had to be exhausted, even if he'd slept from the minute he got off this morning until the moment he called me.

"That'll be good. We can actually have dinner together more than one night in a row and go out on weekends," I said, then took a sip of the warm soup.

"Oh yeah? You planning on taking me out?" I could just see his little arrogant smile, and as much as I liked to pretend it drove me crazy, I loved it.

"I am, yes." I curled up on the couch with my mug of soup balanced on my knees.

"Well that's good to know. I'll make sure I keep my schedule open. What happens after the date?"

"What do you mean?" I took another bite of soup.

"I mean once you wine and dine me, then what?"

I choked on my soup, sputtering and coughing, then finally swallowing and clearing my throat. "Uh, um... a movie?"

CHAPTER THIRTEEN

Rae

He chuckled low and the sound snaked around my neck and settled in my mind, burrowing its way into my memory. I knew, like so many things with Gabriel lately, I'd never forget that rich, delicious sound. "Ok, I'll go to a movie with you."

By Thursday when we'd agreed to meet, I was as close to desperate to see him as I'd ever been.

Ok, that was an exaggeration because me? I didn't get desperate. That was the whole point of keeping our relationship firmly in the dating zone and not in the *progressing* area of relationships. I didn't want progress, at least not when I thought calmly and rationally about it. I wanted companionship and someone I trusted, but not to be sitting at my desk at three pm on the day I was going to see him and feel like I'd crawl out of my skin if I didn't set eyes on him.

My legs wouldn't stay still under my desk, I couldn't get comfortable in my creaky office chair, and I swear people were whispering around every corner.

I'd started to get concerned about all the low voices, the quiet conversations in hallways and off to the side of the building. It was mostly Talcum and his cronies, but I'd heard a few whispers from younger soldiers when I visited the motor pool to find the maintenance company commander and even in the dining facility when I swung by to grab a salad earlier.

Something was going on with Major Toms, and it sounded like he'd had a relationship with a younger soldier. That was absolutely forbidden—the disparity of power in a military unit between a field grade officer and a junior soldier made it both unfair and unsafe. It was a good policy, and the idea that Toms had violated that, even if he hadn't been married, was awful. The fact that he was married, and had been for fifteen years? Despicable.

But then. *But then.* Rumors were just that—unsubstantiated claims. If there was something going on, it'd come out, especially now that the rumor mill had glommed onto it.

I felt disappointment and regret swirl in my gut. *I hope it's all just a rumor.*

On the short drive to the commissary where I'd planned to meet Gabriel to get groceries for dinner, I cleared my mind of all the nonsense at work. I hadn't talked to Gabriel one on one since we'd decided to start dating. After that, we were surrounded by other people at brunch, then I was sick, and then weren't face to face.

"I missed you," I heard just as I stepped out of my car. I turned and there he was, right behind me. I stopped myself from jumping up and giving him a full body hug but did grab his hand and lace his fingers with mine. I stared up at him and took in just exactly how handsome he was.

He was wearing his uniform instead of scrubs, and it looked *good*. I probably preferred nurse Gabriel, but seeing him there in his uniform gave me a trill of excitement.

Ok. Fine.

Attraction.

Raging, blazing, consequential attraction.

"Uniform?" I managed since the other things on my mind were whether I really cared if someone saw me jump him in the parking lot of the post commissary where everyone and their commander was there grabbing last minute groceries for dinner.

"I had to go in for a counseling with my boss—just the quarterly counseling, nothing bad. Sometimes I actually do wear a uniform," he said, and we walked toward the building.

"I've only seen you in your uniform twice, I think," I said, trying to remember.

"Oh yeah? Did you forget I'm a soldier? Is that why you decided to date me?" He said it lightly, but I could see him watching me from the corner of his eye even as he sauntered through the sliding glass doors.

"I didn't forget that." I stopped him with a hand on his wrist. "I didn't forget that Gabriel. If anything, it still makes me nervous, but," I pulled my hand away and started walking to the produce section, "I'm not trying to forget it or pretend it's not part of you."

"I believe you," he said, focused ahead on the display of bananas and plantains.

We made our way around the store, deciding on a meal as we went. We had differing tastes but since I was pickier with food, he was willing to let me decide. I promised we could make dessert if he'd go along with my more spartan main meal.

We checked out with Alice, the checker who'd mistakenly thought we were together all those months ago. *Ironic.* We laughed about it on the way out—she didn't seem to remember us, but that wasn't a surprise since it was a large base and she had hundreds of soldiers come through each day.

We put the groceries in my car and agreed I'd follow him home.

"I'll see you soon," he said, standing right next to me, clearly wanting to kiss me. It was dusky in the late April evening, and I wondered if he would assume no one could see us. I was about to warn him off, but he patted my upper arm as he stepped away. "Ten minutes. See you at my place."

I watched him walk away, laughing at how maddening it was to be so invested in his every move despite myself. I turned back to my car, and as I was getting in, I heard a sound I could only describe as one of *disgust*, then someone say, "pathetic."

I looked around, squinting against headlights coming down the parking lot aisle, then noticed the dome light in the car next to me was on. I saw Talcum getting into his gigantic, fire engine red truck directly across from me. He shook his head, a snarl on his lips, and pulled out of his spot, rolling his windows up.

Clearly, he wanted me to know he didn't like me. *Fine.* I didn't like him. I could remain professional, but this was getting to be a bit much. He was overtly rude, and it was wearing thin.

As I drove, I wondered if he'd been watching me interact with Gabriel. From the outside, was it obvious we were dating? If it was, there wasn't a problem with it. Yes, I outranked Gabriel, but he wasn't in my unit, and we were both officers, so it wasn't considered fraternization.

Still.

It echoed in me as I pulled my door closed and buckled my seatbelt. This was exactly something I wanted to avoid—exactly what I didn't need added to the rumor mill or anyone's perception of me.

The other side of my mind pushed against that—I refused to let Talcum determine my choices. I'd spent long enough letting Brad do that for me. I hadn't given myself time to think about the weekend with Gabriel, hadn't allowed myself to absorb all he'd done and what it meant to me, but I knew I cared for him. I knew he was special and that I wasn't going to just throw him away because he was in the Army—I'd gotten over that impulse, at least.

By the time I pulled into his driveway, I'd talked myself into forgetting about Talcum's aggression. I knew it was time I talked to someone about it, and I planned to do that. But tonight, I'd focus on enjoying dinner with my boyfriend.

Even though the thought of calling him *boyfriend* made me simultaneously smile and cringe. It felt so girly and young, and lately I felt anything but.

He got out of his trusty Subaru as I popped the trunk of my car and gathered the groceries. He came directly to me and took the groceries.

"I can carry those," I said, following him down a dimly lit path.

"I know," he said, not stopping or handing off a bag.

I felt nervous as I walked to the door I assumed was his, following after him as he twirled his keys and carried a beat-up Nalgene water bottle in one hand and the groceries in the other.

He stopped outside the door and leveled me with a serious look I only saw because of the small light over his door—the night was totally black around us otherwise. "I want you to take a deep breath because once you see the luxury and charm that awaits you inside, you're probably going to feel overwhelmed. I'm just trying to prepare you now so you don't totally freak out at what a first lieutenant's housing allowance provides a man with little to no decorating sense. Are you ready?"

"I've been psyching myself up all day. Let's do this," I said with mock determination in my voice.

I had been, in a way. I'd never been to his apartment—he'd always come to my place. At first I thought maybe he had a roommate, but he didn't. For a while I thought maybe he lived in Nashville—a lot of young lieutenants did since that was where the nightlife was, but after getting to know Gabriel it didn't surprise me he didn't opt for city life.

We walked in, and I surveyed the tidy studio apartment. To the left was a couch, coffee table, and TV, straight ahead was a small kitchen, and to the right was his bed. Just... right there.

Why it threw me to see his bed, I couldn't say. It felt so intimate, and yet he'd slept with me in mine on and off while I was sick. But seeing it there, right inside the door, made my heart thud in my chest. The simplicity of the dark wood, the navy comforter, the khaki sheets—it was nice.

The rest of his furniture was equally conservative—a brownish-tan couch, a scuffed wooden coffee table with a few books and remotes and a moderately sized TV.

"It's nice," I said, meaning it.

He walked into the kitchen and set the groceries down.

"It's not particularly nice, but thank you. Now you know why I'm always happy to come to you," he said, unloading the chicken breasts and vegetables we'd bought.

I wandered around for a moment, realizing I shouldn't have been surprised. Everything Gabriel did was purposeful and conservative, even though his personality was generous and ebullient. "I'm not surprised, but why don't you have the typical seventy-inch TV or a big game console? Usually single men are all about that kind of thing."

"Oh yeah? Huh. I guess I'm just not the average guy," he said with a pointed look.

"You know what I mean. It's a nice place, but clearly you're conservative," I pressed.

"I am. I prefer to spend my money on other things. People, experiences, or save it for my future family. I figure it's easier to save now while it's just me and I'm healthy, so I do." It sounded so reasonable, so normal, but it was anything but. How many single men in their mid-twenties thought this way?

"You look surprised. Does knowing that about me surprise you?" he asked as he cut chicken and tossed it in a pan for the stir-fry we'd planned. He turned on a rice maker and turned back to me with arms crossed.

"I guess it does in some ways and doesn't in others. It's not every day you have a single first lieutenant saving up all his money and living so simply. I admire it," I explained.

"Well I'm *not* single, and even when I was, I didn't want to be forever. What kind of man would I be if I wasn't planning ahead? What kind of husband and eventually father would I be if I ignore the fact that those things matter to me and don't plan for them financially?" He turned to the fridge, and I was glad he did. I was sure the look on my face was something near petrified.

Were we doing this now? Were we going to have the conversation about marriage? The one where I told him how I didn't plan to get married, even as much as I cared for him, and I certainly couldn't marry *him*?

"You going to help with dinner?"

Gabriel

I had often thought about having Rae in my apartment—had wondered what she'd think. The place was underwhelming, for sure. But it was comfortable, and clean, and it left me about forty percent of my housing allowance to pocket, or use for Vik, or spend on other things, which was exactly how I liked it. I lived well below my means, and I did that so that when I had a family, we didn't have to worry.

But having her here was surprisingly hard. It wasn't that I felt judged, but I felt hyperaware of what she was thinking. Was she unimpressed? Even though we'd known each other for months now, and I'd recently been at her side through a nasty illness, I still desperately wanted to impress this woman who did nothing but impress me without even trying.

I didn't have a dining table, so we sat on the couch with our bowls of rice and stir-fry in our laps. We'd worked well in the kitchen together as always and had managed not to discuss the whole marriage/kids thing I'd so deftly lobbed into the already sort of awkward conversation when we first arrived.

"How's your week going so far?" I asked between bites of food. I was glad to see her eating eagerly too—her appetite was back which meant she really was better.

"It's all right. Lots of rumors going around in the unit, which is annoying and tiresome." She sounded... something.

"Rumors about you? Is it that guy who's been harassing you?" I sat up straight, already feeling ready to fight this jerk if he was bothering Rae.

"No—no. Nothing about me, fortunately. Though it is about another officer, one whom I've respected, and I'm just hoping they're not true. Talcum has been his typically prissy self, and I'm actually thinking about finally talking to someone about it." She looked down at her bowl and nudged food around with the tines of her fork, not looking at me.

"What happened? What made you decide to say something?" I shifted so I could look at her.

"I wouldn't use the word escalating because it's not like he has threatened me, but I do feel this... feeling. The 'uh oh' feeling, for lack of a better way to put it," she said, then took a large bite.

"The 'uh oh' feeling?"

"It sounds childish, but this guy just gives me the creeps, and I am almost certain he's the one who put the photos on my car. That's a problem anyway. But every interaction we have professionally is antagonistic. I asked him for some numbers for a tracker I manage and he snapped at me. Then the next day I went to grab some papers from the copier, and he was in there and he asked if they were personal copies. Why would they be personal copies?"

My mouth was full so I raised my shoulders to say *I have no idea.*

"They wouldn't be. But why would he assume that, or even ask? Like, what the hell? You know?" She took another bite and chomped the food, her jaw working out her agitation.

"It seems petty, for sure," I agreed.

"But the professional interactions I can handle. It's any *other* time I see him. It's starting to make me more and more uncomfortable. He'll glare at me and keep eye contact until I look away while he says something to someone near him. He's constantly shaking his head or rolling his eyes at me. But then he'll turn around and check me out in this totally slime-ball way. I am positive he's not interested in me—it's like he thinks it gives him the upper hand to look at me like he's imagining me naked."

I swallowed my half-chewed food in a rush. "What? That's completely inappropriate."

"I know. And it's more frequent. Even tonight, he was at the commissary when we were, parked right by me. After you walked away I heard him say *pathetic* and then drive away all pissy. What is it with this guy? What have I done that's so troublesome except have a *temporary* promotion to cover down on Toms' job while he was out?" I'd never heard her frustrated like this. She was genuinely asking, truly trying to figure out what she'd done. It was part of what I liked about her—that she was asking the question, working to find the answer. But the answer was obvious.

"He's an idiot, that's what. I don't know why he's being so passive aggressive with you, but I agree, you need to raise your concerns to someone. He hasn't done anything else like the photo thing, has he?"

"No. Nothing since then, which is why I was going to ignore it. But after tonight, I'm done. I'm going to find a time to meet with the commander. I haven't wanted to sound like

I'm complaining, but I also hate the idea of being willfully ignorant or not wanting to ruffle feathers when I'm being harassed."

"I'm glad to hear you say that."

We finished our food and I took her dirty bowl. We joked around as we cleaned up, washing dishes by hand since my small apartment lacked a dishwasher. Then we mixed up a box of brownies I'd talked her into. While I poured the batter in the baking dish, she wandered around, studying the spare décor of my place. After I started the oven timer, I rinsed my hands, and leaned against the sink.

"You must not know," I said, watching her survey my room as she leaned her back against the front door, one foot propped against it, her hands behind her back. Her blonde hair was still pulled back into a bun at the back of her head in accordance with her uniform. Her green t-shirt wasn't tight but still held my attention. The uniform top had been discarded when we walked in, but she had just taken off her boots, which were now sitting next to mine inside the door.

"Know what?" she asked, looking at me from beneath her lashes.

"How much I missed you the last few days."

"How do you know I don't know?" She folded her arms across her chest in challenge.

"I figured if you *did* know, you wouldn't be torturing me by standing *all the way* over there." I dried my hands on a towel and slowly walked to fill the space in front of her.

"Mm, but how do you know that's not exactly what I'd be doing?" I should have known she wouldn't just come to me. She was the best kind of work.

"I guess I should have known," I said, trying to suppress the ridiculous fluttering feeling I got just looking at her, much less thinking about being near her. Close to her. Alone.

Finally.

She eyed me for another minute, then dropped her foot, reached out, and pulled me by the belt loops to stand closer. "Men need a little torture from time to time, don't you think?" she asked, slowly moving one hand to my chest and pulling me even closer.

"Maybe. Not me though. I'm anti-torture," I said, barely finding my voice. I reached to grab hold of her at the waist and ran my thumbs along the sides of her stomach. "Put me out of my misery," I begged, pulling her the last inch so our lips met.

Her mouth on mine felt right and something in me eased even as the rest of me ignited. Our mouths were an explosion of wanting, our bodies crushed together. We pushed and pulled at each other, stumbling back until my knees hit the bed and I sat. She kept coming, overtaking me with the momentum of our failing balance, and didn't stop until she was *on* me, her small body covering mine, our mouths only separating for breaths and different angles.

My heart was a machine gun in my chest, hammering so hard I couldn't keep track, didn't want to.

Is this happening?

A woman like Rae didn't do anything she didn't want to. And here we were, on my bed, in my apartment, with nothing separating us but our matching uniforms.

I ran my hands up and down her back, then lower, pressing her to me. She made a sound, something pleading and completely unfamiliar to the history of our relationship, and any restraint I had evaporated.

I rolled her over, my body pressing hers into the soft bed. "Eres hermosa." I kissed my way down her neck, only to be met with the olive-green crew neck of her uniform shirt. I cursed uniforms, shirts, and the existence of cotton in general. I cursed anything that kept me from her.

My hand traveled down her sternum, between her breasts, and tugged at her shirt until it came untucked from her belted pants. I pushed the shirt up and let my hands run over the smooth skin I'd seen more than once but never touched without a stethoscope.

Warm.

Soft.

More.

There was nothing headier than wanting something, wanting *this woman*, and finally having her.

Miraculously, or so it felt to me, her eyes were darkened with longing just like mine, her hands leaving nothing untouched, her breathing as erratic and breathless as mine. But too soon, so far from what we clearly both wanted, she pulled back.

"Gabriel. I'm sorry," she held my face in her hands.

I had no words, no response, only a look of confusion and uneven breathing.

"We have to stop, ok?" Her brow was knitted with concern, her face flushed.

"You ok?" I managed, pressing up on one hand to give her room to breathe.

"Yes. But we have to stop." She took a deep breath that I felt against me as her chest rose and fell. "Ok?"

Reason had fled on a space shuttle to the moon the moment my back hit the bed, but it parachuted back to Earth and returned to me. "*Si*, of course." Did she think I'd say anything else? *What else could I say?*

I rolled off to the side and sat up, resting my hands on my knees for a minute to ground myself. I let out a cleansing breath, still working to calm my heart rate and my jumbled mind.

What happened?

She grabbed my hand with both of hers and pressed it to her chest. "I'm not there yet. I'm sorry," she said, earnestness and regret in her voice.

"No, I'm sorry, I thought—"

"You weren't wrong. I do want to... I want to be with you, Gabriel. But I'm not ready for the physical side of our relationship to outpace the emotional side, and for me, sex is a big deal." She squeezed my hand in hers.

"It is for me too, Rae. I'm not taking any of this lightly," I said.

"So, you understand?"

"I'm not sure that for me, the physical would be at a different pace than the emotional," I said quietly, hoping she understood. Hoping she felt the same way.

The shrill beep of the oven sounded loudly in the room, and she immediately went to get the brownies.

CHAPTER FOURTEEN

Gabriel

"Wʜᴀᴛ ᴀʀᴇ ʏᴏᴜʀ ʙʟᴏᴄᴋ ʟᴇᴀᴠᴇ ᴘʟᴀɴs?" I asked, the tone rehearsed in my mind so the question wouldn't feel weighty or too hopeful. I didn't want to pressure her, but maybe she needed something from me to help her see that I was *in*.

We'd chatted agreeably while watching *Modern Family*, a show I knew was one of her favorites—and we'd effectively avoided any more talk of sex and the not having of it, both to my dismay and relief.

"Uh, I'm not sure yet, actually. Normally I go back home, but my mom and her husband are traveling again. I thought about visiting Heath at some point this year, but he's still out of touch. They were looking into finding someone to take the Rear-D over block leave, too, so I might offer," she said slowly, cautiously.

Rear D? That meant she'd be stuck working every day of leave and would be responsible for all of the soldiers and families who didn't travel for the break. It was an unenviable job, and I hated the thought of her taking it simply because she didn't have other plans.

"Oh, cool, yeah." *Smooth.*

"What about you?" She unwound her hair from the bun and unwrapped the elastic that held it all back. I may or may not have been responsible for ruining the look, and she was fixing it. I wanted to mess it up more. I wanted it wrapped around my hands.

"I'm heading home for four days. I have to be back that first Tuesday so I'll just be there a few days. I work the week I'm back, and those should be my last grave shifts for a good while." I could ask her to come home with me. She already knew Victoria, and I had told my parents about her. Somehow I knew she'd totally freak if I did, but I wanted her to want to come with me. I wanted to move forward.

"I'm glad you don't have to work the *whole* leave. It really is different for you guys." She finished wrapping her hair in a ponytail and then let her hand drop and rest against my neck. I closed my eyes against the flood of longing that hit me then.

"Yeah, it is," I said. "Would you—" I stopped myself, nerves slicing my words in half.

"Would I, what?" she prompted, her fingers gliding up and down the back of my neck and into the hair there.

My thoughts bounced between how I needed a haircut and how I hoped she wouldn't stop touching me—it was hard to remember what we were talking about.

Except that I did. Because this was it. This was where I tried taking a step forward.

"I was going to ask if you'd want to, uh, to..."

She turned my head to face her with a hand on my cheek. "Gabriel, what?"

"Do you want to come with me to Texas? For leave, I mean." Dios mio, I'd asked her.

She opened her mouth to speak, but no words came. Her cheeks paled, and I knew I shouldn't have said it. "I—I —I'm just not sure about my plans, so I don't—"

"No, don't worry about it. I just wanted to ask, you know, since your mom is traveling and your brother is gone. You should do something fun." It was a weak effort at covering up the fact that I desperately wanted our relationship to progress, in all senses, and she very clearly didn't want it to do the same.

"Thank you. Really, thank you for the invitation, that's so kind." Her forehead was wrinkled with concern. She sat up on her knees next to me and held my face in her hands. "Truly, Gabriel. You know how sweet that is, right?"

I nodded.

"But you also get that that's a big deal?" Her eyes searched my face, waiting to see that yes, I did understand.

I let out a breath and nodded again, just once.

"I care about you..." she started.

"Don't worry about it. I don't want you to feel bad for saying no." I grabbed her hands from my cheeks and moved them, both to reassure her and to get out of her intensely focused gaze.

"I'm not saying no, I just... it's a really big deal to meet someone's parents." She looked miserable—maybe as miserable as I felt.

"Yeah, no—I get it."

"Do you though?" She didn't believe me.

"I do."

"I'm not sure you do. My mom never met Brad before we got married. She didn't know him. And I—that was a mistake. But I'm not—" she stopped, inspecting her hands now in her lap. "I don't want you to regret introducing me to your family." She was notably *not* touching me even though she sat close, and the inches felt like a chasm.

"I would never regret introducing you. You're amazing and I—" I still had some measure of control over myself, thank God. "I'd be glad for you to meet them. They know we're dating, and it's been a long time since I've been interested in someone."

What I wasn't saying was that my mom had already accused me of being in love with Rae. Vik had told them all about her before I ever mentioned her, and they thought they knew. *Las mamas sienten todo.* And as this conversation was rapidly spinning out of my control, I had to admit it wasn't outside the realm of possibility.

"Thank you. Thank you for feeling that way and for wanting to share your family with me. That means a lot." She put a hand on my shoulder and squeezed. We sat there next to each other for a moment before she squeezed again and then stood. "I should probably get home—5:30 for PT feels early after being sick."

She turned to the door and sat on the ground—again, notably not on the more convenient bed—to pull on her boots, then laced them as fast as anyone ever had and stood again. She shrugged on her uniform top and zipped it up. "Thanks for having me over," she said, and I could hear the sadness in her voice.

"I'm glad you came. I'll see you... this weekend? Or, soon?" *How desperate can a man sound?*

"I'll be around." She leaned up and pecked me on the cheek, a brutal consolation prize after the feast of our earlier interactions.

"Night, Rae."

"Goodnight, Gabriel."

~

Rae

I refused to cry on the way home. There was nothing to cry about. I drove calmly and didn't think. I cleared my mind and just drove—emotional driving was dangerous, after all. It was crazy to feel so bad after such a good night—all good until the last ten minutes.

Well, mostly good.

Why was he inviting me to see his family? What had I missed? I knew he liked me, and I liked him. I knew he cared about me, and I him, but that was huge. *Huge.* Maybe it was because his family was so close. I knew he talked with his parents and grandmother weekly and was constantly in touch with Victoria. Maybe taking a girl home to visit wasn't a big deal.

But being in someone's home was so personal, so intimate. We hadn't even celebrated a birthday together, or given each other presents. Did I want to give him a present? Find a hostess gift for his mother and grandmother? Did I want to have to deal with their disappointment that I wasn't Hispanic, or that I was older than he was, or that I might not be able to have kids and if I did I wouldn't stay home with them?

Pump the breaks.

I was spiraling, and that wasn't usually my response. I was logical, sometimes to a coldhearted degree.

And the almost-sex moment—just thinking about it turned my insides out. He'd accepted my words, but I knew he'd be mining them to see what was underneath. He'd tried to tell me that being together in that way wasn't getting ahead of ourselves, and part of me believed him. *Most of me believed him.*

I walked to my door just in time to see Ann saying goodbye to Dr. Jordan. She waved her off, and even though I wanted to see my friend and hear more about her good news, I needed alone time. I needed to process.

"Hey, looks like she made a decision?" I asked, forcing my boots to still on the walk instead of inching their way to my door.

Ann's face, lit by the porch light, glowed with utter joy. "Yes. She did. I texted you, and I know you saw and replied. But yeah, it's good. We're going to spend a few days of block leave together at my parents' house," she said.

Boxing gloves battered my rib cage as I winced but forced a smile. "That's so great. I'm truly happy for you. Glad she came to her senses."

"Me too. Now why do you look like you just came from a funeral?" She crossed her arms and aimed a look at me that told me I couldn't slink inside.

"I don't know what I'm doing. And I hate it," I admitted.

"With Gabriel?"

I nodded. "I have my crap together in every other area," I said, my defenses bristling.

"Ok—I didn't mean anything by that, I'm just asking. You seemed happy at the brunch with everyone. Did you break up, or... what?" She moved from her little porch and followed the sidewalk around the square of grass we shared as a front yard between our doors over to my doorstep and stood with me under my light. I shivered in the chilly night but knew no matter of cold would keep Ann from getting answers.

"No, we didn't. At least I don't think we did. He invited me to go with him to Texas when he goes on leave."

"Ah. And that freaked you right the hell out, I'm guessing."

I wrapped my arms around my bag in front of me, shielding me from her insistence that I be truthful with her and myself. "Yes. Big surprise."

"Well the surprise was you agreeing to date him. But I'm glad you did. He's a good guy, and if he was only interested in you physically, he wouldn't have stuck around and held your head while you puked your guts out." I'd given her an update on the weekend, just like she had me, since we hadn't seen each other again.

"He is," I said, the words scraping my throat. "I think he's... more invested than I am though. I hate the thought of hurting him." I leaned against the brick wall to one side of my front door.

"I wouldn't be surprised if that's true. But are you sure you have to hurt him?" she asked, her eyes not letting me duck and cover.

"It's going to end at some point, obviously."

"Why *obviously*?"

"Because if it didn't *end* that would mean we'd... what, get married?"

"Yep. That's one option, sure." Ann nodded, her voice placating like I was a child. I felt irritation climbing my spine, each disc a rung.

"Great. So I marry the first guy who comes along after Brad?"

"Is he the first? He's the first you've given a chance, but I think there's a reason for that. And it's not like you got divorced six months ago. It's been six years, or more, right?"

"Maybe," I grumbled.

"I can see you're not in the mood to hash this out. If and when you are, you know where to find me," she said with a pat to my arm, and then an infuriating pat to my cheek. I jammed my keys in the lock and let the door shut just a little louder than I normally would.

Why did I feel so upset by his asking me? He wasn't pressuring me—he was just offering. And I could admit that part of me did want to go–I wanted to see what his brothers were like, how they all interacted together, and how his parents treated him. But I felt an unsettling fear too—there were so many implications to that. It set us on a path to a far more serious relationship, one I was in no way prepared to be a part of.

In truth, I didn't believe he was either. He didn't know me. He didn't understand I wasn't going to stop, wasn't going to stay home, wasn't going to follow *him* around the country. And everything I knew about Gabriel told me he wasn't going to be satisfied staying home either—he'd been raised by parents who'd instilled the importance of the *man* providing. I wished I felt like that didn't matter to him, but the way he talked about *his women* and how he supported his sister—never mind the fact he'd talked about saving money to provide for his family earlier tonight.

But when I closed my eyes, I didn't see the stress of meeting his family or his unspoken but clearly ever-growing expectations. No, I saw him brushing my hair back from my face as I got sick over and over again. I saw him drying and braiding my hair, not once but *twice,* that weekend. I heard him calmly telling me I'd be ok, that he wasn't going to leave me. *I'm right here, baby.*

Even in the sick stupor I was in, I'd felt that word, that endearment, slice through my professed indifference. I'd felt his affection for me, his care, and his refusal to give me space. I wasn't even able to be embarrassed because he wasn't awkward or tentative. He took control and told me what to do, and I believed him and did it. And I got through it much more easily than I would have without him.

He'd given up plans for me. He'd called in sick to work. That wasn't nothing. That mattered. I understood that wasn't a small thing—it wasn't like he was staying with me to do something fun.

But where could this go? He was younger. He likely had at least another year, if not another three or four years, depending on what he tacked on to his initial commissioning obligation during college, before he could get out. If all went to plan, I'd be leaving for a new assignment in as little as eighteen months—I'd be through my accelerated master's and off to the next place by then. What kind of time did that give us?

And how was I even thinking of this? I shook it off, marching into the kitchen and gulping down a glass of water. I'd go to bed, and wake up, and take on the day feeling focused and right. I'd see Gabriel that weekend, and hopefully the awkwardness of my declining his invitation —*and him*—would be fine.

It *would* be fine.

What wasn't fine was that Talcum was pissed at me for no good reason, and he let me know it from the moment he stepped foot in the building. He harrumphed his way around the office, stomping too loudly and breathing too irascibly to be ignored. When he actually threw a folder of documents at me, which sprayed out over my desk and the floor as he did, I asked him point blank what his problem was.

"My problem? It's you." His face was a permanent sneer.

"What is it that I've done to you?" I sat in my chair, not standing, not leaning forward, and in no way making myself the aggressor.

His face twisted into an ugly smile. "Oh, I think you know." Then he turned on his heel and tromped back to the end of the building where he worked.

I looked around, wondering if anyone had witnessed his outburst. It was early afternoon so many people were at lunch, and a few were in meetings. Just my luck, no one would have witnessed his confrontation. I flipped to the notebook I kept of every encounter we'd had. I logged the one from the night before and now this latest run-in. I emailed Major Toms and LTC Basto asking for a meeting.

Later that afternoon, Basto replied he could see me midday on Tuesday—Toms would be out the next week, and they couldn't meet with me before then. I set a reminder in my calendar and wrote down a few notes about how I'd address the issue. I was tired of wondering if or when Talcum's behavior would escalate—tired of feeling like I had a secret when I had none and had done absolutely nothing wrong.

~

The weekend arrived with all the glory of a sixth-place finish. I hadn't been sleeping, hadn't seen Gabriel because I was working and then he was working (except the night after our date, but neither of us initiated contact until Friday morning), and now I faced a long weekend of interminable days, mild anxiety over my meeting with Basto and how reporting Talcum would go, and mostly, incredible confusion over where I stood with Gabriel.

I wasn't a person who reveled in the drama of a relationship—I had minimal tolerance for it and didn't want to *have* to think about it. At some point along the way I'd learned to compartmentalize my feelings, which was one of many things that made me an effective soldier, kept me calm in heated situations, and caused me to outperform peers when it mattered.

But this skill was also potentially poisoning me.

It kept me from being able to shut down my logical self, and if I was honest, my fearful self that had been hurt by Brad, hurt by the insinuation that by being a woman I was less than, and hurt by my own expectation to be hurt by Gabriel.

I asked if he could come over on Saturday before work, but he messaged to say he was in Nashville with Victoria. That wasn't unusual, but he'd said we'd see each other that weekend. I assumed that meant he'd stop by Sunday before work, or we'd meet for dinner. I waited for him to say something or show up.

When I didn't hear from him by late afternoon, I asked if he'd stop by. I then swallowed the bowling ball-sized hunk of pride stuck in my throat and called him. He didn't answer but texted back that he was going in early and would try to stop by on Tuesday when he was off.

I hadn't expected him to avoid me. I hadn't thought he'd make excuses, and I *knew* in my gut they were excuses. He would have tried to see me if he wanted to see me.

Was he angry? Embarrassed? Hurt?

It could be all of them, and I couldn't blame him. I'd rejected him on more than one front, and I couldn't exactly expect him to keep coming at me if all I did was hold up the *Stop* sign.

Monday was cruel, as Mondays so often are, but it was a relief to be back at work and have something to do with myself. For some reason, Toms was gone again—more emergency leave, and I stepped in to cover down again. By Tuesday, I'd worked myself up about Gabriel, but I'd also gotten extremely nervous about my meeting with the battalion commander.

I sat in his chair as he closed the door—an unusual move since he was always an open-door kind of leader. I wasn't uncomfortable, but I was surprised when just before he shut the door completely, the brigade's lawyer stepped in and sat next to me.

"Captain Jackson, I'm glad you scheduled this meeting," Basto said as he folded his lanky body into the seat in front of me. He had to be six foot six at least.

"Me too, sir. It's been a long time coming, I'm afraid." I kept my hands folded in my lap, resting on my manila folder full of the logs I'd kept and the original folder that had been left on my car.

"Major Justice, our brigade JAG, is here, just so we have covered our bases." Justice nodded to me and clicked a pen, then clicked again. I might normally have enjoyed the man's last name lining up so neatly with his chosen profession, but something about the tension in the room, and Justice's presence, felt off.

"Is that typical, sir?" I asked Basto.

"Not always. I thought it best to have reinforcements here, particularly in light of some of the rumors floating around." Basto cleared his throat and lifted his chin in Justice's direction.

"I'm going to keep an informal record of this meeting for

now, Captain Jackson. Should things escalate, we'll deal with sworn statements," Major Justice explained.

"Ok, that sounds reasonable. I'm seeking direction here, and if you think a sworn statement is right at this stage, then I'll do it."

And then I told them. I told them how Talcum had always been aggressive, spoke about me behind my back when I was in the room and would be sure to overhear, had made a suggestive gesture to me more than once, and looked at me inappropriately. Then I showed them the folder, and Basto was angry I hadn't brought this to him before.

"I should have, sir. It's why I'm here now."

"I have to tell you Rae, I hear you, I see these records you've kept and this alarming evidence, and I have no reason to doubt you," Basto said.

I could hear it in the air, though. That rippling, zinging effect that doubt had on a small, enclosed room.

"But, I also have to tell you there are now rumors flying around about *you*, and someone has filed a complaint."

My heart jumped off the starting line, and I sat up straighter, if that was possible. "What? What rumors?"

"I'd prefer not to say," Basto said with a purse of his lips like he thought the whole matter was distasteful.

"I have a right to know what's being said if it involves me in any way."

Basto nodded silently and leaned his elbows on his desk. "Rumor has it that *you* and Major Toms are... involved."

The air had been sucked out of the room, I was sure of it. I could hardly breathe. I took a moment to find the oxygen and slurp it in with one long gulp, then spoke. "With all due respect sir, people were saying that I'd traded sexual favors for the cover-down on Toms' job when he was gone, and you and I both know that's not true." I gave him a hard look and he met me breath for breath.

"I don't buy it, but I'm letting you know. You're an excellent officer, and I don't want to see this go bad. Why don't you work on a sworn statement for JAG here and then take off. Shake it off, and we'll work on next steps."

"Roger, sir. See you tomorrow. Major Justice, I'll have that emailed to you within the hour." I'd already written up the sworn statement. It was just a matter of formalizing it.

As I walked back to my desk, my mind reeled. Did people really believe I was involved with Toms? Yes, there'd been rumors he was involved with someone, but *me?* Wouldn't we be more... friendly, at least?

It had to have been Talcum, just like I'd heard him suggest I'd worked out a *deal* with Basto for Toms' job. And the formal complaint—that had to be him too. It wasn't that I was universally liked, but I was professional, cooperative, and unapologetically excellent at consensus building and the team dynamic. The idea that any one of the other people in this building except for the few that hung on Talcum's every word had any issue with me was just not likely.

He was setting me up to look like a fool, and I'd given him the space to do it.

CHAPTER FIFTEEN

Gabriel

I'D SPENT the weekend *away* from Rae. I wasn't sure if I was motivated by the need to get space from her for *myself* or if I was hoping she'd realize she had deeper feelings for me while I was gone. *Or something.*

I'd made plans with Vik on Saturday before work, then got on shift a few hours early on Sunday, and that kept me from going over to her house—I'd felt practically magnetized by the pull in her direction, but I stayed strong. I'd told her I'd come to her on Tuesday, and there I was, pulling into her little townhouse driveway, right next to her car.

I'd pushed her the last time we were together. I'd put myself out there, both in wanting her physically, but it wasn't like that was a secret, and in asking her to come with me to Texas, which *was* a step. I'd known that, and that was why I'd asked.

Her suggestion that we weren't *there* yet was not a shock, but it was a deep disappointment. After feeling that acute disappointment stinging like an open wound for about twenty-four hours, I shifted into problem solving mode.

What I came up with was essentially more pushing. But it came from an honest place.

On Saturday, a woman was wheeled in on a gurney with a neck brace and a black eye. She had long blonde hair that, when they stopped by the desk to get a bay for her bed, slipped over the side of the bed. For a heart-stopping ten second moment, I thought it was Rae, gravely injured.

I practically ran to the bed, but the minute I got closer, I saw it wasn't her—hair too close to platinum, much different face, younger by about ten years. Really, they were nothing alike, but my mind had made one thing clear—I was irrevocably in love with Captain Rae Jackson.

Vik had been telling me all afternoon that I was, and I'd half-heartedly denied it. "You know you want her for good. You want to marry her and have little Raebriel babies."

"Raebriel?"

"It's your couple name. Accept it and move on." She gave me one of those imperious looks that said there was no point in further discussion on the matter.

"Uh, fine. But that's a ways down the road, don't you think? We haven't even been dating a month," I said, resisting the know-it-all affect Vik so easily adopted.

"Yeah, but you've liked her for months, and you've been good friends that whole time. It's not like you just met and started dating—you were already good friends. That speeds up the dating timeline. Next stop, wedding bells." She laughed at my face, though I wasn't sure what she saw on it —hope? Longing? Annoyance?

But that evening at work, I couldn't ignore Vik's words or my own mind because in the same moment I thought she was hurt, I saw my own life play before my eyes, and I saw it empty. My mind linked her injury or illness with my future potential happiness. And while that was just about the most inane and selfish thing it could have done, it made it clear as a Las Vegas sign post.

When I knocked on her door, I wasn't sure how I'd get there, but I was going to get her to tell me how she felt. I'd do it.

I can do this.

She swung open the door, and I could tell immediately she was exhausted. Maybe she'd had five sleepless nights (or days, in my case, sure) like I'd had. Maybe she was as worried as I was about all of this. Hope stirred in my chest.

She held the door knob, effectively blocking my way into the house, but she gave me a small smile. "Hi," she said, almost shyly.

"Hi. Can I come in?"

"Of course," she said and stepped back to make space. She didn't move to hug me, but I supposed my choice not to come over the weekend had made her question things.

That was exactly what I wanted, wasn't it?

I followed her into the house, straight to the living room where she sat in the large chair and I took the seat nearest her on the couch.

"How was your weekend?"

"I don't want to talk about that. I want to talk about us," I said. I knew I'd lose my nerve if I stayed and we batted around small talk and reports of mundane things.

"Today was a tough day for me..." she started, studying the arm of the couch.

"I'm sorry for that. But I think we need to talk. I think we need to figure out what's going on here so I can stop feeling like I'm tiptoeing around."

"You feel like you're tiptoeing? When did that start?" Gripping the arm of the chair, she swallowed hard.

"I—that's not the point. The point is, I care about you. And I *know* you care about me."

"That's true, I do," she agreed, her eyes meeting mine.

"But you're holding me at arm's length. We just barely started dating, yes, but we've been getting to know each other for months. I thought we'd gotten to a new place, that we'd moved forward a little, but the other night..." I trailed off, not sure how to describe my disappointment with the scent of embarrassment still fresh in my mind.

"I didn't handle things well, and I'm so sorry if I said anything that hurt you," she said as she stood and came to sit by me.

"I'm not here for an apology, Rae. I'm here to figure out where we go from here. I want to move forward, but I don't think you're going to let yourself do that with me."

"I don't know how to do that with you." Her shoulders slumped and her posture was the picture of dejection.

"You just... do. We keep seeing each other. You think about coming to Texas with me—and if that's too much, that's ok. We can go another time. And you tell your mom about me, if you haven't yet. At some point, you know, things keep progressing." I put my hand on top of hers. "I don't know what's going on in your head, and I wish you'd tell me what's making you back away."

She stared down at our hands, and her breathing was audible as she pushed out a breath through her nose like she was calming herself. "I can't do this with you right now. I'm sorry, Gabriel, but this day has gone to hell and I can't sit here and try to console you. I'm getting crap from all angles, and you coming here, it just... it basically confirms my concern that you are in a different place than I am with all of this."

The doorbell rang and she jumped, then asked me to wait a minute while she got it.

∼

Rae

I couldn't have been more surprised to see Captain Talcum standing at my door if I'd tried. My mind was reeling from Gabriel's arrival, caught between wanting to yell at him for pushing me and cry to him about how bad my day was and just let him comfort me.

But here was *this guy*.

A rage so cold it nearly stole my breath crashed over me at the sight of him.

"What are you doing at my *house*?"

"You are a complete *bitch*." He spat the word, and I heard Gabriel say something from the living room.

"You need to leave," I told him, my muscles going rigid and my jaw hardening.

He swore at me, tossing nasty words in my face. "I can't believe you reported me. Got your panties in a twist because I'm not in your fan club bowing down to your tits and hair."

"What the hell? You don't talk to her like that," Gabriel said from behind me, placing a hand on my shoulder and pulling me back a step into the house.

"Gabriel, let me deal with him."

"Oh this! This is perfect. You're screwing Toms and then you're over here with some other poor sap of a soldier doing him too, huh? Why am I not surprised, you little beauty queen bimbo—"

Gabriel lunged at Talcum, and I pulled hard on his arm. He didn't hit Talcum, didn't hurt him in any way, but Talcum flinched, and his tirade died on his lips. "Get out of here, now." I'd never heard fury from Gabriel, not even when he'd been at Victoria's after she was attacked.

"Talcum, get out of here. Don't ever come to my house again."

I stood there and watched him go. He didn't run, but he moved fast. When he got into his truck I threw the door shut and pushed the heels of my hands to my eyes. I grit my teeth and let every muscle in my body tense against the wave of emotion crashing over me.

This was exactly why I couldn't move forward.

Gabriel was at my shoulder. "Are you ok? What the hell was that guy doing here? Talk to me, Rae—what's going on?" He pried my hands from my face and I exhaled long and slow before speaking.

"You need to leave. This is exactly why I can't be with you. I need you to leave." My voice shook, my hands were unsteady, and my lungs had shrunk at some point in the last five minutes.

Gabriel stepped in front of me and ducked his head to catch my eye line. "What are you talking about?"

"He thinks that because he's seen you here, he knows something about me. He thinks I'm predatory because I'm with a first lieutenant, and so why would I stop there? Why not sleep with Toms too?"

"That guy is an idiot, and he's the one in the wrong. He has nothing to do with us." Gabriel ran his hands through his hair and reached out to me again, but I stepped back.

"Listen, please. Hear me." I waited a beat, making sure his attention was on me, though it hadn't been anywhere else since he'd arrived, however long ago that had been. "I need you to leave. I need us to take a breath because I care about you, but I can't take this risk. I'm seeing this implode in front of me, and I will not ignore that or feel bad about doing something to stop it."

I watched his face as my words sunk in, the initial pain, and then the total shut down of anything but cold compliance. He nodded silently for a moment, then said, "Whatever you say, ma'am."

He was out the door before I could take a breath or register the welling pain and regret flooding my mind, my body, everything.

～

Gabriel

It had been two days since Rae dismissed me. That was how I thought of it. I'd been *dismissed*.

I knew she was driven, and I knew she wasn't going to change. It was one of the things I liked about her, that I found most attractive. And yet, being on the receiving end of her scalpel of professionalism was a kind of brutality I hadn't experienced in my life to that point.

I care about you, but I care about my career more. She hadn't said those words exactly, but she might as well have. I shut my eyes against the memory, but her face was there repeating the words back to me, slicing the rejection into my mind so I'd never forget it.

I hadn't realized that to be with her would mean I'd always be *second*. I guessed that was what she'd been trying to tell me—that I was moving rapidly toward the time when I'd want to put her first, and she would never get to that place. I'd always be second to her career.

She'd warned me, after all.

It was two weeks until I'd be in Texas, and I didn't want to tell my family that not only was Rae not coming with me, but this woman they all assumed I was in love with—who I *was* in love with—was no longer a part of my life.

I'd requested to work every night I could until I left, but as I got off work on Friday morning, Robert told me that Rebel was coming in for her shift and didn't need me to cover her that night anyway. I'd never been so disappointed to have a night off.

When I woke up that afternoon, I had a missed call from Ann Richards, who'd never called me. I threw my phone into the couch cushions and leaned back, not sure if I wanted to listen. The pathetic part of me that wanted to hear from anyone close to Rae wanted to hear the message.

The burnt, crumbling, rejected part of me wanted to smash the phone with a sledgehammer.

Since it was so unusual to hear from Ann, I listened to the message. *"Gabriel, it's Ann. You need to go see Rae. I don't know what happened between you, and not that I don't care, but it can't matter right now. She's in a bad place—she got put on involuntary leave because Talcum openly accused her of sleeping with Major Toms, and, as he put it, 'several other junior soldiers.' It was a serious enough accusation that Basto had no choice to put her on leave while they investigate. Hopefully it's only this week, but... just, man up and go see her. Whatever else is happening, you guys are friends."*

What the hell?

I was out the door before I'd even thought about changing clothes, my basketball shorts and t-shirt proving to be completely ineffective against the stormy May wind and rain. I pulled into Rae's in eight minutes and banged on her door. How could she not tell me this had happened?

"Oh. Gabriel," she said from behind the door, her face clear of makeup and her hair pulled back in a ponytail. On the surface, she looked normal, but the way she shielded herself with that door was the first clue something was not right.

"I'm coming in, and you're going to tell me what the hell happened this week. You're on involuntary leave?" I barged past her, not willing to deal with false politeness when she was hurting and maybe in trouble.

"Yes, please do come in," she said to the empty doorway and shut the door after a beat.

At least she still has a sense of humor.

I paced around her living room, waiting for her to tell me what had happened.

"Why are you here, Gabriel?" she asked, sounding exasperated I'd showed up. Was she that over our whole relationship she didn't expect me to care what was happening with her?

"Ann called. She told me you'd been put on involuntary leave. I came as soon as I got the call."

"Why?" Her voice was small and she was hugging her arms around herself. She didn't look disheveled or like she'd been crying, but she seemed... fragile.

"You have to ask that?" I stepped closer to her, though we were on opposite sides of the room.

"I'm upside down right now. I'm questioning everything." She ran her hands along the back of the couch, picking off imaginary lint and not looking at me.

This wouldn't work.

I walked to her and stood next to her. I wanted to hug her, or shake her, but I stood right next to her, my hip against her hand on the couch. "I'm here because I care about you, Rae. I don't understand what's going on with us, but right now, I'm here because you're my friend, if nothing else, and I know whatever is going on is messed up. I wanted to be here for you in case you need me." I set a hand on top of hers on the couch and watched the muscle in her jaw tighten.

"I appreciate that, but I'm fine," she said, her shaky voice betraying her.

"You can't be. This is insulting and there's no way you're ok with this," I said, pressing against her hand, trying to get her to respond.

She snatched her hand away and crossed her arms across her chest. "I don't have another choice, do I?" Her chest rose and fell, and I *finally* saw the signs that she was hurt, but also furious. It was far better than the quiet mouse who had opened the door.

"I don't know, do you?"

"No, I don't. I have to wait, and pray that it goes my way, because Talcum is lying. In the end it's going to be his word against mine. If he says he saw something, and Toms was already under suspicion, then the only other person involved is me, and it's my word against his. In theory, that should be no contest, but I never would have dreamed I'd be here counting the hours of my *third* day of involuntary leave while they investigate my character, my relationships, my work, *my entire life*." Her voice rose at the end, and her cheeks flushed with anger.

"This is insane. There's no way they'll find against you."

"Isn't there? I've been dating a junior officer, haven't I?"

She looked at me, her jaw clenched, her whole body a live wire of frustration.

"I'm not in your unit. I'm not one of *your* lieutenants! You have no input on my records or evaluations. That makes no sense." What universe were we living in if our relationship was going to get this woman in trouble?

"It doesn't matter. We *were* dating, and Talcum included that as evidence—whether it's a black mark on my character or not, it's something true and lends legitimacy to all of his claims. And ultimately it makes me look questionable." She shut her eyes and exhaled, then stretched her neck from side to side.

"If that's the only thing he has a shred of proof of, it's going to be fine," I said, working to reassure her even as I ignored the ripping sound in the fabric of our relationship. She'd said it in the past tense.

"I need you to leave." She wasn't looking at me anymore.

"I'm here to support you."

"I really need you to leave, Gabriel," she pleaded, and it was then I heard the first shred of emotion in her voice. Just a ripple of it when she said my name, but it gave me hope.

"I'm not leaving when you're dealing with this. I'm your friend and maybe more than that, and I'm not leaving *you*." I crossed my arms, hoping my bravado and determination would stick around.

She shut her eyes tight and shook her head. "I cannot be with you. Can't you see that?"

"This has no bearing on our relationship. I refuse to let Talcum and his lies change anything. If we're not going to be together, it needs to be for reasons beyond this ridiculous situation." I heard the anger in my own voice but couldn't stuff it back down.

She sucked in a breath, the sound sharp in her quiet living room. "You want my reasons? Fine. First, you're a junior officer, and I should never have started dating you anyway, especially since I had a personal rule against dating someone in the military."

"Someday, at *some* point, that's not going to be a good enough excuse. It never has been for me, and one day you'll realize it's not enough for you either." I scrubbed my hands down my face and blew out a breath to calm myself.

"If we did stay together, then what? I go home and meet your family and they realize I'm not Catholic, I'm several years older than you, I'm going to keep working, and that life as a dual military couple is *hard*. No mother wants that for her son, especially not you—they won't want that for you, and neither do you." She'd started pacing, ticking off the different disqualifiers as she went, but she stopped right in front of me.

"I don't care about *any* of that." Dios mio, this woman!

"Yes, you do. You think you don't, but you'll expect me to stay home. Or you'll say it's fine, but when there's a sick kid at home, it'll be me who's expected to take off work instead of you. It's just... it'll happen. And then what about deployments? I will be my own breadwinner, and that's not the kind of woman you want." Her hands were on her hips, her cheeks flushed, her eyes piercing with anger.

"Well, you definitely seem certain of me. I guess I should have been asking you what I wanted all along." My voice was all bitterness.

"I'm not trying to be hurtful, but I don't want us to keep going down a path I see as a dead end. I don't want either of us to get hurt," she said, her hands wrapping around herself again now.

I looked at her, searching for some kind of...*something*.

Some sign or flashing light that would tell me this wasn't it. This wasn't the end of us, the end of something I'd hardly realized I wanted so much until it was gone.

"Yeah. Better stop now. Wouldn't want anyone to get hurt." I pulled my keys from my pocket on the way to her door. "I'm sorry this happened to you Rae. I'm sure it's going to resolve in your favor."

CHAPTER SIXTEEN

Rae

THE TUESDAY after I met with LTC Basto the first time after I'd submitted my sworn statement, I was back at work. Word came down at the end of the day on Monday that I was exonerated, or cleared, or whatever it was that happened when you'd been placed on leave, totally humiliated amongst your colleagues and community, and then set back in place as though you could pretend you hadn't just been suspected of having no integrity and being a lying whore.

That might have been my own choice language, but who cared? Someone had jabbed me with a needle to the heart and broken off the syringe—could I recover from the wounded pride, from the hurt, from the embarrassment?

Talcum was now on leave—he'd started his summer block leave early and wouldn't be back for weeks. Lieutenant Colonel Basto assured me he'd been formally reprimanded for his fabrications. In the meantime, Major Toms had been found guilty of having an affair, but it was with a staff sergeant from one of the companies. He'd lose his job and be forcibly retired early.

What a mess.

I renewed my offer to act as rear detachment commander while everyone was on leave, and Basto happily accepted. Because of that, I at least had something to do other than wander my apartment and wonder what I was doing with my life.

Because that was what I was doing—wandering around second guessing every single choice I'd made in the last few months. And maybe it wasn't *every* single choice, but every one having to do with Gabriel.

Gabriel, who I hadn't heard from—nothing, not even a *Happy Memorial Day* on the day or anything for weeks after. I knew he'd been back in town for work those last few days of leave, and every atom I owned was begging him to message me, to stop by, to break the silence.

But he wouldn't. I knew that, but it didn't stop my stupid heart from hoping.

Because what I had realized, in the blazing clarity of a "not guilty" verdict from the investigation, was that I'd messed everything up. *I* was to blame for the way our relationship imploded, and that was because I was constantly expecting it to.

I couldn't let myself relax into the time with him and just look forward. I'd spent so many years closing myself off to anyone else that I didn't know how to consider someone else—I was wretchedly selfish and that left me wretchedly alone.

The cohabitating horrid reality check was that I'd almost lost everything I felt mattered to me in my career, and it was through no fault of my own. Someone had it out for me and did his worst, and it was only by grace that I hadn't ended up kicked to the curb by my one true love.

Ann had called it that—*my one true love*. When I told her that was a horrible thought, she asked me why. "When you give up everything for someone else, it *must* be your one true love. Your someone else just happens to be your career."

Ann was pulling no punches, and I could tell she was angry with me. I couldn't wade through that because what I wanted to do was get on my knees and cry at her feet. What she'd done for me in the days of my involuntary leave was proof of her excellence—not that I'd needed proof, but prove it, she had.

She'd rallied my troops—my people, who I didn't realize existed until she gave me the list. Luke Waterford, Lieutenant Colonel Wilson, and Major Flint from Rambler Battalion, and Gabriel Marquez… yes, even Gabriel. They wrote letters outlining my character, what they thought of me, and how it was impossible I'd done anything like what I'd been accused of.

What Gabriel's letter said, I didn't know. I was afraid to know in many respects, but I knew he had stuck himself way out on a limb for me. I'd been harsh and angry with him —he'd borne the brunt of my frustration and panic at both Talcum's visit and then the ensuing time at home, and it wasn't fair to him.

It wasn't fair to *us*.

I had no idea how to get back on course, and I had the sense that if I didn't change the way I lived and *soon*, I could end up married to my job. I wanted a successful career, but at what cost? And why had I insisted on keeping Gabriel at arm's length when he was nothing but supportive.

I also kept having this thought—what if that disdain I had for my mom, the idea that she'd given up so much of herself, was misplaced? The thing that had paired with compromising myself with Brad and grew into something ugly and hard inside me—what if I'd been wrong. Because in seeing Gabriel support me, even when I was shutting him out, and in seeing *myself* get tunnel vision and cut everyone out, I realized maybe she'd compromised the first time, with my dad, but that didn't mean she didn't have purpose, and it didn't mean that her choice to focus on enjoying life with Jerry was wrong.

Did I have that in me? Was I capable of enjoying life, of finding a balance between being myself professionally and finding middle ground in a family?

We needed to figure out a way forward, but I had to figure out a way to start again. I wasn't sure he'd give me the chance—I imagined that if I'd been shut out as completely as I'd shut him out, I wouldn't even look at the person, much less listen and give them a chance.

So my nights, weekends, and any time I spaced out at my computer were spent thinking about him. About the reality that I loved Gabriel, that I wanted to be with him, and that I had absolutely no idea how to get him back.

Gabriel

It was the worst summer of my life so far, bar none.

Call me melodramatic, but a heart sent through the meat grinder had that effect on a season. My family tried to console me, and I was able to take the distraction here and there. I'd expected a lecture from my mom about it—about being more tenacious about getting what I wanted, and if not that, about bucking up and moving on because there were plenty more pretty blonde girls in the sea. Somehow she'd known I couldn't stomach anything other than soundly ignoring the subject.

My abuelita, like so many sensible Mexican grandmas, prescribed her usual for heartbreak—tequila. I'd followed her directions resolutely.

All I wanted was Rae and to stop thinking of Rae. All I wanted was to be with her, and then yell at her, and then make love to her.

Pendejo.

The only good thing to come out of the visit was that just before I got there, Rip was arrested on assault charges—apparently he'd found another woman to beat up on and was finally jailed. Vik could rest easy knowing he couldn't get to her, no matter where she was.

I wished I'd had more time in Texas, more distance from Clarksville and post because I was waiting to see her. Around every corner, in every parking garage, in every line of traffic, I was looking for her, simultaneously eager and terrified to see how she was doing.

Robert texted. Rebel messaged. Ann even messaged once. I sent vague replies and steadily avoided actually interacting with anyone who would make me deal with real life.

I launched into a routine of playing video games and drinking tequila and cheap beer as though it would assist my attempt at closure. I kept a count of how many days it'd been since I'd seen her last (currently twenty-seven since it was now late-June) and often had one-sided conversations with her in the car or the kitchen telling her all the ways she was wrong about me and even her and certainly us.

Vik came by to check on me on July first, and I knew what she saw scared her. She must have thought it was just the initial breakup with Rae getting me down while we were in Texas, plus she'd had her own concerns to deal with while there. But when she saw me unshaven, hung-over, a walking pile of misery weeks after the fact, the look in her eye changed.

She'd been to visit me every weekend since. Today, she was making me buy vegetables and other preservative-free items at the store. I pushed the cart, all stiff robot interacting with humans in the aisles, and mulled over the only thing I mulled anymore.

I didn't have anything else left to give was the problem. Because not only was I hurt by Rae's refusal to place any value whatsoever on our relationship or even our friendship, but I felt my confidence in general ground to dust.

Had I read her so wrong? Had I believed there was so much more there than was there? Had I misread her body language, the sounds she made when we kissed, the way she touched me when I was near her, almost despite herself?

I didn't think I had, and yet here I was, shopping for a box of brownie mix to bake just so my apartment would smell like it had the last time we were together and *together*, before her perpetual brake-pushing and my Rae-pushing had halted progress.

No, not just halted progress. Made progress something requiring an EOD squad.

I didn't tell Vik that was why I wanted brownies because she wouldn't have let me buy them. She'd have told me that was too sad, and she'd have been right.

"Goob, put the box in the bag and let's go. I'm going to melt!" Vik's impatience oozed from her popped hip and her tapping toe, all the more because she couldn't stand being hot and July had arrived with a heat wave. She stood a few feet from the check-out counter, glaring at the brownie box I gripped in my hand. "You are so spacey. Tune in! We've paid. Let's get home so you can make your precious brownies, all right?" She spun, her long black hair a curtain closing.

I cleared my vision with rapid blinks and grabbed the last remaining bag, slipping the brownie mix in and lumbering out to the car. I looped the bag around my hand and then let the pocket of my hooded sweatshirt warm both hands. I didn't need a sweatshirt, but it was comfortable, and comforting, and eventually we'd be back in my air-conditioned apartment, so it wasn't worth changing out of it.

When I got to the car, Vik shoved the cart at me. "Put that back. I'll get the car going." She was in tough love mode, which was fine with me. I was being sappy enough for both of us.

I steered the cart with one finger peeking out of my sweatshirt, cursing myself for not being a normal human who wore t-shirts and shorts when it was a hundred degrees and sunny. I gave the handle a hard push into the bay, enjoying shoving the metal frame against the stack of other carts and hearing the crash and screech of metal on metal.

"Oh, hi," she said before I could register Rae was standing two feet from me, steering her own shopping cart to the drop off I'd just turned from.

I immediately lost the ability to speak or move but swallowed and forced out a "hi." Could she see my chest rising and falling, working to recover from the gunshot that went off in my body the minute I turned to see her behind me.

"How—how are you," she said with a wince.

"Me? Fine. You?" Single syllables were all I had access to.

Wisps of her hair whipped around her in the blow-dryer-hot breeze, and she caught a few and tucked them back behind her ear. My fingers itched with the need to do it for her.

"I'm all right. But, hey, I'm glad to see you. I need to thank you for what you did—the letter for the investigation and everything," she said, reaching out for me and taking a step closer, then letting her hand fall before she touched me.

At her step, my heart stuttered and hands tingled, but I clenched and released my fists and cleared my head with a small shake.

Nothing but a thank you, that was what this was. She didn't want me—just wanted to thank me for helping her. Helping her job.

Of course.

I shouldn't have been disappointed, but somehow seeing her there, her cheeks pink in the heat, her eyes lustrous in the late afternoon sunshine, felt like a drill to my spine.

"Don't mention it. Hey, I'll, uh, see you 'round." I was already backing away as I said it, hands forced inside my hoodie pocket to keep them from reaching out and touching her because that was what I desperately wanted.

That pathetic, needy part of me wanted simply to run a finger over the cap of her shoulder or catch a strand of her hair and let it stray over my palm.

I didn't run away, but I walked faster than I had in a long time and slammed the car door when I got in.

"Whoa!"

I huffed a breath, then grabbed my hair and let out a string of curses.

"What just happened?" Vik asked, not shifting from park and squealing out of there like my mind demanded.

"She was here. I just want to go. Will you go?" I felt like tucking my head between my knees, the swell of heartache-induced nausea overwhelming me. Good thing I knew there was no such thing.

Rae

He ran away from me. He didn't actually pick up his feet and run, but he moved at a pace equal to what I do for a long run, his long legs pounding the pavement. He'd gotten in the car on the passenger's side—who was he with? Who'd be driving his car?

I hadn't recognized him from behind as I approached the cart return—his sweatshirt's hood covered his hair and he was hunched over until he pushed the cart and turned once it crashed into the other. But it took me less than a second of seeing him for my heart to lurch out of my body in recognition.

He was closed off from me, distanced, and I shouldn't have been surprised, but the missing warmth that was so *him* was excruciating to experience. He'd looked awful—dark circles under his eyes and his sweats completely out of place in the summer heat.

My mind raced on the drive home, as I made dinner, as I paced my living room, unable to relax and enjoy the weekend—not that I had enjoyed anything since we'd... whatever it was we'd done. Broken up, I guessed, but it felt like more than that.

Detonated.

By the end of the night, an idea had materialized in the midst of my pacing. Gabriel had risked himself and his pride for me more than once. He'd *tried* to get me to see him and see the possibility of us.

I finally did. I'd been confronted with the emptiness of my life, of the instability of what I'd created by pinning all meaning and value to my success in a career that could be torn from me by one small man having a series of bad days. That wasn't enough anymore.

Gabriel wasn't trying to tear me away from work, or keep me from doing what I wanted. My excuses for not wanting a soldier had officially worn out—that rule I'd applied after the failure with Brad was obsolete.

My life was more than work, and I'd never have much of a life at all if I wasn't willing to be open to someone who clearly cared for me and meant so much to me. No more excuses now—it was time to trust myself *and* Gabriel with my future.

I called Ann and asked for her help, silently praying at some point I'd be able to repay all the favors she'd been doing for me these last few months.

"He doesn't know I'm going to be here, right?" I ran my fingers through my hair, which I'd curled a few hours earlier. I smoothed my royal blue dress down my sides and let my fingers slide into the pockets of the flared skirt. I looked around Alisha's house and searched for the best spot to stand.

"No. He thinks it's a hospital party, and Alisha mentioned I was the only non-hospital person coming." Alisha and Ann were hosting a party—and I was using it as an excuse to corner Gabriel. "I guess he agreed because his sister has been begging him to get out of the house, so he *should* be here."

"Good. I hope he doesn't turn around and leave when he sees me." I had been anxious since I'd had the idea the night I saw him at the grocery store. It'd been two weeks since then. Ann had mentioned earlier that day she and Alisha were having a party, so I asked if they'd help me get Gabriel there. Maybe if I could get him alone, but on neutral ground, he'd be willing to listen to me.

"I don't know what he'll do, but I'll try to help if there's a way I can," Ann said, patting me on the arm and giving me a reassuring grin.

"I owe you. I already did, but now I do, double. You tell me when you need me and I'm there."

"I'll remember that. But you know that's not how this works, right?" she asked with a glint in her eye.

"Yes. I know. But still, I owe you."

"You're going to be fine. Stop being so nervous." She widened her eyes to impress me with her words.

I pulled her in for a hug and then held her away by the shoulders. "Thank you."

"Ok, enough. Now go get some water, or go to the bathroom, or whatever you need to do to stop internally freaking out until he gets here," she said with a lifted eyebrow showing me just how well she knew me.

I took her advice, and before I knew it, he and Victoria walked in. I was glad I knew she was his sister because my heart and hopes would have bottomed out if I'd seen them together without that kernel of information.

I stayed out of sight once I saw him, hiding away in the back of the kitchen, making sure he wouldn't see me until he'd gotten a drink and had a minute to get acclimated.

My whole body fizzed and popped at the sight of him—he'd styled his hair, which was longer on top, and wore a dark button up with the sleeves rolled to just below his elbows and nice jeans. He looked so good—far better than he had at the store weeks ago, and even then, when he looked a mess, he was beautiful.

My heart bounced around my chest as I worked to calm my breathing. As soon as I walked into the living room, his head snapped up.

"Rae?" He stepped back, and Victoria crossed to him and put a hand on his arm. She said something in a low voice in Spanish I couldn't understand.

I moved to him quickly and clutched a wine glass so I wouldn't reach out and touch him. "I would appreciate it if you would give me five minutes to speak with you in private," I said, looking at him and doing my best to avoid the wrathful stare emanating from Victoria's face.

His eyebrows pinched, and he gritted his teeth. It took him more than a normal beat to answer, but eventually he said, "Sure." Vik put a hand on his arm, and he nodded to her before she dropped it and he followed me.

I wasn't sure what to expect from him other than resistance. I knew going to knock on his door would yield nothing—he wouldn't answer. I knew this because I'd done it over the break, twice. Whether he knew it was me, or just wasn't answering the door at all, I didn't know. His car was in its spot, and the light was on in the room, but no answer came.

I knew, too, that I couldn't approach him at work. As much as he hadn't insisted on the physical separation at work like I had, I didn't want to harass him or distract him while he was working.

I'd set up a semi-elaborate plan to get him on neutral

ground—a place I knew he'd been before based on conversations and surrounded by people he knew and liked. The fact that he'd said *sure* was good, but his body language brutalized me. He wasn't standing tall and loud and gregarious, wasn't smiling at everyone in the room and chatting with them like an old friend.

He was a husk, and I was the one who'd pried out the delectable middle.

I nodded over my shoulder and turned, but moved slowly, making sure he was following me. Alisha had suggested her office would work well, so I led him to the third room on the left and held the door open for him. He stepped inside and walked to the wall where Alisha's diplomas hung, and I shut the door and leaned against it. If he was going to leave, it wouldn't be without hearing me out.

"I owe you an apology, Gabriel."

He turned slowly, a beer in one hand. He took a sip and shook his head. "You don't owe me anything, Rae," he said in a low, cool voice. It wasn't distant, but it wasn't warm, friendly, lovely like I'd gotten used to.

"I do. I hurt you, and I can't forgive myself for that. I am sorry for the way I spoke to you in our last few conversations. I am deeply sorry for making you feel anything but exceptional."

He inhaled a long, deep breath and took a swig of beer. "Thank you for saying that." His voice, again, wasn't remote, but it wasn't engaged. He was keeping all of his walls up, and I wasn't sure I had the conversational prowess to knock them down, especially with my heart at a gallop just being near him.

I left the door and walked to stand in front of him. I set my wine glass on the desk next to me and crossed my arms.

"I don't know how you're feeling, but you have every right to be angry, or hurt, or—"

"—I have a right to those emotions? Oh good, I'm glad I've got your permission." He took another drink of his beer then crossed his arms to match mine. He tilted his head down to look at me, and I wished I'd worn higher heels so I could meet him eye for eye.

"That's not what I mean. I just mean, I know I hurt you, and I don't blame you for hating me. But I don't want that— I don't want it to stay there."

"I don't hate you," he said, his eyes rolling to the ceiling like I exasperated him.

"Ok. Good," I said, feeling some relief, although unsure what that meant.

"But I don't think I can be around you. You did hurt me, and it's going to be a while before I can be your friend again." He took a step to me and I followed him. His eyes skated down my body, over the dip of my waist and flare of the skirt and down my legs to my shoes. His eyes shot back up to mine and his nostrils flared in annoyance.

"I don't want you to be my friend," I said, looking him directly in the eye, willing him to understand.

He leaned back against the wall and shut his eyes, his face looking just as pained as when he first saw me. He shook his head back and forth like I was wrong for saying that. "What do you want, Rae? Just tell me. I've clearly failed to figure that out every time I've tried, so please just tell me so I don't make a fool of myself again."

Before I could speak, the door banged open. "All right, I gave you five minutes, and you've had your say. Let's go, Gabriel," Victoria said, marching past us, grabbing him by the wrist and pulling him past me.

I wanted to grab him but thought better of it. "Wait, Victoria, please. We're still talking. Gabriel—"

"I told you what would happen if you hurt him. I liked you Rae, but... you're done." Gabriel let himself be led out by his petite sister who walked in stilettos like she'd invented them herself. She cat-walked her way to the front door and left, slamming it just as soon as they were out. He'd only looked at me and not said a word.

I swallowed the rocks in my throat, shook my head at Ann as she came to check on me, and left as soon as I could get out of there without seeming like I was running after him.

I *was* going to run after him. He was worth that. But I wasn't going to do it when Victoria was there to witness it. She had his best interest at heart, and somewhere inside I recognized that as a valuable thing. But right now I wanted to slap her pretty face and scream at her to let me explain things.

After that, I waited. I hoped I'd hear from him *this* time since I'd made the effort—I'd put myself out there or tried. But nothing.

I knew that was only fair. I knew the ball was still firmly in my court, not that this felt anything like a game, and I knew I had to keep pushing.

I got takeout from his favorite Mexican food place despite its inferiority to my favorite place, and I showed up on his door that Sunday at five. I hoped that would be late enough in the day that Victoria would need to go back to Nashville if she'd stuck around for the weekend and before he'd done anything about dinner. If he wasn't totally convinced he wanted to talk to me, then he might at least be tempted by dinner.

It was blazing hot out, the sun blaring down on the back

of my neck while I stood at the door. I knocked with a firm knock that left my knuckles feeling raw—or maybe that was just how all of me felt lately.

A minute passed. I knew from the last times I'd tried I wouldn't be able to tell what was going on inside—I couldn't hear movement or anything from outside the door. I resolved to wait a full two minutes, then knock again. Just before I knocked again, the door jerked open.

His shoulders rose and fell and his gorgeous lips pressed into a flat smile. "Rae."

"I brought you dinner," I said, holding out the bag of food to warm the chill between us.

He eyed the bag, then me, but hesitated. "We eat, then talk." His voice was gruff and unused. I wondered if he'd been home all day without Victoria, or if he was just tired. He wore low-slung sweatpants and a shirt that said "Kiss me, I'm Irish."

"Ok. That works for me," I said, relieved he would want to spend that time together.

CHAPTER SEVENTEEN

Gabriel

SEEING her stand there with a bag full of food from my favorite place tested me. It tested the resolve I had to talk through all of the things we needed to talk through. I didn't know how I'd get through that without begging her to kiss me.

I know. It had gotten bleak.

But seeing her at that party and knowing she'd set it up so I'd come and not know she was there fertilized the hope that had all but died in me.

She didn't have a chance to answer when I asked her what she wanted. She was about to, but Vik stormed in and pulled me away, and part of me was glad for it. Another part of me was internally kicking and screaming, but I knew that if she wanted to talk with me, she could work for it.

Rae followed me inside and her coconut-fresh smell

wafted behind her as she moved in front of me to set the food on the coffee table while I got forks from the kitchen. I sat down next to her, letting my eyes follow the trail of her hair over her shoulder and past the swell of her breast to brush her ribs. Had it gotten longer?

It was true I felt in some small way I had the upper hand. I felt the ugliness of that in me hovering right there with my hurt and sadness. I didn't want to make her feel bad, but another less evolved part of me wanted to know she'd suffered like I had.

She handed me a heavy clamshell, and I popped it open to find my favorite dish ordered exactly the way I liked it. It was piping hot and the smell made my mouth water and register that I was actually hungry.

I hadn't been hungry in months.

I sliced into the tacos al pastor, careful not to pierce the bottom of the container, and knew I should have dumped it onto a plate. But it was too late now. I could feel her watching me as I shoveled bite after bite.

"Glad to see that hasn't changed," she said, a small smile tugging at the corner of her mouth. She took a bite and chewed, never taking her eyes off me.

"This is the first time I've been this hungry in a while." My fork paused over the food for a second before I dug back in, hoping she wouldn't realize that missing her had created a hollowness in me that was never sated, and I'd stopped worrying about eating except for the sheer fuel of it. There'd been no joy in eating, that was for sure.

We continued eating quietly, only the occasional squeak of Styrofoam propped on our legs striking out into the room.

"I like your shirt," she said, setting her food on the table and wiping her hands on a napkin draped over her leg.

"Ah, yeah. Vik thinks she's funny." I wiped my mouth with a napkin and set my container down next to hers. "I didn't even offer you water. Do you want some?" I'd gotten nervous somewhere between wiping my mouth and recognizing my total failure at hosting the woman I'd thought about more than pretty much anything.

Granted, I wasn't expecting her. And she showed up on my doorstep with my favorite takeout looking hopeful and somber and simply, painfully beautiful.

"Sure. Thank you." I heard the rustling of the plastic bag and saw she'd packaged everything up. She watched me warily as I approached and handed her a glass. "Are you..."

"Am I, what?" I knew I was being a jerk—I knew what she wanted. But I was an injured animal, scared to be helped by someone it no longer trusted.

"Can we talk now?" Her voice was soft but not timid. She wasn't begging me, but she was calming me with her smooth tone.

"Ok." I sat down on the other end of the couch, though it wasn't a large couch so we were only a foot or so apart. I crossed my arms, giving her the universal sign for *closed for business, emotional appeals, and impervious to your blinding beauty.*

Ok well maybe all that wasn't universal, but that was the vibe I was laying down.

"Ok, then. I'll just... get right to it." She searched my face for something, and I was sure she didn't see anything. I'd pulled my anger and hurt up like a shield against her, unwilling to be walked down the aisle toward peaceful friendship and apology acceptance. I'd hoped, for something like forty-four hours, that if she came here it'd mean something. I wasn't ready to show her that yet.

She exhaled, wiping her hands down her jeans. "On

Friday, before Victoria came in, you asked me to tell you what I want."

I sat up. Was she going to be that direct? She wasn't going to draw out the torture? "I remember."

She pinned me in place with her eyes. "I want to be with you. Again. Or, for the first time, because I've finally figured out what I want, and why, and why I've been afraid."

My eyes fluttered and I looked at her like she was losing it. "What?"

Could this be real?

"I, uh, I want us to date, and, you know, be together again. I've missed you, and I care about you," she explained, folding her hands together in her lap.

I shook my head, my eyes searching hers. "Sorry, what?"

She wasn't speaking a different language, but I could tell she felt like she was, glancing side to side for something to aid her with getting her point through my thick skull. I saw the flush creep up above her shirt, up her neck, and into her cheeks. I bit the inside of my cheek to keep the smile I felt growing in my gut from blazing across my face.

"I want you to be my boyfriend, and I want to be your girlfriend."

My eyebrows shot up in surprise and I shook my head again. "I'm sorry, I'm sure I'm not understanding you." I'd admit later, I was torturing her.

"I want you, Gabriel Marquez, to be with me, Rae Jackson, and I want us to stay that way, for a long time," she said, her voice insistent.

My heart was racing, roaring in my chest. Couldn't she tell?

I watched her pick up her water and take a sip, then set

the glass down again. I kept my face still and her face fell. I bit my lip to hide a smile.

"I could potentially be interested in that position," I said, pressing my lips together to keep the smile at bay. I had to give her *something*. I didn't want her losing hope and storming out of here—I had better things in mind.

"Yeah?"

"Yes. I'd be interested." I grabbed her arm, then pulled her to me. Our lips met and I pulled her into my arms, into my lap, pressing her as close as she could get. She clasped her hands around my neck, leaning up to strengthen the kiss. A surge of relief and excitement pushed through every vein in my body.

I kissed her ravenously, like it was the first time I'd tasted in weeks. And despite the meal we'd just shared, maybe it was.

I pulled back and settled her next to me. "I'm interested, but we have some ground to cover before I accept your offer."

She was breathless, her eyes dark, but she nodded. "That's fair. We do have a lot to talk about, and I'm still me. I haven't magically shed all of my concerns. What I *have* done is realize that I love you, and I don't want to keep ignoring that."

"You love me?" I pulled her closer again, my heart a firework. A freaking menagerie of colors exploded inside my chest—the stuff of fairy tales.

She nodded, not looking away, and I relished taking in the face I'd missed so desperately the last few months from just inches away.

"Thank God," I said, and then wrapped her in another kiss. I released her, and then looked around like something was missing. "I don't know what to do with myself, or you. I mean, I know what I *want* to do with you, but..."

"I want us to go slow, ok?" A worried look creased her brow.

"I can respect that. I'm not sure we'll agree on the pace, but I understand a little bit better now that's what you need. I'm sorry I pushed you," I said, stroking her hair back from her face.

"One of the things I love about you is that you push me, but on *that*, I'm going to need time. I'm nervous about this because I don't know what I'm doing." She looked at her hands instead of me when she said it, and my heart ached to make her understand there was nothing I wouldn't do for her.

"Tell me." I leaned to kiss her forehead, her cheek. "What are you worried about?"

"If we stay together..."

"We are staying together, so talk about it like *when* not *if*."

"Ok." She brightened. "Well, at some point, you're going to want to get married."

"Yes. And you don't think you will?" I braced for the response.

"It's not that I'm against marriage, but would you really want to be married to me? I can't stay—" I cut her off with a kiss.

"I want *you*, carita. *You*. I don't think you've understood when I talk about us that way, but I know you're not going anywhere. I love that you're ambitious, that you know your place in the Army and want to rise up. I don't want to take that away from you."

Her eyebrows quirked and she looked surprised.

"Why would that surprise you? You've made it clear since the beginning you're not going to stop working, and you don't want to be a stay at home mom if we have kids. I get that you want to stay in, and I support that. I told you I thought it was awesome when you told me about your goal to be an O6—why wouldn't you believe me?"

"I guess I just... didn't. It seems too good to be true. You want to be the provider and caregiver—that's such a part of who you are. I didn't think you'd want someone like me if I'm not easy to take care of, I guess."

"I love taking care of you. You're not hard to care for, not at all. That's why we're in this mess—I started caring about you the second you begrudgingly agreed to be my friend. I don't care if I'm the one paying the bills. I can still take care of you, and if we have kids, of them too."

Her face darkened at that. "I don't know if I'll be able to, you know that, right? I don't know." She squeezed my hand.

"I know, Rae, and we'll deal with that." I kissed her temple, feeling a pull of anxiety. I wanted to see what a child we made would look like, but I knew we'd handle whatever came.

"We could look into adoption." Her voice was so small, and it made me want to crush Brad of Before into pieces for wounding her and creating so much doubt about this.

"We're going to adopt whether you get pregnant or not," I said, realizing I'd never told her my plans.

"Oh, we are? That's good to know," she said, her face lit with amusement. She ran a hand up and down my arms and my body tracked the movement of the pads of her fingers with impatience.

"Yeah. And I'll be a stay at home dad while they're

little. I'll probably work a few hours a week to keep my licensing so it's not so hard to go back when they're bigger."

She turned to look at me straight on, even though we were smashed against each other on the couch. "What?"

"I figured I'd stay home if there are babies, and then we can figure out daycare, or whatever." I gave her a half smile, knowing she was just catching on to my explanation.

"The Army doesn't give that much paternity leave," she said, hope in her eyes.

"No. But a lot of civilian hospitals do. And if not, I'll quit that job too if I need to. You can be my sugar mama."

She chuckled at that. "If you're working as a nurse at a non-military hospital, you'll probably be my sugar daddy, at least for a while."

"True. I'd planned to coast it out in the Army as long as they put me places I wanted to be, but now that I have the motivation to consider other options, I've done some digging. I can definitely out-earn what I make now if I go civilian, especially if I don't have to deal with health insurance."

"Really?"

"Yeah, civilian nurses make pretty good bank, depending on where you live. They're not raking it in or anything, but once you factor in the moves and lack of flex-ibility—"

"I believe you on that. Most medical people I know just want to serve their initial commitment and jump ship unless they are passionate about staying in. But, I mean, you've been thinking about all this, even while we were broken up?"

I straightened and faced her head on. "Rae, I don't know how to tell you this without freaking you out, but I've known I wanted something serious with you since we decided to date. Easter made that more apparent, then taking care of you when you were sick, then seeing you handle the tornado of BS thrown at you before leave. Me wanting you is not news."

She leaned in to kiss me gently once, twice, again. "It's news to me, but I'm so glad to hear it."

EPILOGUE

Rae

I KNOCKED on the door and stepped back, clutching Gabriel's hand in mine too tight.

"Baby, chill. She's fine, and this is going to be great."

"I will chill when she has accepted my apology and doesn't look at me like she's going to find a way to shank me when you're not looking." I took a deep breath and told my heart to calm down. If I was going to be with Gabriel—which I was, so there was no *if* about it—there was no way I could avoid this.

The door swung open and Victoria, typically magnificent with her long hair flowing over each shoulder and a stern look on her face, raised her perfectly arched eyebrows. "*Hola.*"

"Hi, Victoria," I said, summoning all the wartime courage I'd need. "I'm here to apologize to you."

"To me?" It sounded like a question, but her body language and expression said *it's about time.*

I did feel bad that it had been weeks since Gabriel and I repaired our relationship. I'd been busy prepping a field training exercise, then was gone for the exercise, and then Gabriel had worked weekends. As generally unflappable as I could be, Victoria wasn't someone I was about to face alone for the first time after seeing her at a party where I ambushed her heartbroken brother.

Yeah, no.

"Yes, to you. I told you I wouldn't hurt him, and I did." He squeezed my hand to reassure me, but I didn't look at him. I'd get even more nervous and fidgety, which I didn't like, but he looked astoundingly attractive today and it was distracting. I needed to focus.

"I'm a big girl. If you two are fine then I'm fine," she said, her arms now crossed against her body, her hip jutting to the side to hold her door open.

"I appreciate that, and I know you and Gabriel have talked so you know everything." I searched her eyes, waited for her to open the door wider, or do something other than stare back at us with arms crossed.

"Hita, invite us in." Gabriel moved forward as he said it and pulled me along behind him. Victoria stepped back out of the way and closed the door behind us but didn't follow us in.

"Give me a minute with Rae, Goob," she said from against the door. She leaned against it, arms crossed again, her face sharp and serious and beautiful in a fearsome way. She was a young woman to be reckoned with, even at twenty-one.

I released Gabriel's hand and he moved to the patio door but paused before he exited. "Be nice," he said with a pointed glare at his little sister.

We watched as he slid the balcony door closed and stretched in the late summer evening heat. August had flown by and it was nearly time for the heat to give way to fall.

I turned my attention to Victoria who hadn't moved and waited.

"You hurt him," she said, her voice cold.

"I did. I was an idiot. I regret it."

"You will not hurt him again." She clenched her teeth shut, cutting herself off from saying something more.

I stepped closer to her so we were only a few feet apart. "I can assure you that no part of me intends to hurt him. But I can also say that if we stay together, which I plan on us doing, then I probably will. I'm human, and so is he. What I can tell you is that I won't ever take him for granted, and I won't ever stop loving him."

Her brows rose at this and she studied me a moment. "So you're like... thinking marriage?"

"I am. We are. It's a ways off, but not as far as I would have thought," I said, unable to keep one side of my mouth from rising with a small smile at the truth I'd shared with her.

"You going to take our last name?" She pushed off the door and came to stand right in front of me.

"Uh, we haven't talked about it," I admitted.

"He's pretty traditional about that kind of thing," she said, her voice a small warning.

"I'm aware. I guess we should talk about it."

"Do. Today. And don't forget we have lunch next week at Robbie's Kitchen. You guys better be on time."

"Oh, I thought that was just you and Gabriel—"

"No, you too. If you're going to be my sister, I should get

to know you better." She gave me the barest hint of a smile, and then went to rattle around the kitchen.

When I slid open the door, Gabriel was watching. "What'd she say? She lay down the fighting words?" He was joking, but I knew it mattered to him if Victoria and I got along. It mattered to me too.

"I think we'll be fine. She had a few questions, and I gave her honest answers that seemed to appease her for now."

We walked into the apartment and he hugged Victoria goodbye. We shared a peace treaty-like smile, and then we were gone. I was glad we hadn't planned to stay and press the détente tonight.

"So what did she ask?" His hand was warm on my back as we walked to the car.

"She asked whether I'd take your last name when we get married."

"When?" His voice was high and disbelieving.

"We've talked babies and marriage already—is this a surprise?" I asked, baffled by his shock.

"No, it's not, I'm just... you said you wanted to take things slow, and I—we—we have been. But if you're talking last names with my sister, you mean it," he said in a huff, his eyes bright in the late afternoon light.

"I do."

He turned the key and started the car, then turned it right back off.

"Do you think you will?"

I leaned against the car door to see him straight on. "You'll have to wait and find out."

~

15 years later
Gabriel

"Gabriel, honey, we're running late!"

I heard her voice from the kitchen, the impatience and nerves. "Carita, I know, but your growing children are apparently still incapable of dressing themselves." I peeked into Tori's room.

My newly-teenaged daughter frowned at me from her bed where she fought with a buckle on her sandals. Her black hair rushed in curled waves over her shoulder.

"Don't say it. I know. I'm coming. I had an incident with a necklace and my hair, but I'm fine, and I'm coming." Tori's frustration was palpable as she straightened her navy dress and hopped out of the doorway behind me as she pulled the other shoe on. Her hair, perpetually long like her mother's used to be and like her aunt and namesake's still was, was usually an issue.

"Heath's going to wonder where we are. He's already there," Rae hollered from below. I knew she'd be pacing, waiting on me. She'd been ready for half an hour, but I knew once she put on her jacket, she'd be particularly antsy. She must have slipped it on when I'd gone up to check on the kids.

"Matthew, Michael, *come on.*" I hustled back down the stairs, straightening my charcoal suit and stopped short at the sight of her standing in the kitchen.

I knew the boys would also be in gray suits, and they'd look like twins, even though they were almost a year apart, one arriving after six hours of labor, the other a gift who came to us only months later when he was hours old. Like their sister, they had dark hair, their skin somewhere between mine and their mother's, their features a miraculous combination that said the three of them belonged to each other more than either of their parents.

I got to see Rae in her blues more often than I had in years past, but I felt my heart nudge my rib cage a little faster at the scene before me. She stood at the counter in the kitchen of our house on post at Fort Campbell. Her head was ducked and focused on what she was scrawling on a pad next to the microwave.

We'd traveled the world, but for this, she'd landed back where she felt at home. In many ways, I did too.

It was, after all, where we started.

She was tiny, but looked sharp, fierce, and more than ready to take command.

Brigade Command.

She'd promoted to Colonel not too long ago, and then we'd moved yet again to attend the next level of Army education in a distinctly non-military place that made us feel like we were on vacation from military life in some ways and yet right in the thick of it in others. We'd decided I wouldn't work—not for a year while she was in school and the kids had afterschool activities.

Usually, I picked up hours at the on-post clinic when I could get a position there or found something in family practice off post with predictability. But not lately.

Like most military spouses, my career hadn't looked like a traditional career—sometimes I worked, and sometimes I didn't. I was often the only male spouse in the room at family readiness meetings or other gatherings. But Rae never let me feel anything but essential, and I knew that was true... even if my brothers continually gave me hell for not being the breadwinner.

And now I'd take another few years off because Rae was about to take command of the sustainment brigade, the second of two women to ever have such a command. She'd have long hours, incredible stress, insane responsibility, and was likely to deploy. I'd be the stay at home dad for now while they were still here. I knew the years before they'd be out of the house would slip by, just like so many had already.

I thought I'd puke, there was so much pride welling up in me.

For her.

For the kids.

For myself.

We'd done it. And I knew, whatever she said in the speech as she accepted command at the ceremony today would be short and sweet, but eloquent, and it would remind us that we'd done it *together*.

Our kids were growing, and despite the challenges, they were amazing. At thirteen, ten, and nine, they were big enough to feel the full effect of the changes we took on. They were wise enough to know that stability was a ways off. But they also knew we were a team, and we couldn't do it without *them*.

Dios mio, I was sappy, standing there staring at a smaller version of that same blonde bun I'd been unable to avoid so many years ago, that same compact body I'd always been drawn to.

I shook myself, ungluing my eyes from Rae's still-spectacular behind. "I just yelled for the boys, but I don't hear them. Let me run—"

"No, they're in the car already. You didn't see them? They must have run past you when you were getting Tori." She wrote one last thing, most likely a few notes for her speech, stuffed the paper in her pocket, and turned to face me, her eyes skating over me from head to toe.

We heard a yelp. "I'm going! Don't do your thing yet," Tori said and scuttled out of the kitchen with a slam of the garage door.

"Our thing?" I said, inching toward Rae.

She smiled and shook her head. "She's referring to our being affectionate. I think it humiliates her delicate teenaged sensibilities that her parents like each other." She reached for me.

"I more than like you, Colonel Jackson." I dipped down and pressed a soft kiss to her lips.

She tilted up on tiptoes and pressed her lips farther into mine. "That works out well. I more than like you too."

Her fingers slid up my chest, over the collar of my shirt, and took my face in her hands. Her bright blue eyes shifted between mine and her brow furrowed. "I cannot thank you enough for getting me here."

Immediately, my throat thickened and emotion welled. I was getting soft in my old age, and I didn't give a damn. "Rae, I'm so proud of you. It has been—"

"No. It has been *my* honor. There is nothing I can say in my speech that will properly express the debt I owe you or the depth of my love for you. No one knows how well you've loved me—sometimes I don't even see it. Everything you've done for us—"

"We make a good team," I said, smile wobbly.

She swallowed, took a breath. "We do. Thank you, my love."

"De nada, carita."

The End.

∽

Thank you for reading Rae and Gabriel's story! I hope you enjoyed it as much as I enjoyed writing it. The Rambler Battalion series continues with Major Reese Flint's novel, Home With You. Keep reading for a sneak peek, or grab your copy now!

Almost Sure, Book 3

Almost Home, Book 4

ACKNOWLEDGMENTS

First, thanks to God, who loves unconditionally. That reality is incredibly freeing, and I thought of it often as I wrote this story.

I couldn't have written this book without the insight and honesty gifted to me by the women who responded to my female service member survey in 2017. To all of you, who represented each of the five services, thank you for sharing your experiences—the good, the bad, the ugly. You truly inspired this book (and much more than this one, to tell the truth).

Special thanks to Monica and her family for providing insight into Gabriel and *his* family. All the best parts of Gabriel, particularly his care-taking and generosity, are directly inspired by you, dear one. Thank you for sharing yourself, your culture, and your cascarones with me.

Jamie, Karen, Denise, and Julie, as always, thank you for putting up with me droning on about my angst, especially with this book. I love you. WWW ladies—you rock my world. Thank you.

To the brilliant beta readers, Christy, Allison, Victoria, Gricel, Kirsten, and Lauren, thank you for being insightful readers willing to share your thoughts and help make this book stronger. This book is better because of you.

To Judy Roth, my amazing editor, for being patient with my indecision and wise in the small moments that made big differences. I love this book so much, and it is thanks to you.

Rainbeau, my amazing designer and photographer, I can't thank you enough, especially on this one. It was an extra challenge finding the models, but you did it! You continue to amaze me and I'm just delighted to get to continue working with you.

Thank you, Ma and Da, for your uninhibited support. Thank you, Tots 1 and 2, for being unendingly impressed that I write books. Thank you to Matthew, who loves me so very very well, and who makes me proud to be a part of the team.

For all of the people reading, thank you. I can't tell you what it means to that you spend some time with my book—I can literally think of a thousand other things you could have done, so thanks. Cheers. Rainbow glitter explosion for *you*.

ABOUT THE AUTHOR

Claire Cain lives to eat and drink her way around the globe with her traveling soldier and three kids, but is perhaps even happier hunkered down at home in a pair of sweatpants and slippers using any free moment she has to read and cook. Or talk—she really likes to talk. She has become an expert at packing too many dishes in too few cabinets and making houses into homes from Utah to Germany and many places in between. She's a proud Army wife and is frankly just really happy to be here.

You can join Claire's facebook reader group for exclusive content and fun: https://www.facebook.com/groups/clairecain/

Website: http://www.clairecainwriter.com

E-mail: Claire@ClaireCainWriter.com

Newsletter sign-up for new releases, exclusives, and freebies: http://www.clairecainwriter.com/newsletter

facebook.com/clairecainwriter

twitter.com/writeclairecain

instagram.com/clairecainwriter

pinterest.com/clairecainwriter

amazon.com/author/clairecain

bookbub.com/authors/claire-cain

goodreads.com/clairecainwriter

SNEAK PEEK

Want more? Here's a teaser for The Rambler Battalion Series Book 4, *Home With You*, starring Major Reese Flint and Erin Kelly, available now!

Erin

"Hello?" A gruff voice rang out across the yard, penetrating the blaring music in my headphones.

I pulled the stalk of a weed, patted the soil into place, and pushed back from my knees onto my feet. Swiping at my damp forehead with the back of my glove, I wondered if I should go get my straw hat, and who'd just arrived. I'd been in the shade all morning but the sun was cresting over the house now. At least, I'd need to reapply sunscreen.

Straightening to full height and looking around, I spotted him. His gait had always been directed and almost aggressive, even though he'd been mild and quiet around me all our lives. He stopped ten feet from me, the sun beating down on his dark brown, short hair. More dark hair covered his face and cheeks—it was more facial hair than I'd ever see him with. I couldn't see his eyes yet, but I knew they'd still be that paralyzing gray-green that made my stomach drop out.

"Sunny?" His voice was harsh, disbelieving as I pulled out my headphones.

I laughed. We'd been e-mailing for months—nearly a year at this point. He'd always greeted me as Erin. Now he was calling me Sunny?

"Pieces?" I said, smiling at the old name I hadn't said aloud in more than a decade.

We both paused to assess each other a moment, and then something came over me and I couldn't stop myself. I jogged to him, pulling off my bright green gardening gloves and sticking them in the back pocket of my shorts.

I stopped short of crashing into him and raised my hand to his scruffy cheek. He stayed still as I pressed my warm hand to his face and smiled up at him. His eyes were wide, his mouth barely open with no sound or breath escaping.

I looked in those eyes, always full of a rainstorm, and a small piece of me that had been floating out in the ether was called back to me. The sense of belonging was there, right behind the foolishly long dark lashes.

And, of course, it would be. He'd known me all my life. I don't remember a time when I didn't know him or love him in some way.

"Sure enough," I said, unable to hold back the smile swallowing my face. I wrapped my arms around him and pulled him to my chest. I squeezed him tight and let the joy pulse through me for a moment, inhaling the clean scent of him. Then I remembered I'd been out doing yard work for something like three hours and probably smelled like sweat and sunscreen and dirt at *best*, so I pulled back.

When I saw his face, heat jumped to my cheeks. Instead

of smiling back at me, he stood there, just as he had when I'd approached. He was frozen, though his expression edged more toward horror or even, *oh, no, is this happening?*, disgust.

He hadn't put his arms around me. He hadn't smiled at me. He hadn't said a thing past my name. Had I grossed him out with my all-out gardening sweat assault?

Why do you do this to yourself, Erin? Why?

"I'm sorry, gosh. I'm just so happy to see you. I... it's been so long since I've seen you and I've been looking forward to it since your mom suggested I house sit for you. I didn't mean to make you uncomfortable just now. I don't want you to feel like I'm going to attack you every time I see you, I'm just—"

"It's fine."

His voice was sharp when it came, but not angry. Just... sharp.

"Good," I said, the embarrassment burning through me. If the sun hadn't turned me red in the last few minutes then this fresh and glowing humiliation should do the trick. Might even match my hair, so at least there was that.

"It's been what? Ten years?" He remained stock-still, his feet planted in the gravel driveway, towering over me at six foot four, based on the last time I heard. But his voice wasn't so insistent or forced.

"Yeah, it has. I was sixteen the last time I saw you," I said, pasting a small smile on my lips so he wouldn't see the tremor run through me just thinking about the last time I saw him. I was sure he had no idea what'd happened just before he found me, but I was grateful to him. My way of thanking him was to ensure he never knew.

"You're—you—." He let out a breath and ran a hand through his hair, turning away from me a few degrees.

My belly flipped when I saw his fingers cut through that thick, dark hair. He'd always had gorgeous hair, and I'd always wanted to touch it. Never mind the fact that this move drew my attention to his t-shirt, or more specifically the sleeve of his shirt that rode up on his arm as he moved it, revealing large, sculpted biceps.

Was my mouth watering? What was happening to me? I was standing here incurring the sun's wrath for being pale and ogling my old friend-turned-boss's biceps.

Really, Erin? You're that lonely?

I was, but that was beside the point. He'd always been tall, and dark-haired, and muscular. He was more muscular, more filled-out, like he'd been just a boy the last time I saw him, though if I was sixteen he would have been twenty-seven. He'd been a man for years by that time.

Maybe he'd spent his deployment eating protein powder and lifting weights. We weren't technically even at war, right?

You are a ridiculous human being and you need to chill.

"What?" I said, anxious to hear what would come out of his mouth. He'd turned away from me while I mentally spiraled down the path of arm muscles but shifted on his heel and turned back toward me.

"You're devastating."

I blinked.

And again.

I swallowed, my pulse skittering in my veins.

"What?"

"You're just... uh, well. All grown up, of course," he said, turning away from me again.

The pit of my stomach took a dive. Ah, yes. He'd remembered me as a charming little child and now he was faced with the grown woman and it was all a little less delightful.

"Tends to happen to the best of us," I said, taking a few steps closer to the main house, and closer to him.

He must have heard me approaching, my feet crunching in the gravel drive, and glanced sideways at me with a squint, then jerked his head back to study the ground.

Ok then.

"I'll finish up weeding tomorrow before it gets hot again. I left all the mail for the last few weeks on the kitchen counter, and I'm sure Wallace has found you—he's been murdering mice in anticipation of your return." I smiled at the thought of Wallace, a fat mutt of a cat who looked like he'd fallen in different puddles of brown and black paint and come out a speckled mish-mash. He was affectionate to the point of being annoying, but he got along with my prissy Siamese mix cat Bleep well enough, so we'd done fine while Wallace's master was away.

Or, since we were talking cats, Wallace's loyal subject.

"Thank you," he said, walking to the side entrance of the house, just next to the garage. It was the same door I took to get to my little apartment over the garage. There was a small hallway, maybe six feet long, inside the door that separated the stairway that led to my apartment entrance and the door that led to the kitchen of the main house.

His kitchen, I corrected myself. He was home now, and he'd be home. It was time for me to start looking for places of my own.

"I've been looking for apartments—nothing yet, but I'm sure something will come up soon once September really gets rolling. I'll be out of your hair before you know it, and until then, you won't know I'm here."

~

Reese

What. The. Hell.

My grandfather said swearing was the sign of a weak-minded man, and for much of my life, he'd been my idol. I'd made it a habit to keep my mouth shut when I was angry, especially because when I was much younger, opening it when I was flustered or upset meant my stutter would be more unmanageable than usual and that typically made things worse for everyone.

But I was not prepared for this situation.

I'd been blindsided.

I'd been communicating with this girl—this *woman*—for upwards of ten months now. If you included the six weeks since I'd arrived back home, readjusted to being home while she was traveling visiting her last remaining relative in Maine, and then the time I'd been on block leave for nearly a month once I took all the time I needed to use or lose, it'd been a year.

And at no point had I imagined that sweet Erin Kelly, little carrot-haired rug rat of my youth and awkward teen full of angles at our last meeting, would have turned into that.

That.

And that was probably a good thing. Because had I known that *that* was who I'd been talking to, my mind might not have been able to handle it.

No, it definitely wouldn't have in the context of the deprivation and loneliness and boredom of deployment.

I knew this for certain since it was most definitely not handling it now. I'd had to look away from her for fear of embarrassing myself if she met my eye and saw the sheer and immediate *wanting* I felt.

I'd parked in the garage last night and figured she was home but didn't want to disturb her. I spent the night in ignorance, clearly, because I had no idea who was just feet away in the garage apartment.

I didn't want to interfere with her Saturday morning on a long weekend. I knew she worked, on top of acting as caretaker for my house while I'd been gone, and thought maybe she slept in. She was in her twenties after all—why shouldn't she?

So, I'd wandered out this morning, ready to greet this old friend of the family and thank her, maybe catch up a bit and hear how my needy little bastard of a cat had done without me, when I saw her.

On her knees in the dirt of the flower bed, two braids a familiar color of red trailing down her back. It was slow motion as I called hello, and she slowly stood, turned to me, and my breath caught in my throat.

She was like every farm girl fantasy wrapped in one. Cut off jean shorts left miles of her toned, pale legs exposed until they plunged into her worn, dirty tennis shoes. Her tank top, if it could be called that, was cut off at her midriff, her taut stomach glistening in the heat of the morning.

Fricking *glistening*, I'm telling you.

Her shoulders were bare and slightly bronzed, though the rest of her was pale but for the light freckles that chased each other in places.

Her braids had hung over either shoulder once she was standing, and I had half expected to see little ribbons tied in bows at the ends of them, just to make the picture complete. But no, just small elastics, or whatever held them together.

A burst of longing hit me so hard I'd almost gasped.

The picture she'd made was assaulting, but it was her face that caught me, had me calling out her old nickname before I knew what I was doing.

"Sunny?" I'd said, sure she could hear the strangled way my voice crept out of my throat.

"Pieces?" She'd said, though her voice held a laugh, clearly enjoying calling out *my* nickname in the way I had hers. She knew exactly who I was, but I was still standing there like an imbecile gaping at her when she approached me and touched my cheek.

I was amazed I stayed standing when I felt her warm palm on my cheek. All the sounds around us must have stopped, because the only thing I heard was her skin scraping against the hair covering my jaw. All I could think was that I'd do whatever she wanted me to do if she'd just keep smiling at me with her bright green eyes and touching me.

Something I never thought about before I joined the Army was how little physical contact there was during deployment. You might occasionally shake hands with someone, but that was quite unusual considering any military greeting would typically necessitate a salute. You might play a game of basketball and clap someone on the back or bump against them in the heat of the game. If things went wrong, you might end up holding someone in your arms, trying to stop something or start something or beg them to hold on.

But no one touches you on purpose.

So even though I'd been back in the United States more than six weeks, I'd spent most of that time first in reintegration briefings and check-ups, and then backpacking the Appalachian trail. I'd gone to see my mother the first weekend, and hugged her, but nothing since then.

Until *she* touched my cheek with that smile on her face and then pulled me to her and hugged the life out of me.

Although really, that hug did nothing to drain the energy from me and everything to make my awareness of her, of the situation, break out of the tentative hold I had on it. I'd breathed her in, trying to stay as still as I could so she wouldn't feel uncomfortable. She smelled like lemon, dirt, sweat, and something sweet that, I kid you not, made a lump rise in my throat.

What the hell was happening to me?

She pulled back and apologized, and I managed to fumble around until I called her devastating.

I shouldn't have said it, but that was what she was. She was absolutely and completely devastating.

She was *sunshine*. Her dad had called her that, and we'd all adopted it because as a kid, she was so sweet and light and endearing, it was the perfect way to describe her. She was Sunny.

But now, my God, she was glowing with the life and vitality of a grown woman. I felt like one of my old graying paperbacks, dusty, discarded and losing its pages from time and inattention.

My astute observation that she'd grown up was met with humor, thank God, and she didn't immediately run away and move out for fear of my creepiness.

What am I doing?

I heard her when she said she was looking for an apartment, and everything in me revolted at the thought. I'd just now gotten to see her—just this once. Now she was going to move?

"We'll talk about it. I'm not worried," I said, my voice still gruff. I hoped she didn't see me glance at her legs again,

again, taking in the smooth expanse of the back of her thigh slipping up into her frayed shorts.

Holy mother of all idiots, you have got to get a grip man.

She turned back to me and smiled, then waved as she disappeared into the door. I stood there, not entering the house, waiting for the inconvenient pulse of wanting and familiarity, of shame and confusion, to quell.

This was not going to work.

Grab Home With You today!